"I'd hardly call this our first date."

"I promise, our next first date will be better."

At that, she actually grinned, and her body relaxed back into his, and he could breathe again. "That's not what I meant and you know it."

"Well, how many dates would you say we were at, then?"

"I have no idea! Why does it matter?"

"Because if you don't put out on the first date, then there's a schedule. And I need to see where we are in it." Gently, he cupped one hand over her left breast. "Are we far along enough for this?" he asked, rubbing his thumb back and forth across the nipple that poked through the fine cotton of her dress.

"Oh." Her lids drooped and her breathing went slow and soft. She squirmed on his lap and instantly his dick reacted, sucking all the blood from the rest of his body. "Oh, yes. We definitely are," she murmured.

"Excellent." He took her mouth, tasting the wine mixed with that unique sweetness he'd noticed the very first time he'd kissed her. Slowly, he lowered her back until he was lying next to her, him on his side, her on her back, leaving his hand free to coax the buttons of her sundress loose from their holes.

It was like unwrapping the most delicious package ever. Each button revealed more tantalizing, tempting flesh, and each time he had to touch, to feel, to taste. Beneath his ministrations, her body arched and she moaned.

PRAISE FOR LAURA K. CURTIS

Twisted

"Sexy small town suspense, with finely drawn characters that will tug at your heart and keep you up at night turning pages."

—Dee Davis, bestselling author of the A-TAC series

"The writing is strong, the characters come to life, and it's a treat to have an interesting, complex female character who sends the message that she can solve her own mysteries and who doesn't exhibit TSTL behavior. Ethan is a well-drawn hero, but this is really Lucy's story, and she absolutely owns it."

—Sunita at Dear Author (DA Recommended Read)

Lost

"Lost succeeded for me both in terms of the romance and the suspense. Tara and Jake had chemistry and their love for one another was built on a solid layer of mutual respect, which was a plus. They came across as smart and mature and that is always a pleasure for me to read. At about the 70% mark, the tension ratchets up and I was completely invested in the outcome and worried it wasn't going to work out. (It does. It's a romance. But in good romantic suspense, you should be worried, I think.)"

— Kaetrin from Dear Author

ALSO BY LAURA K. CURTIS

ROMANTIC SUSPENSE
Twisted
Lost

CRIME FICTION ANTHOLOGIES
"The Jaws of Life" in
Feeding Kate
"Only People Kill People" in
Murder, NY Style

TOYING
with his
Affections

LAURA K. CURTIS

This is a work of fiction.

Names, characters, places, and events are either the product of the author's imagination or used in a fictional fashion. Any resemblance to actual persons, living or dead, any business establishment, company, event, or location is purely coincidental.

COVER
Cover Design © Seductive Designs/Carrie Divine
Couple Image © Illustrated Romance/Jenn LeBlanc
Landscape image © Dreamstime/Digitaldarrell
Hair image © BestPhotoStudio

eBook ISBN:
Paperback ISBN: 978-1-941097-04-5

For Jessica, who believed even when I did not.

ACKNOWLEDGMENTS

For this book, more than in any other I have written, I have leaned on a crew of supportive people. First and foremost, I owe a great debt to Clare Toohey, who explained to me the fact that sex toy home parties *existed.* And who came to the one I had in order to research this book. And for the phrase "if my hand were a clitoris...".

Also, the wonderful woman who did our "Passion Party" and explained things to a group of red-faced toy party newbies who were primarily writers and agents, and so had a lot of questions. To all the people who drove up to my house to attend that party and tried out products and played games...I owe you all.

Once the research was done, I had to write the book. To all the people who helped me, let me lean on them, let me scream at them, and encouraged me along the way, I thank you. I know this list is missing some people, as is the nature of any list, but among those I remember best are K.M. Jackson, Elyssa Patrick, Clare Toohey, Ros Clarke, Karen Stivali, and the members of my wonderful CoLoNY RWA chapter.

This is the first book I have undertaken to publish "on my own." What a ridiculous thing to say. Without Isobel Carr, Bria Quinlan, Meghan Hogue, Carrie from Seductive Musings, Jessica Faust, and so, so many others, this book would never have become a physical product. And you, dear reader, would have been subjected to a text riddled with bizarre comma placements.

And last, but never least, my gratitude to my husband. He knows why.

Thank you so much, everyone.

CHAPTER 1

THE PALE, PINK LIGHT OF dawn should have made the familiar house with its weathered grey clapboard and neat white trim appear charming. Welcoming, even. But it didn't. All Evie felt as she pulled into the driveway was dread, and all she noticed was the darkness of the shadows hiding the deep front porch.

No welcome home light here, though her aunt had known Evie would be arriving overnight.

Maybe the bulb's out. Or she wants you to know you don't have to bother stopping at the main house yet.

Or maybe Patricia was no happier to have her than Evie was to be here. Though she'd spent most of her childhood living with her aunt, Evie had never been able to read the woman. And it hadn't been Patricia herself who had called. No, that had been left to Evie's cousin, Candace. No matter, Patricia needed her, and Evie owed her far too much to deny her anything. So here she was and here she'd stay.

She turned her attention to the detached garage. In the ten years she'd been away, an apartment had been built atop it, precisely matching the style of the house. Candace had sent her the key, so at least she could shower and change out of the sweats she had worn for the long drive from Vegas before facing her aunt.

As she slid from the car and stretched, joints popping and cracking, her eye caught the boxes in the back seat with their prominent markings. She didn't feel like hauling them up the stairs to the apartment—especially as they would likely remain unopened the entire time she was there—but unless she wanted the whole town talking about how she sold sex toys for a living in Las Vegas, she had to get them out of sight.

The garage would do fine. With her broken leg, Patricia wasn't apt to be driving any time soon. After all, that's what she had Evie for.

The boxes weren't huge, but they were heavy. Her boss and best friend, Benny, had slid them into the back of her Civic as they said goodbye. "You never know," he'd said with a wink, bussing her on the cheek, "they just might come in handy."

Right. Like the upright citizens of Fairview, Tennessee, would be so eager to be seen buying sex toys from the prodigal daughter. Or prodigal niece. Or whatever.

Shake it off. You're here. They'll just have to deal with it.

With a sigh, she opened the garage. No fancy electronics here, just twist the handle and raise the door. Beside Patricia's ancient, maroon convertible Chevy there was plenty of room in the two-car space to store the cartons. Evie dragged them out of the car and plopped them down behind the various gardening implements Patricia's injury would prevent her from using.

That project complete, she pulled the suitcase from her trunk and climbed the stairs to the apartment where she'd be staying for the next several months.

A multicolored area rug covered most of the floor in the single, large room. Along the right side, beneath the windows that looked toward the main house, a built-in counter functioned as a desk. A big fireplace took up the far wall, with doors on either side that turned out to lead into a bathroom that had been divided into two sections, each tucked into a corner under the eaves. One held a tub and vanity, the other a toilet and sink.

On the left wall was a full-sized bed, hidden behind a needlepoint screen. A memory assailed her of her mother sitting on the couch in their little Nashville apartment stitching a canvas of a ballerina. "All the women in my family do some form of needlework," she'd said. "It may be the only thing I actually have in common with them." Evie had been seven or eight at the time, and that ballerina, framed the minute she could afford to do so, was now packed away with some of her most precious possessions. A well-worn loveseat provided the sole place to sit in the room, and a closet-sized kitchen just left of the entry contained a dorm-room refrigerator, a toaster oven, a two-burner electric stove, and a sink.

But no coffeemaker that she could see. That was going to be a problem. *Think about it tomorrow. Just get through today.*

She put her clothes away in the built-in drawers on the back wall of the closet and hung up her lone dress and two nice shirts.

The sun was fully up now, streaming through the windows, hurting her tired eyes. She dropped the matchstick shades to dim the light and give herself a bit of privacy. Her aunt would be expecting her. Time to clean up and face the day.

Because of the slope of the roof, there was no shower in the bathtub under the eaves, and Evie's long hair slid down the drain when she tucked her head beneath the faucet to rinse out the shampoo. By the time she'd gotten most of the conditioner out, she'd resolved to spend a few of her remaining dollars on a hand shower.

She wound her damp, wavy tresses into a loose knot and stuck a pair of chopsticks into it. She'd left her blow dryer in Vegas, knowing she had no one in Fairview to impress. The dress she'd hung in the closet was more than a bit wrinkled, but Evie didn't own an iron, let alone an ironing board, so she pulled it on and hoped her aunt wouldn't ride her too badly over her sloppy appearance. At least the dress gave her self-confidence a bit of a boost.

As she walked from the garage to the main house, her eye caught on the masses of roses on both sides of the birch steps. She'd planted those bushes with her uncle half a lifetime ago, in the first days after she'd come to live in Fairview after her mother's death. They'd searched nursery after nursery for the perfect color. Patricia had suggested yellow because Emma, Evie's mother, had been so cheerful, but when Evie actually saw the flowers she'd burst into tears. They were too happy, too bright. And pink were too girly. Red too somber. Finally, they'd found what the nursery owner called a "Tracey Wickham" rose with pale yellow petals that darkened to deep pink at the tips.

In the six years Evie had lived with her aunt and uncle, the roses had been her responsibility. Harry had taught her how and when to prune and fertilize the bushes, what to look for when it came to deciding whether insects were good or bad. At the memory, a sick pang went through her.

"I'm so sorry, Harry," she whispered, touching one of the flowers and inhaling its rich, sweet scent. "I wish I could have been here for you."

Shaking off the melancholy, she climbed the porch steps and rang the doorbell. She heard the thump of crutches approaching from the other side and reflexively stood straighter.

The close-cropped curls of the woman who opened the door had grayed slightly since Evie had last seen her, but the intervening years had left few other marks. Evie straightened even further, well aware the same could not be said for her.

"Hello, Aunt Patricia."

"You're a little old to be calling me Aunt these days. Patricia will do fine."

"Oh. Okay." Evie stilled her fidgeting fingers. "May I come in?"

Patricia winced—either at the boldness of the

question or at the reminder of her own lack of hospitality, Evie couldn't be sure—and swung the door wider. "Of course. Please. I was just taking you in. You haven't changed much despite the years."

Really? Evie certainly felt different. Or she had, until she found herself fidgeting under her aunt's scrutiny. "I told Candace I'd be here last night or this morning. And the apartment was all set up. I needed a few days to get my things together and contact my boss about a replacement at work." Benny had been in New York dealing with an issue in his Times Square store when Evie had called. He was none too pleased to have to return to look after the Vegas shop which, under Evie's supervision, usually "took care of itself."

"But all that foolishness is over now. You're back home where you belong. Let me make tea and we can discuss the plan for the day."

Evie shoved away her immediate, defensive reaction to Patricia's dismissal of her job as "foolishness," focusing instead on the second half of the statement. Tea. Good grief, she'd have to drink a gallon of the stuff to come even half-awake.

"I can make the tea, Au— I mean, Patricia. I'm here to help until your cast comes off." And not a moment longer. No matter that Patricia seemed to take for granted Evie had returned for good.

"I'm not an invalid, despite what my daughter may have told you. I can make my own tea. We'll drink it in the kitchen so we don't need a tray."

Evie dutifully followed her aunt through the swinging door into the kitchen. This, too, was both familiar and new. They'd eaten at the miniature trestle table in the center of the room every night. Strange how small the table seemed to her now. The bare oak cabinets remained, but they'd been whitewashed and distressed, and the Formica countertops replaced with gleaming green composite stone.

No sooner had Evie settled into one of the well-worn

ladder-back chairs and allowed herself to get comfortable, however, than the doorbell rang.

"That'll be Sheriff Barstow," said Patricia. "He stops by in the mornings to check on me. Invite him in for a scone."

The words brought to mind the picture of the scowling, bejowled man who'd issued Evie her first and only speeding ticket. She'd gotten it on her way out of Fairview at age eighteen. Hard to believe he was still sheriff.

She braced herself for an unpleasant blast from her past and got…something else entirely. Not Bertram Barstow at all, though it took her a minute to identify the stunning specimen behind the crisply starched khaki shirt with the badge pinned to its pocket.

Griff Barstow had been all angry young rebel the last time she'd seen him. He'd worn his chestnut hair too long, his jeans too baggy, and his leather jacket like armor. His every muscle, ligament, and tendon had virtually vibrated with defiance. Evie had idealized him. More than that, she'd wanted to *be* him, to crawl inside his skin and find out how it felt to break every rule, to shrug off every expectation.

And he'd gotten out. Two years her senior, Griff had disappeared one day the summer after he graduated high school. Rumors abounded, but the sheriff refused to confirm any of them. By the time Evie herself escaped, people had even stopped talking about him.

So what had happened to turn the rebellious hero of her teenage fantasies into this buttoned-down, buttoned-up, crew-cut cop?

"You must be Evangeline," he said, a smile cutting deep grooves in tan cheeks. Dammit, even his teeth were perfect!

"Call me Evie." She thrust out her hand. "When Patricia said the sheriff was coming by, I expected your father."

He grasped her fingers, and the rough slide of his

flesh over her own sent such a surprising shock through her that for a moment she entirely missed his words.

"My father had a heart attack four months ago. I was appointed to fill his position."

"Oh, no! I had no idea! I'm so sorry."

"I'd hardly expect you to have heard. I know you and your aunt don't talk much." The censure in his tone erased any lingering frisson of pleasure from his touch, and Evie spun away to lead him toward the kitchen.

"Patricia said to invite you in for a scone and some tea," she tossed over her shoulder, not waiting to see whether he would follow.

WELL. PUT HIM IN HIS place. Griff admired Evie's take-no-prisoners attitude almost as much as the sway of her lithe figure beneath the filmy sundress as he trailed her into the kitchen. He didn't remember her as a particularly attractive girl, but then it had been a long time since he'd seen her, and in those days he'd been more interested in Candace, whose wildness had almost matched his own. And now, Candace was an attorney while good-girl Evie had become a showgirl. Of course, who'd have believed, given his own reputation, that he would take his father's place as sheriff?

"Good morning, Patricia," he said as he entered the kitchen on Evie's heels. "What have you cooked up for me today?"

"Blueberry scones. And you know Beth Ann does all the baking."

"Yes, but they're your recipes. And she doesn't give me freebies." Not that she wouldn't. Beth Ann Wheeler had set her sights on him the minute he'd moved back to Fairview, and while she embodied everything he'd eventually want in a wife, being a quiet woman, diplomatic, conservative, and a force in the community in her own right, he wasn't ready to settle down yet, and he wouldn't lead her on.

"Now that Evie's home, you don't need to worry so much. She'll take me to the store in the mornings, and you can get your breakfast there if you still feel the need to check up on me."

Patricia, he knew, considered Beth Ann a perfect match for him. Her invitations to the store had more to do with his unacceptable marital status than the state of his sweet tooth. Not that she'd ever admit it. Patricia maintained an absolutely unruffled, stoic exterior and would be mortified to know he saw through to her good-hearted matchmaking.

"In fact, Evie and I are going in this afternoon and regular hours will resume tomorrow." She plunked a pot of tea in the center of the table, where a plate of scones already lay. Three delicate cups designated the spots where each of them was intended to sit, and Griff helped Patricia lower herself into her seat before taking his own.

"Beth Ann's cousin Leah has been keeping the store open eleven to three while her son is in school, but I need to get back to my normal schedule before people in town forget about me entirely and start going to the chain store in Greeneville." She aimed a pointed glare at Evie, filled with condemnation for not stepping up as quickly as Leah.

Not exactly polite, but Patricia had her reasons. After all, Evie hadn't showed up for her uncle's funeral, nor any time in the four years since.

"We can't have that," Evie replied with a shark-like smile. "The retail gods would never forgive me if I let a big box store swallow you whole. Especially not with my retail experience."

Huh. He didn't understand the return swipe, but Patricia's lips thinned. Round one to the newcomer, which was pretty impressive given Patricia Bell Stewart's legendary poise.

"My gloves and hat are on my dresser," the older woman said. "Run up and get them so we can get moving. We don't want to be late for church."

Griff watched with interest as Evie flinched, then controlled herself. Round two to the pro. This could be more entertaining than anything that had happened since his return to Fairview.

EVIE COULDN'T BELIEVE SHE'D FORGOTTEN her aunt's insistence on Sunday services. It had constituted one of the major changes in her life when she'd moved to Fairview. Before her mother's death, she'd never been to a formal religious service of any kind, but Harry and Patricia attended church every Sunday, and Candace and Evie were expected to dress accordingly, in frilly dresses, fancy bonnets, and white gloves that prevented Evie from chewing her fingernails. As she gathered her aunt's sophisticated straw bowler with white lace trim and white gloves from the dresser, she caught sight of the nails that had so offended her aunt. No longer shredded and torn below the raw tips of her fingers, they were now long, strong, and painted a bright, carnelian red.

Patricia almost certainly didn't approve of the color any more than she had the gnawed remnants, but Evie couldn't afford to care. Literally. If she didn't make some money, she wouldn't be able to pay for a simple manicure, let alone the complicated highlights she'd taken to wearing in her hair. And what, she wondered, did Griff think of her new look? Not that it mattered. She was who she was, after all, but the question of how others—especially her teen self's ideal—would see her transformation was irresistible.

When she returned to the kitchen, Griff stood at the sink rinsing the tea cups. *Some rebel.* He turned and flashed that killer smile again.

"Perfect timing." He laid the final piece of china in the drying rack. "I'm going to be the talk of the town this week with two such lovely ladies on my arm."

"You're coming to church with us?"

"'Course. I always bring Miz Patricia. Gotta keep my hand in with the Ladies' Auxiliary if I hope to be elected in a couple of months."

Evie looked to her aunt for an explanation. "When Griffin's daddy had his heart attack, the County Commissioner appointed Griffin to the position. But come November, he'll be elected without any problem."

A grimace Evie couldn't interpret flashed across Griff's features before he grinned once more. "Your aunt's one of my biggest supporters."

"Griffin's really made something of himself," said Patricia, and Evie's stomach muscles clenched at the obvious implication.

"Well, we should get a move on," said Mr. Made-Something-Of-Himself into the increasingly awkward silence. "Being late to church won't help my reputation, especially since Candace and Jim will be holding seats for us in a pew near the front."

Of course they would. The knots in Evie's stomach tightened and twisted as the big, black Suburban with SHERIFF painted on the side rolled through town. Just as well she hadn't had any coffee that morning. She'd probably have puked all over the nice, clean leather.

Griff assisted Patricia up the stairs to the church door, and Evie hesitated for a moment below them, dreading what was to come. As a child, she'd sensed the town's pity, a palpable force every Sunday for at least a year. They'd sat in the front then, too, and she'd practically heard the whispers of "poor child" echo at their backs. Evie had always felt herself shrinking, becoming tinier and tinier as she trailed her aunt and uncle up the aisle until by the time they slid into their pew, she was a mere speck, a mote floating in the air. Apparently, Candace had stepped right into her mother's low-heeled pumps, but this time Evie refused to disappear.

With a little mental prod, she joined the others as they passed through the doors. She felt a bit like a bride, slowly making her way up the aisle while those seated in the pews watched her every step. She met their stares with her own, daring them to pity her now. Unfortunately, no handsome prince of a groom awaited her at the end of the procession. Just Candace, her husband Jim, and their twin boys, Billy and Teddy, age five.

"Are you our aunt?" asked Teddy in a loud whisper.

"I am," Evie replied, holding out her hand. "And you must be Teddy. Your grandmother sent me pictures of you."

"She didn't show us any of *you*," Teddy said with an accusatory scowl at Patricia. "We only found out about you after her accident." Both boys solemnly shook her hand.

"Well, I live very far away. I doubt she thought it mattered you had an aunt until we were going to meet."

"Are you Mommy's sister? My teacher says an aunt is Mommy or Daddy's sister." Teddy was obviously the talker of the two.

"That's true," Candace said, "but Evie is *not* my sister. She's my cousin. Which makes her your cousin once removed, but that's hard to say, so we call her your aunt."

Billy wrinkled his forehead at the explanation, but Teddy forged ahead.

"You can't be our cousin. You're too old."

"Teddy!" Patricia glared, but for the first time since leaving Vegas, Evie laughed aloud. Of course, church wasn't precisely the best place for such a thing, even if the service hadn't yet begun.

"It's okay, Teddy," she assured him. "I *am* too old. That's why I'm a cousin once removed instead of a regular one."

"Now, hush," said Patricia, rapping once on the pew. "Here comes Reverend Masters."

The minister in Evie's youth, Reverend French, had been ancient and doddering. His sermons had been gentle, if exceedingly boring. Reverend Masters took a different tack, exhorting his congregation in a harsh and booming tone against the evils of pride. By the time the sermon was over, Evie's jaw ached from gritting her teeth.

They made their way outside—slowly, because of Patricia's crutches and the crowd in front of them—and Patricia began to urge Evie toward the minister.

"You don't want to do that," Evie muttered, trying not to draw attention.

"Don't be ridiculous. You have to meet Reverend Masters."

"No, I don't. And, honestly, Patricia, you don't want me to. Because I'm likely to remind him about stones and glass houses." She heard a gasp behind her, but didn't bother looking to see who she'd offended.

Rescue came from an unlikely corner. "I must admit, Miz Patricia," Griff interjected, flashing that killer grin, "today's wasn't one of the Reverend's more inspiring sermons. Perhaps Evie should wait until next week."

Evie very much doubted the smug minister would improve in a week's time, but she did appreciate the reprieve. She gave Griff a warm smile and he blinked a couple of times like a rabbit caught in the beam of a flashlight.

"I'll just take you ladies home," he continued at last, as if Patricia had agreed. He took one of her crutches and held out an arm, and Patricia conceded with more grace than Evie would have expected.

WHEN THEY ARRIVED AT THE house, Patricia recommended Evie change clothes. "It's dusty in the bookstore these days. I couldn't very well ask Leah to clean for me, so we'll do it today. You run up and change, and I'll get lunch started. I made egg salad. I hope you still like that."

"I don't like your egg salad. I adore it. I can't believe you remember my favorite foods."

"Of course I do. I'm not senile." Patricia peeled off

her gloves and handed them to Evie along with her hat. "Before you change, please put these back where you found them, will you?"

"Of course."

Evie laid the gloves and hat back on the bureau, then gave in to temptation and walked down the hall to peek into the room she'd shared with Candace as a child. The pale mauve walls had been repainted sky blue, and denim covers, rather than the floral prints of her memory, encased the fluffy duvets on the twin beds. A big box of toys and trucks held pride of place in the far corner. It had clearly become a boys' space, and Evie wondered how often Candace's children spent the night with Grandma.

Closing the door on her past, she headed back to the garage apartment. It took her only a couple of minutes to change out of the sundress and into jeans, a tee shirt, and a pair of scarlet high-top sneakers, but by the time she was done Patricia already had sandwiches on the table. She'd even bought Evie's favorite vegetable chips to go with them, and Evie found herself forced to blink away tears. She really hadn't gotten enough sleep. She shouldn't be reacting so strongly to such a small thing. Her reserved aunt wouldn't thank her for such sentimentality.

So she swallowed the lump in her throat and, at Patricia's instruction, grabbed the pitcher of iced tea from the refrigerator. Which reminded her of something she'd forgotten to check while changing.

"Is there a coffee maker in the apartment? I didn't see one when I looked."

"No. We built the studio over the garage for Harry's father when he came to live with us after Martha died, and he didn't drink coffee. If you want coffee, you can get it at the café in the mornings when we go into the store." Patricia thumped over to the table and set a plate in front of Evie, then got her own.

"I'll buy a machine. They're cheap, and I'll want

caffeine before I see anyone in the mornings. But that brings up a subject we haven't had a chance to talk about." Evie took a deep breath. "Salary."

For the first time in her life, Evie saw Patricia's jaw literally drop. Her facial muscles seemed completely frozen, her mouth unable to close. It lasted only a moment, however.

"I'm not planning on paying you. I don't need an employee. As I said to Candace, I only need a hand here and there. I'm supplying you with room and board; what else do you need money for?"

"It's not here and there, Patricia. I'll be driving you everywhere you need to go, working in the shop, helping out around here. It's a full-time position, even if only a temporary one."

"The cast comes off in a month. Surely you can help me out for a *month*."

"A month until your cast comes off, and then at least another of physical therapy before you can drive. I've known dancers with breaks like yours. It's not an easy recovery." And Patricia, unlike most of Evie's friends, was of an age where bones were starting to become brittle anyway.

"Two months is nothing. You'll be staying in the apartment. I'll stock the kitchen up there and you know you can always come down here and get anything you want."

"It's not just food. I have bills. I have a *life*." And a pile of debt. But she refused to confirm the beliefs of all those who'd whispered about her feckless mother. They'd expect her to fail, expect her to go broke. They wouldn't care about the reasons.

"A life?"

"Back in Vegas. Yes, I found a sub-letter who'd take my half of the apartment furnished so I didn't have to sell everything before coming back here, but I only had a week to find someone, so she's not paying my full share. I still owe a bit on that, and I have ongoing bills." She didn't want to talk about the biggest, so she waved a hand vaguely. "Cell phone, stuff like that."

"Don't you have savings? How could I raise a child who lives paycheck to paycheck? Candace—"

"Don't go there. I don't need a big salary. I can manage on a couple hundred a week."

"You expect me to pay you two hundred dollars a week? I could hire someone for that!"

"You could try, but even kids don't work that cheap these days. You're stuck with me."

"And what if I don't happen to have a spare few hundred a week to donate to the cause?"

The question might have been rhetorical, merely another way for Patricia to express her disgust at being asked to pay for something she considered her due, but a hint of desperation lurked beneath the words. It resonated with a dreadful familiarity, sending a shiver down Evie's spine. Patricia wouldn't appreciate being confronted, however, so Evie kept her tone as light as possible while privately resolving to examine her aunt's finances as soon as possible.

"If you don't, then my job will include making the store more profitable, won't it? So why don't you finish your sandwich, and we'll get started."

CHAPTER 2

MOST OF THE STOREFRONTS ON Main Street were dark, and Evie found a parking spot right in front of The Book Nook. She noted the "back to school" display in the window with a critical eye. It should have come down no more than a week after the school year started. Once parents had purchased their children's required reading, the focus should have switched once more to attracting adult customers. But of course, Patricia couldn't crawl around fixing up the window in her condition.

Inside, Evie's practiced eye spotted more changes she would need to make. How many of the oversized paperbacks at the front of the store could her aunt be selling? They cost more than the smaller ones she bought for herself, and the few she read the back cover copy on all looked the same: family or romantic trauma leads to journey of self-exploration, which ultimately results in richer and more satisfying life. It was the kind of thing Evie wanted to live, not read about. And she had. Granted, her journey had taken her down a few side roads, but that's where the most interesting scenery lay, anyway. And she'd found a good, fulfilling life, regardless of what other people thought of her profession.

She picked up one of the novels and held it out. "Is this doing well for you?"

Patricia sighed. "Not particularly. It's too bad. I read

that one and it was good."

Evie wouldn't be distracted. "What about these?" She pulled three at random from the display and held them up.

"Umm…I've sold a few copies of the middle one. They made a movie out of it."

"If they're not moving, why are they here?"

"They get reviewed, written up. Oprah recommends them, so people expect to find them when they come in."

"We need to use this space for books people actually buy," Evie said, "not waste it on those they won't spend money on. You can send them back, right?"

"Well, not exactly. I can get credit for them by sending back the covers as proof I've destroyed them. But not having those books—it would be like opening a cheese shop and not selling brie."

"And if people in this town don't eat brie, you'd drive yourself into the poorhouse tossing old wheels and buying new to keep it nice and fresh. You'd be better off becoming famous as the cheese shop with fourteen kinds of cheddar."

Patricia frowned, but nodded. "I suppose. I keep meaning to start a book club to get people reading, but I can't seem to work up the energy."

"That's a great idea for the future, but for now let's concentrate on the store itself. If people don't buy these, what do they buy?"

"Mostly romances."

Evie headed for the romance section in the back corner. While Patricia tidied the check-out area and went through the notes Leah had left for her, Evie examined titles and placement.

"What happened to the children's section?"

"The old Red Barn Boots out on the highway went out of business. A young couple bought the building and turned it into one-stop shopping for children. It's called Kiddie Barn now, and they sell toys, clothes, and books, so everyone goes there for children's books."

"Okay, then." A nebulous plan was beginning to form in the back of Evie's mind, but she couldn't accomplish it on her own. She stepped outside and used her cell to call Benny.

"Please tell me you're coming back already," he said by way of greeting.

"Nope. I need a favor. I want you to come down and give one of your 'how to' talks in my aunt's store. We'll sell the books, you can sign them. Everybody wins."

"My books do just fine without me haring off to the middle of nowhere. Is there even a decent hotel in that town?"

"Yes. A lovely bed and breakfast." At least, Evie hoped it was lovely. She'd never actually set foot in the place, but they'd driven by it on the way to church and it looked adorable.

"Oh, God, Evie. You know I don't do the B and B thing."

"Then you can stay in my apartment and I'll stay in the main house for a couple days. You know you want to. You'll be The Book Nook's first celebrity guest. I've got the promo worked out already."

"You're going to promo me? Now that's an enticement I can't refuse. When do you want me?"

"Give me a little while to generate interest. How about two weeks? Not this coming Sunday, but next? But send me a half-dozen of each book overnight, will you? I need them for the promo."

"Done."

Evie flipped her phone closed and went back inside to find Patricia, who had moved to the café area and was counting receipts.

"How long does it take you to get new books in after you order them?"

"Depends on where they're coming from."

"On average. Or better yet, the ones that come in fastest. Since romance is your biggest seller, we need to pump up that section—it's looking a little tame."

"I am not turning The Nook into some kind of porn shop!"

"I sure hope not." Griff's amused voice cut into their conversation.

"What are you doing here?" Evie knew she sounded surly, but she hated to be sidetracked when she was gearing up for a pitch. Her aunt needed to make major changes, and Evie wasn't about to discuss them in front of Griff Barstow.

"I knew Patricia hadn't been in for a bit," he answered easily, "so I stopped by to see whether I could help with any heavy lifting."

"No, thanks," Evie began, but Patricia interrupted her.

"Actually, there are a couple of light bulbs that need changing. The ladder isn't too stable, so if you'd hold it while Evie climbs, I'd appreciate it. I'd hate for her to fall the way I did!"

"No problem." Griff, clearly comfortable around the shop, let himself into the storeroom and came out with an ancient aluminum ladder and a pack of bulbs. He set the ladder beneath one of the burnt-out bulbs, then stepped so close to Evie she could almost feel his broad chest brush against her nipples which—suddenly and humiliatingly—puckered in anticipation.

He glanced over his shoulder at Patricia, who'd gone back to her work in the café, and then down at Evie. "Need a boost?" he asked in a hot, honey-smooth whisper.

She stepped back quickly, almost tripping over her own feet. The flash of amusement in his quicksilver eyes cleared the sensual fog from her mind.

"No, thanks." She stepped around him, grabbed the ladder, and began to climb.

WOW. GRIFF REFLEXIVELY PUT A foot on the bottom rung of the wobbling aluminum ladder to stabilize it, but his attention was all for hot woman, not cold metal. With each step, sleek muscles flexed and stretched beneath worn denim that caressed every curve. She might be the very worst thing for both his newfound peace and his political career, but she sure was sexy. And free. And probably not interested in a long-term relationship, given she'd be moving back to Vegas. He could take her out and she wouldn't expect a commitment, unlike the other women in Fairview.

"Bulb," she demanded, holding out a hand with the one she'd unscrewed. He took it, deliberately brushing his fingers over hers, and handed her a fresh one. She fixed him with an evil stare. Once she'd installed the new light, she came down, he moved the ladder, and the process was repeated. This time, however, as she stepped off the last rung, he trapped her between the ladder and his body.

"Have dinner with me?"

Her muscles stiffened until she practically vibrated. "Why?"

Okay, he hadn't expected that. "Why not?"

She put a single, scarlet-tipped finger in the center of his chest and pushed him away. "Not good enough. By that logic, why not run naked down Main Street?"

"Because it's illegal and I'd be forced to arrest you?" But, damn, the idea of her naked in cuffs sent all the blood in his body rushing straight to his groin. Thank goodness he was no longer close enough for her to feel his reaction.

"Fine. Then why not parade down Main Street in a thong bikini, which I am pretty sure isn't illegal since Thompson Pool is only a few blocks away and even here in Fairview some girls must be wearing bikinis."

That image didn't help cool Griff down at all. He was going to have to take a dip in Thompson pool himself. He forced a casual response. "Well, to start with, behavior like that would probably give people the wrong idea."

"Which is precisely why I shouldn't go to dinner with you."

She was right, of course. If he expected to be elected sheriff, he had to remain even more respectable than other candidates because of his checkered past. Clark Devane had begun making noise about running against him, and not only was he a member of the local Lion's Club, but he'd never once colored outside the lines. He'd certainly never taken up with a showgirl who didn't consider family important enough to show up for her uncle's funeral. No, Devane's wife was just as unimaginative and utterly respectable as he was.

He stuffed his hands deep into the pockets of his jeans, resisting the urge to coax Evie into agreement with a touch. He'd been living like a monk since returning to Fairview.

At first, he'd just wanted to prove to the town—and his father—how much he'd changed. And then, when he'd been appointed to fill his father's shoes, he hadn't wanted to let the old man down. When had it become so much more? Fact was, he loved being sheriff, watching over the town, and he couldn't toss it away over a fling. No matter how hot she might be.

"Ah, well." He stepped further away from the temptation she posed. "If that's what you want."

"It is." She made a little shooing motion with her fingers.

The easy dismissal infuriated him, but he didn't respond. Instead, he folded the ladder and returned it to the storage room.

"Anything else you need?" he asked Patricia.

"Not a thing. Thank you so much."

"No problem. You know you only have to ask."

"SUCH A NICE BOY," PATRICIA said once Griff had left, and Evie, having learned her lesson, had locked the door behind him.

Evie had no desire to talk about Griff Barstow, so she shifted the conversation back to her aunt's profit margin, or lack thereof.

"Look at what you have here, Patricia. I was reading Georgette Heyer in Middle School. I love her, but she doesn't exactly exemplify modern romance. I'm not talking about bringing in a whole slew of erotica, just raising the level of sensuality a bit."

"Fairview isn't Las Vegas. Just because trash sells there, doesn't mean people here will buy it."

"What will you lose if they don't? You can get credit if the books don't sell."

"My reputation! If folks walk in and see shelf after shelf of barely clad men and women, what will they think?"

That you've joined the twenty-first century?

"Tell me what publishers you can get quickly, and I'll find spicier books without offensive covers." It should be easy enough. One call to Celia, her room-mate in Vegas, who was an inveterate romance reader and had written one of her own that she was currently trying to sell, should net her the information she needed.

With obvious reluctance, Patricia agreed.

"So if you sell a lot of romance, you must have primarily female customers."

"Women buy more books nationwide."

"Okay. I can see that. But without children's books, we need to find a way to bring in the men."

Patricia huffed. "I carry all the current thrillers and non-fiction."

"I know you do. We just need to entice them in to see that you carry stuff for them, too."

"Good luck," Patricia muttered. She limped to the storage room and began to drag out a vacuum.

"Hey! Let me get that!"

The rest of the afternoon was devoted to cleaning and stocking. Several shipments of books had arrived in the two weeks Patricia had been incapacitated and then on short hours, and she hadn't been able to get the books on the shelves. Although conversation lagged occasionally, Evie resisted bringing up her plan for attracting men to the store. Patricia had enough to get used to already.

MONDAY MORNING, THE CAFÉ HAD a steady stream of customers. A few came over to the bookstore side, but most bought coffee and pastries and went on their way. Those who did wander into Evie's orbit were less concerned with books than with gossip, but Evie had prepared for that. The night before, she'd called her room-mate, Celia. Celia owned every Vegas- and showgirl-themed romance on the market and happily listed them all. Before they even opened the doors, Evie dragged a wire display rack out of storage and put every book Celia recommended that Patricia had in stock into it. Whenever someone asked about how she'd been or what she'd been up to since leaving home, Evie sold them a book.

By the end of the day, her voice was shot and her jaw ached from keeping a pleasant smile on her face, but she'd sold every romance in the rack along with a couple of Vegas-themed mysteries Patricia had recommended. Once they locked the door, they stayed for half an hour to go over the list of new titles and publishers Evie had drawn up—with help from Celia—and Patricia agreed to order almost all of them.

Tuesday, the books Benny had shipped arrived. Most of the gossips had satisfied their curiosity the day before, so Evie had plenty of time to put the next phase of her plan into action. First, she went to the copy shop and had the cover of one of the books enlarged to poster size. Then she headed down the street to the five and dime— now a five and ten *dollar* store, she noticed—and bought a roll of craft paper and a couple of markers. Back at The Book Nook, she covered the entire front window with craft paper, then removed and re-shelved all the back-to-school items. She dragged risers and a wire rack into the space and filled it with Benny's two books: *Dirty, Sexy Business: Getting Down to the Nitty-Gritty of Making Money*, and *Kinky Business: Ironing Out The Wrinkles On Your Path To Success*. On the poster, she wrote "Come ask a millionaire about making your business successful, no matter what it is!" Then she wrote the date and time of Benny's appearance.

"You think men will come in to hear a stranger tell them how to run businesses they've been running for years?"

"When I'm done, they will," Evie replied. "But I'm not revealing the window just yet. I'll come back late tonight and put on the finishing touches when no one's around." She made Patricia promise not to answer any questions about what was behind the paper.

Not that anyone asked. Foot traffic was a mere trickle, and Evie wondered, though she'd never admit such a thing to her aunt, whether the business might be too far gone to save.

Evie waited until after eleven that night to head back into the store. Once there, she laid out a piece of craft paper the size of the front window on the floor and drew a large, triangular bulls-eye in the middle. Each point of the triangle had a dot at the tip, and each dot formed the base of a question mark. Along the top of the paper, she wrote in large block letters: WANT TO SEE SOMETHING… and then along the edges of the triangle, she wrote DIRTY? SEXY? KINKY? Finally, she cut the center of the triangle out, creating a peephole.

With a long look up and down the street to be sure no one was walking by, she peeled away the original craft paper and replaced it with her new, improved version. Once it was securely attached, she stepped back in the small space to be certain everything lined up, so anyone who put their eye to the hole could see all the information about Benny's visit. She straightened the wire rack supporting the poster, then looked back at the hole.

Only to find an eye staring back at her. With a shriek, she stumbled back into the display.

"Damn! Damn, damn, damn," she muttered, disentangling herself from the rack as someone began pounding on the front door.

"Evie? Evie?" Fantastic. Griff Barstow. The very last person she wanted to deal with tonight. "Evie, open the door so I know you're okay."

"I'm fine." She opened the door, but blocked the entrance with her body.

"You're sure?"

"Of course. You just surprised me, is all. What on earth were you up to?"

"Looking. That's the whole point of the peephole, right?"

"Well, yeah, but I didn't expect anyone to be walking by at this hour."

"Driving, actually. On my way home from a call. I noticed the lights and stopped to check it out. Sorry if I frightened you."

Evie shrugged. "At least I can already tell the promotion is working."

He chuckled, and the sound sent a warm shiver through her. It was really a shame he'd gone and gotten all uptight.

"I'm frankly surprised Patricia agreed to it."

"She hasn't seen it yet." Evie leaned against the doorjamb, attempting a casual stance. "She knows about Benny's visit, of course, but I wanted her to feel the full impact of the window."

His warm smile disappeared, replaced by a combination of disgust and disdain that squashed any soft feelings she'd begun to harbor toward him. "What's the matter with you? Are you trying to give the poor woman a heart attack as well as to ruin her business?"

"I would never, ever hurt my aunt or her business." Evie drew herself up to her full five-foot-eight and gave him her best stink-eye. "You stopped. You looked in the window. Others will, too."

"Oh, yeah? Well, I have news for you. I'm not the old biddies who shop in your aunt's store. They *won't* put their faces to a peephole."

"Which is precisely the point! Old biddies don't pay the rent. When did people in this town last stop to look, honestly look, at Patricia's window display? I could put up all the signs I wanted advertising Benny's books and the fact that he's willing to share his expertise, but most people still wouldn't know about it because they're so used to walking by this window, this store, and ignoring it."

"What makes you think Fairview's citizens will be willing to be seen looking into this kind of thing?"

Evie rubbed her temples. "They trust Patricia. They know she wouldn't sell anything truly sordid, so the contrast will seduce them in."

"Not everything in life is about seduction."

A wave of exhaustion almost knocked her down. Too much change, too much work, and now, too much disapproval. "Go home, Griff. I still have work to do here and I'm not up to explaining the basics of marketing."

"I apologize. I shouldn't have said that. I've had a long day."

"Whatever."

"Seriously. I'm not usually so thoughtless."

"Yeah, okay. Apology accepted. But I meant what I said—I still have to put the racks back together now that I've made a huge mess, so go on home."

"Can I help?"

"No. Really. I'll do this faster on my own."

"Okay."

BUT EVEN AFTER HE LEFT the store, Griff stayed for a full ten minutes sitting in his SUV parked at the corner, watching. Only after Evie was safely in her car and on her way did he pull away from the curb. He didn't expect trouble. The town had little enough crime to speak of. The only reason he'd been out at all was that Mrs. Branck always insisted on him, personally, rather than any of the deputies. One day, an actual crime might prevent him from answering one of her calls, which usually occurred when she woke in the night convinced a prowler was creeping around her yard, but until then he preferred to keep her happy.

Evie's sign had cracked him up, and even though he was dog-tired, he'd just had to peek through the hole. And given that the view at the time had been of Evie's extremely shapely rear end, he'd just kept on looking.

Until she'd caught him at it. Only then, while he waited for her at the door, did the rest of the window register. How in the seven hells did Evie decide that Benny "The Sex Toy King" Silver was a good in-store guest? She'd implied that Patricia had agreed to it, but Griff couldn't imagine Patricia even knowing who the guy was.

He climbed out of the car at his house. His father's house. Griff had moved out of his own apartment after the old man's heart attack. For the first month, when things had been touch and go, he'd spent most of his non-work hours at the hospital. Once Bertram had been shifted to a rehab facility, Griff had moved into the house to take care of it until his return. After rehab, his father had surprised everyone by taking retirement and going on an extended vacation. First he'd visited family in Arizona, then decided to go on a cruise. In a few more weeks, though, he would be home again and Griff would need to find a new place to live.

His mind returned to Evie. How had she ended up in Vegas? Most people who left Fairview headed for Nashville or Memphis. But then, by the time she left, he'd been gone two years, and considerably further than Vegas. Of course, he hadn't had a whole lot of options.

He stuck his head into the fridge and found four beers and two slices of leftover pizza. Not precisely gourmet pickings, but they'd do. He popped the cap on a beer and stuck one of the slices in the toaster oven. When the smell of pepperoni filled the kitchen, he pulled it out and ate standing over the sink.

Hell of a life, Griff. But for the moment, it would have to do.

CHAPTER 3

AS THEY DROVE PAST THE store Wednesday morning to get to the town's central parking lot, Evie saw a line outside the store, apparently waiting for the café to open. A knot she hadn't even recognized in her stomach relaxed. No way did all those people just want a cup of coffee. Her promotion had begun to work already.

Patricia was not so sanguine. "What have you done?" she asked in horror when she saw the sign. "The minute we get inside, that's coming down."

"No, it isn't." Evie pulled into one of the village permit parking spots. "I didn't change a single item inside the window. There's nothing racy or raunchy, just books about business written by a self-made millionaire who's been on Fox, MSNBC, CNN, even Oprah! He's as mainstream as they come. Most folks in town have probably already even seen him interviewed a time or two."

"That's not what your sign implies!"

"Come on, Patricia. Give it a chance. It's funny, not nasty." She thought about her encounter the night before. "Even Griff laughed when he saw it."

"He did?"

"Yes." Evie helped her aunt out of the car and they made their way toward the crowd.

"It is rather exciting," Patricia admitted with a small grin. "I don't remember the last time we had more than one or two people waiting for us to open.

"We'll be open in ten minutes," she called out as they slipped inside. "Just have to get the coffee going!"

Beth Ann was laying pastries in the case on the café side. "I take it this was your idea," she said to Evie.

"Yup," Evie replied cheerfully.

If Patricia noticed the tension between the two women, she ignored it. "We're going to be busy this morning. Maybe Evie should start the day on the café side."

"That won't be necessary! People don't mind a bit of a wait." Beth Ann was defending her territory. Evie sympathized with the emotion, but her own defenses rose immediately. Luckily, Patricia spoke before Evie could.

"If you're sure." She cut a glance at the café window.

"Of course I am. It's just coffee and pastries. And if they have to wait, that will give them an excuse to pop over to your side, which is what they want to do anyway."

"Won't do them any good," Evie said. "I've blocked off window access from the inside. If they want to know what's behind the craft paper, they'll have to suck it up and peek through the hole."

"It's time," Beth Ann said. Patricia stationed herself behind the register while Evie and Beth Ann unlocked the doors. People flooded into the café. A few boldly stepped through the bookshop door, making no pretense of wanting coffee. Once inside, however, they faltered. Where there had once been an open space allowing customers to see into the window display, Evie had placed a wire rack filled with bargain books and backed with craft paper. Even if customers removed the books, they wouldn't be able to view the inside of the window.

The entertainment had been in progress for about fifteen minutes, and Evie was just beginning to enjoy herself, when Candace arrived.

"What the hell are you doing?"

"Candace! Don't make a scene!" Patricia tried to

shush her, but Candace was on a roll.

"Make a scene? Me? What about her? She's turning your store, your life into a scandalous joke!" In a move that would have made Evie's dance instructors proud, she spun on one leather-clad toe, yanked the discount book rack out of its spot, and tore away the paper.

"Hey!" Evie stepped forward.

"Stay out of my way. This is a *family* business, something you clearly don't understand."

"You're going to lecture me about family?" Evie could practically feel steam rising from the top of her head. "That's rich. Really—"

"Girls! This is neither the time nor the place! Candace, go back to work. You can come by the house this evening and we'll discuss matters then."

"I have to take care of the boys."

"Jim can handle them for a few hours." Patricia turned her glare on Evie. "Put the store back together. We have customers."

Customers who'd gone dead silent as they watched the drama unfold and now, unwilling to be seen as mere busybodies, picked up the nearest book and brought it to the register. A giggle rose in Evie's throat as Sharon Davies paid for a thriller set in eighteenth century France, and Mary Williams bought War and Peace because she happened to be standing next to the Classics section. Both of those books would turn up at the next library sale.

Just before one, an older man Evie didn't recognize came into the store chuckling. "That's quite a window you have there, Patricia," he said. It was the first time anyone had addressed the issue directly, and Evie tensed as she waited for Patricia's reaction.

"Do you think it's too much?" she asked.

"Got me in here, didn't it? Does that fella really know his stuff?"

"You'll have to ask my niece. Evie Bell, Martin Waters. Martin owns the hardware store down the street."

"And I'm always looking for new marketing ideas." He gestured to the window. "Was that his idea or yours?"

"Mine. But Benny gave me my start in business and I've learned a lot from him over the years. I'd encourage anyone who wants to sell more to show up next Saturday."

"Hardware's not exactly thrilling."

"That's basically the subject of his first book—how to sell just about anything better, whether it's a sexy product or not."

"Maybe I should buy that. How much is it?"

"Fifteen ninety-five."

He nodded slowly. "That'll be fine. You ring me up for one."

Evie got one of the books she'd put in the back and Patricia made the sale.

"Now don't you go giving away the secret of the peephole," she joked as Waters tucked the bag under his arm.

"Not on your life," he said with a wink.

OVER DINNER, EVIE TRIED TO get a sense of her aunt's feelings about the display, but Patricia shut her down, claiming the topic could wait until Candace's arrival.

"I don't want her to feel as if we're ganging up on her. After all, you're living and working with me, so she'll already be at a disadvantage."

Evie didn't pursue the subject, though she wished she could. Once she went back to Vegas, mother and daughter would have to work out their issues on their own. Still, sooner or later, they'd need to talk openly about Patricia's future. Why couldn't Candace see that her mother needed help?

Calm discussion, however, wasn't on Candace's mind when she arrived. No sooner had Evie brought them all tea in the living room than she launched into a set of arguments she'd clearly been preparing all day.

"This is going to destroy you, destroy the store. You spent your whole life building that place up and you're going to let Evie tear it down with that…monstrosity of a display?"

"Tear it down?" Evie's temper flared. "Do you have the slightest idea how the store, how your own mother is doing financially? I know you're terribly busy with your husband and your kids and your high-powered career, which is why you had to call some under-educated, trampy relative to help out, but did it never even occur to you to ask whether she needed a hand?"

"Of course things are tough since her injury…"

"That's not what I meant." Evie braced herself and confronted Patricia. "How long has the store been running in the red?"

"In the *red*?" Candace's shock almost gained Evie's sympathy. She'd assumed Candace knew Patricia couldn't afford other help, which was why she'd called Evie. But maybe not.

"It's not in the red. Business has fallen off over the past several years, but we're still making a profit."

"On books? Or is the café artificially boosting your balance sheet?"

"I own both businesses and each benefits the other," Patricia said, her voice as stiff as her spine, "separating the money would be artificial. Keeping it together makes sense."

"No, it doesn't." Candace shook her head, frowning at her mother. "You need to have a handle on what's making money for you and what's not."

"Exactly," said Evie, latching onto Candace's argument to make her own. "Which is why I set up that display. Patricia wasn't getting men into the store and she needed a change of pace to make people sit up and pay attention to the store again."

"I can speak for myself," Patricia said.

"Well, obviously you didn't," Candace replied, "or you would have torn down that tacky display the moment you saw it!"

"It is tacky," Patricia agreed. Candace smirked. "But it is also funny. And Martin Waters came into the store today and bought a copy of one of the books. I don't think he's set foot in the Nook since they moved to town five years ago. So it works."

Evie resisted her own desire to smirk.

"But your reputation. Don't you care what people will say? I can't even tell you the number of phone calls I got today. Imagine what Billy and Teddy will hear at school."

"If people were calling you at work," Evie put in, "the damage is already done. In a town this size, the word's already out. Leaving things as they are for a few more days won't hurt."

"A few more days?"

"I planned to take the paper down on Saturday anyway, so people would have a week to read about the event without standing at the peephole."

Candace chewed her bottom lip. "Can you do it Friday? I'd rather people had all day Saturday to see the truth before we have to go to church on Sunday."

Part of her wanted to deny Candace's request out of sheer spite, but she had no legitimate grounds. And she would doubtless need Candace's help later in order to keep tabs on Patricia's well-being. "That sounds reasonable."

"As long as you don't plan to put up another, equally offensive display once your friend has given his little talk?"

Evie drew a deep breath, and was—literally—saved by the bell.

"I'll get it," she said, heading for the door. She took her time, though, counting up to ten and then back down to cool off before opening the door.

Griff stood outside, dressed in jeans and a black tee.

Evie drew another deep breath, for a completely different reason. Why did the man always show up when she was at her worst? Dusty from cleaning, damp from a bath, frustrated from dealing with her cousin; he inevitably looked cool and collected, even amused, while she felt flustered and out of control.

"Hey there," he said with a smile.

"What's up?"

"Griff," said Candace from behind Evie, "come on in. How are you?" She stepped forward and kissed Griff on the cheek, and Evie's hands clenched involuntarily, her fingernails digging into her palms. She forced herself to relax them. So what if Griff and Candace were friends? It was only to be expected. Hell, they'd been tight as teens, too, and they'd both changed their stripes from wild child to upstanding citizen, so she should have expected them to stay close.

But no matter how much she lectured herself, she couldn't stop feeling slightly betrayed by the ease of their friendship as Candace drew him toward the living room.

"Come on in and sit with us for a while. Mama will be so happy to see you. Don't tell me our little drama at the store this afternoon brought you over tonight."

"Candace, it's settled. And it's a family thing. Don't involve Griff."

"Don't be foolish. Griff is practically family himself. At least *he* came to Daddy's funeral."

"Candace!" Patricia's shocked admonition only increased the physical and emotional exhaustion already dogging Evie.

"What? You know perfectly well that it doesn't take all that long to recover from an appendectomy. You and Daddy practically adopted her, and she hasn't been home *once* since he died."

Evie sucked in a breath. She'd made light of the surgery at the time, not wanting her aunt to worry when she had so much on her plate with Harry's sudden death.

It had never occurred to her that Patricia might believe she was simply making excuses because she couldn't be bothered to come to the funeral.

"I'm sorry I didn't make it clearer back then," she said, "but there were complications. As you can see, everything worked out fine, but I spent two weeks in the hospital and even once I got out, getting around was difficult."

As long as she was spilling her guts, she might as well put it all on the table. "Plus, I had huge medical bills. Still do. That's why I can't afford not to work; I have a payment plan with the hospital, but I have to keep up with it."

She glanced at Candace, expecting pity or disgust, but instead found chagrin.

"What do you owe them?" Patricia asked.

"Believe me, you don't want to know. But the payments are manageable. It will just take forever to pay off."

"And you're okay now?"

Okay. Okay had a lot of definitions. Evie pasted a smile on her face and patted her aunt's hand. "I'm fine. As you can see." But when she peeked over at Griff for the first time since beginning her tale, his eyes ripped through the mask. He knew she wasn't telling the whole story and a promise to uncover her secrets lurked somewhere behind his dark gaze. She shifted away and made a production of pouring herself more tea.

"But enough about the past. On to the future. And better things." She raised her teacup in a toast and her aunt and cousin followed suit. Griff nodded, but she noticed his eyes never left her face.

THE CROWD THE NEXT MORNING as Evie and Patricia approached the store had a different temperament than the previous day's.

"I don't like the look of that at all," Patricia said.

Evie didn't, either. People were muttering and tense in an indefinably different way. When they got close, they realized why: overnight, someone had sprayed black paint across the glass, obscuring both the writing and the peephole.

Evie thought for a moment she might be sick. Sure, she'd foreseen a bit of disapproval, even counted on it, but she hadn't expected anything like this. But all the years of performing on stage, sick or healthy, rain or shine, kept her back straight and her legs moving forward even when all she wanted to do was run home and cry.

The crowd stilled when they realized she and Patricia had arrived, but no one said a word. Evie unlocked the door, then locked it behind them.

"I was going to call and warn you," Beth Ann said, "but I figured you would have already left your house. Guess someone didn't care for the new look."

Beth Ann's flip attitude pissed Evie off, but she wasn't up to snapping. Her face hurt and a lump had formed in her throat. Were Candace and Griff right about the promotion being too much for the town? Could she really have been that wrong about how people would react?

Patricia came to her rescue. "That is *not* helping, Beth Ann. We need to present a united front here. I'm sure that paint will come off with a scrub brush. We have one in the storeroom."

"I'll get it," Evie said. "You deal with customers, I can handle the manual labor."

But inside the storeroom, she sank to the floor with her back to the wall and dropped her head into her hands. If she had the money, she'd hire someone to take care of Patricia and go back to Vegas in a split second. She'd never fit into Fairview. Not that she particularly wanted to. When she'd left at eighteen, she'd sworn never again to suppress her own instincts and desires to please someone else, and for the most part she'd stayed true to that oath.

The storeroom door creaked open and she rubbed her face to scrub away the tears that had managed to escape. "I'll be right there, Patricia."

"Not Patricia." Griff settled on the floor beside her.

"Oh." Well, that sounded brilliant. But what else was a girl to say when found crying in what amounted to a closet? She started to stand, but he wouldn't let her. Instead, he slid one long arm around her shoulders and pulled her close against him. She wanted, perhaps more than she'd ever wanted anything in her life, to curl into that warm strength and let the rest of the world fade away, if even for only a few minutes. But weakness wasn't an option, so she held herself away from him.

"I need to get up so I can get that paint off the window. Patricia's probably wondering where I am."

"Who do you think sent me in here? The window will wait."

"No it won't. You don't understand."

"Then explain it to me."

"People were supposed to be a little shocked, but not furious. Furious sucks as a marketing strategy."

"So this didn't turn out quite the way you expected." He shrugged. "You'll come up with something else. Or you could just leave the store alone, let Patricia run it the way she always has."

"No, I can't." The dreaded tears fought their way back up, choking her throat, blocking her nose, pooling in her eyes.

For a long time, Griff didn't say a word. Finally, he asked, "Is the Nook in trouble?"

"I can't talk to you about the business." Patricia would consider even that much a betrayal, but Griff had trapped her with the direct question.

He chewed that one over for a while, stroking her hair until she gave in to the overwhelming temptation and leaned against him. Soon, his strength and solidity were all that supported her. If she let herself, she could sleep right there on the floor, leaning against a man she barely knew, who didn't approve of her lifestyle. And he didn't even know the worst of it.

"Do you know what I do for a living, Griff?"

"You dance. And sing, maybe? I'm not exactly sure what a showgirl does."

"I haven't been a showgirl in almost five years."

"Your aunt never mentioned you changing jobs."

"Because she never asked me explicitly what I had gone into. She didn't want me to tell her. But here's the thing. I'm a saleswoman, just like she is. Only, I don't sell books. Or, I don't sell many books. I sell sex toys."

He choked, and the arm around her shoulders convulsed. "Sex toys?"

"Yeah. I work for Benny Silver of Goody's Goodies. I run his flagship store."

"Oh, cripes."

"So you can see why she might be a bit hesitant to mention my profession to people around here."

"Yeah." He let her go and tucked his arms between his knees, and she immediately missed the warmth of his embrace. She'd expected the reaction, but she already felt bruised by the day's events and his defection hurt more than it should. In response to the pain, she wrapped herself in her stage smile, a cheery persona that reached from tip to toe, and stood up.

"So you see, I'm accustomed to dealing with disapproval. I can handle this, too. It surprised me, is all."

He stood, too, and shifted so he blocked her access to the door. "I don't believe you."

"Excuse me?"

"Unless you've changed a whole lot since you were a kid, I doubt you're used to having people disapprove of you. Of what you sell, sure. But that's different. I remember you as the one who was never in trouble."

"I'm surprised you remember me at all." And wasn't *that* just a bit too revealing? But there was no unsaying it.

Griff merely grinned. "Of course I remember you. You and Izzy starred in every damn dance recital they made us go to at school from the moment you moved in with your aunt. Plus, Candace and I dated for a while, so I got to hear just how well-behaved you were."

"Goody Two-Shoes."

"I wouldn't say that."

"You didn't have to. I heard it from others. Along with 'poor orphan girl.' Which isn't even true. My father left us when my mother was pregnant. He didn't die."

Griff tilted his head to one side and examined her. "What are you up to, Evie?"

"Pardon?"

"You're trying to push me away."

"Don't be absurd."

"I'm not. Why else would you rub your profession in my face?"

"I didn't mean it that way. I was trying to explain why you have to get out of the way and let me go back into the store and get to work. And then you should leave by the back door. You don't need to be seen coming out of here with me. Word may not be out yet about my true profession, but once Benny comes to sign books, everyone will know. And if you think that window ticked them off, just imagine how horrified they'll be to have a woman who sells sex toys in their midst.

"Putting yourself by my side would effectively ruin your political chances. Even if you don't mean anything other than offering a supportive shoulder."

Griff hesitated, and Evie took the opportunity to step around him and out of the storeroom. She hadn't found the scrub brush, but she couldn't stay in that confined space with Griff any longer. He was wrong for her in every way.

GRIFF LET HER GO. HE wanted to reach out, to keep her with him, but she had pegged his situation perfectly. Looking at himself through her eyes left a bad taste in his mouth, however. Surely he could help her and still win his election come November. When he'd seen her sitting there on the floor, her despair had sucker-punched him. In every other encounter, even when he'd deliberately backed her into a wall, self-confidence had radiated from every pore.

He dug around in the back until he came up with a scrub brush and bucket, then stepped into the miniscule bathroom and filled the bucket with soapy water. He stepped out into the store, expecting it to be filled with customers, only to find it empty but for Patricia.

"What's going on?"

She gestured to the brush and bucket. "You might as well put those away. Martin Waters sent his son over to clean off the paint. Evie's outside talking to him."

Griff played pool with Jimmy Waters on occasion. He liked the guy, but he sure didn't care for the idea of him outside helping Evie, gaining her gratitude. He shoved the feeling down deep and concentrated on his job.

"You have any idea who might do something like this, Patricia? Anyone seem particularly put out yesterday?"

"No. They were more curious and a bit shocked and titillated than anything else."

Rachel Jennings stepped inside. "Hey, boss. Hey, Miz Stewart."

"Didn't you work last night, Rachel?"

"Yeah. I wanted to catch up with you and tell you. I came by here when I first got on shift at midnight because, of course, I'd heard about the famous display and wanted to see it before I started patrol. I cruised back down Main a couple more times overnight, once around two and once maybe an hour later. Both times, the window was clean. So it must have happened after three."

"Okay."

The door opened and Evie stepped in. Her face glowed, all signs of sadness gone. "Officer Jennings! I didn't notice you arrive. How nice to see you again."

"Call me Rachel. I'm off duty as of twenty minutes ago."

"Oh! Then can I sell you a book?"

"No," the woman hesitated, then slanted a look at Griff. "But I wanted to ask you about the display?"

Evie stiffened slightly and Griff had to hold himself back from stepping between her and the petite Rachel, who could not possibly mean her any harm.

"What can I tell you about it?" Evie asked, her voice completely steady.

"Well, um…" Rachel looked over at Griff and then leaned in to whisper something into Evie's ear. For a moment, Evie looked shocked, but then she grinned and her smile sent every nerve in Griff's body into high alert.

"I hadn't really considered doing that," she said to Rachel. "But if you have, um, interested parties, I have no objection. Can I get in touch with you in a day or two?"

"Absolutely." Rachel wrote her name and number on a piece of paper from her notebook and handed it to Evie. "Can't wait!"

"I didn't realize you'd met Rachel Jennings," Patricia said.

"She actually pulled me over the night I got to town. I was tired and not driving carefully enough."

"And on the basis of that you've become friends?"

"Not exactly. I know it sounded like that, but she was actually asking me to help host a party at her place. Can we talk about this later?"

Griff had a sneaking suspicion he knew what kind of party his deputy had in mind. He felt his skin turning red.

"If there's nothing more you can think of, Patricia,

I'll take off. You seem to have the problem under control, but I'll be back later with paperwork for you so you don't have to come down to the station."

Outside, he stopped to talk to Jimmy Waters.

"Boy, was dad pissed off when he saw the mess," the younger man said. "He told me he respects both Patricia and her niece and he couldn't believe some intolerant asshat would vandalize Patricia's property like that. He sent me over straightaway. Gotta say, I agree with him."

"Yeah, me, too. If you need any help cleaning up, give me a holler."

"Nah. I'm almost done. They used regular spray paint, so it's coming right off. They must have had it sitting around in their garage, though, 'cause we haven't sold any in weeks."

"That'd be far too easy," Griff sighed.

"She sure is pretty."

No need to ask who Jimmy meant. "Yeah, she is. You ask her out?"

"Hell, no. She's a showgirl and I'm a twenty-seven-year-old guy who works in his father's hardware store. One day, I'll inherit that shop and move from being a clerk or partner to a small business owner. Hardly Mr. Right for a girl like her."

"She's not a showgirl anymore. She's a shopkeeper in Vegas. Not so different from you." Maybe if Evie hooked up with Jimmy, Griff could put her out of his mind.

"Really? Maybe I'll give it a shot, then."

"You do that." Griff patted Jimmy on the shoulder and left before he took back all the well-intentioned advice and told the boy to stay the hell away from Evie.

"I'M REALLY HAPPY AT HOW many people came by when I was outside to show their support," Evie told Patricia once both Rachel and Griff had left. "And how lovely of Martin Waters to send Jimmy over to clean up.

He wouldn't even let me help."

"Perhaps we should invite them to dinner as a thank-you," Patricia said.

"Maybe. But just dinner, Patricia. No match-making. I'm only here for a little while."

"Of course! That's all I meant."

"Besides, imagine how they'll react when they find out what I've really been doing in Vegas for the past few years. You never told people I quit dancing."

Patricia shrugged. "I always assumed you'd go back to it. You loved it so much."

"My mother loved it. And I loved her. I took all those classes so I could dance with her. When I moved here, the classes, I guess a shrink would say they gave me a sense of continuity. And success. So, yeah, I enjoyed them. But I never intended to spend the rest of my life doing two shows a day."

"You were going to be an actress. I remember that from your first letter. You were just stopping in Vegas to make enough money dancing so you could move to California and find your way into the movies."

"Yeah, like every other halfway cute, blonde, eighteen-year-old in the world."

"That's exactly what your uncle Harry said when he read your letter. But you figured it out yourself. You always were a smart girl. Which is why I cannot understand how you ended up in the position you're in now."

"I could say the same to you."

"I have a savings cushion I can live on for some time if I am careful. And I'm not destroying my life selling…you know."

"Sex toys, Patricia. I know, it's hard to say. But in ten days, when Benny comes in to give his seminar, he's going to say that and more. What I sell doesn't hurt anyone."

"But you already anticipate decent people like Martin and Jimmy being offended when they find out about your true profession. So deep inside you know it's wrong."

"That's not it at all. I don't want to lead Jimmy on, or have you lead him on, and then find out he can't live with the real me."

"And Griff?"

"What about him?"

"You don't want to lead him on, either?"

"No, I don't. Which is why I told him up front about my job. It would be deadly for his political ambitions."

"Really. You told him already." Patricia leaned her chin into her hand on the counter and examined her niece. "I heard him ask you out the other day. I'm old, but I'm not deaf."

"Then you also heard me turn him down. As I said, I love working for Benny, but I'm not under any illusions about what it would mean for Griff's career to be linked to me once the truth is out."

"Mmm-hmm." But Patricia was smiling.

"Patricia, don't go there. I mean it."

"Of course not, dear."

CHAPTER 4

FRIDAY AFTERNOON, AS SHE'D PROMISED, Evie tore down the craft paper in the window so passers-by could easily see the contents. She'd spent the last couple of days stocking the new romances as they came in, covers frequently faced out so people could get a sense of the different stock. Patricia had taken one of the historicals home herself and come back the next day to place an order for all the woman's work. Celia had rated the books "sexy but not sleazy," and Evie couldn't have been more pleased with her aunt's reaction.

Regular customers had noticed the change, too. Patricia said sales had gone up. Not much, but every little bit helped Evie's cause.

Just before closing, she sold one copy of Kinky Business to a man in town for the day who said he wished he could be there for the seminar.

"Benny Silver's a genius," he said. "My wife hosts Goody's parties and I can't believe the income she's bringing in with it. I hope you get a big crowd."

"Me, too," Evie agreed, waving to him as he left.

"Goody's parties. Is that what Rachel Jennings meant?" Patricia's voice could have frozen fire.

"Yes. She saw the box in the back of the car when she pulled me over."

"The box your cousin and I assumed to be full of your clothes and personal items?"

"Well, they are personal items."

"Evangeline Lorraine Bell! Don't you smart-mouth me!"

"No, ma'am. Benny gave me the box when I was leaving. He thought I might need to make some money. He was right. I called Rachel last night, as a matter of fact, and I'm going to go over to her place Sunday evening. I planned to talk to you about it over dinner tonight."

"By talk to me, I assume you mean inform me. You certainly didn't plan to ask my opinion."

"No, I didn't. Goody's Goodies is a huge business. The parties are popular everywhere, for women of all ages and in all income brackets. They're today's Tupperware parties."

"That's repulsive."

"I'm sure a number of people think so. But one of the reasons the parties are so successful is that people who feel that way don't have to have the product on display in a store in their neighborhood. Only people who are interested show up at the parties."

"And did you discuss this aspect of your life with Griff?"

Way to twist the knife, Patricia. "No. But, then, I don't usually host parties. Benny pays me very well to manage his store. It never occurred to me I'd really move into the home party realm coming back to Fairview."

"Do you imagine he'll approve?"

"You're missing the point. I don't—won't—live my life begging for someone else's approval."

"Well. I guess there's nothing more to be said." Patricia sniffed.

"No, there isn't." Their usual closing routine was fraught with tension, and Patricia barely spoke at all over dinner. Instead of sitting with Patricia after the dishes were done, Evie went straight up to her own apartment.

Her head pounded, and she made herself a cup of tea. She still hadn't had time to purchase either a coffee pot or a hand shower. She was getting used to walking around with her hair in a damp knot, but when winter arrived for real she'd need to buy a hair dryer, too.

It seemed only moments after she fell asleep that the phone rang. Oh, how she wanted to ignore it. But she couldn't. What if Patricia needed her? Who else would call at…four in the morning?

"Yes?"

"Evie?" Griff. Why did it have to be Griff?

"What can I do for you, Griff?"

"I'm afraid I need you to come down to the store."

"Not again."

"Yeah."

"Did you call Patricia?"

"No. I didn't see any need to wake her when it's so hard for her to get around."

"Okay. Let me throw on some clothes and I'll be right there."

Exhaustion dragged at Evie, but she couldn't blame that alone for the time it took her to get to the Nook. Reluctance held her back, too. What had they done this time?

She pulled into a parking spot just behind one of the Sheriff's Department cruisers and immediately Griff jogged up. He wasn't dressed for work—he looked as if he, too, had rolled out of bed to get there. Rachel Jennings, however, wore the uniform she'd worn the night Evie had arrived in Fairview. Obviously, she'd been the one to discover the problem.

"Sorry about this, Evie," Griff said. He put an arm around her shoulders and guided her toward the shop.

At first glance, things didn't look nearly as bad as Wednesday night's painting. Tonight's vandal had merely put up a large piece of poster board on the window. In the dark, the words on it were hard to ascertain, but then, one arm still firmly hanging on to Evie, Griff played his flashlight over the lettering.

SMUT SOLD BY A SLUT.

Evie began to shake. "They're business books," she said, her voice a mere squeak. "Can't people read?"

Griff snapped off his flashlight, shoved it in his back pocket, and hauled Evie into a tight embrace. She tried to fight—if the damnable sign showed nothing else, it proved how poisonous she'd be to his ambitions—but he refused to let go.

"I'm sorry as hell you had to see this, but I wanted you clear on what it looked like in place so you could see what we were dealing with." As he had before, he let one hand wander to her crown to stroke her hair. She hadn't even bothered putting it up, and it fell in a mass of tangles halfway down her back.

"Rachel, take that thing down and see whether we can get any prints off of it. Not that I have much hope. I figure the person who did this knew we'd have more patrols out, so rather than taking the time to spray paint the window again, she made the sign in advance."

"You think a woman did this?" Evie couldn't imagine such a thing.

"Yeah, I do. Men don't tend to use either smut or slut in a pejorative way. Also, this has always been more a women's hangout than a men's. It's much more likely that your window, or your job, offended a woman than a man."

"Oh, God," said Rachel. "I hope it wasn't me telling a couple of my friends about the Goodies you have and the possibility of a party that caused this."

"You didn't cause anything," Evie said. "I should never have come back."

"Bullshit!" Griff drew a deep breath, let it out. "Go on, Rachel. Evie and I have some talking to do."

"On my way." Rachel pulled on a pair of purple gloves, then carefully removed the sign and stowed it in the back of her car before leaving.

Griff maneuvered Evie to the front stoop of the Nook, then sat her on the step. He took the spot next to her, and captured her hands in his, but didn't speak.

Eventually, he eased one arm back around her and urged her into him.

"You said we needed to talk," she said at last, when her body had stopped shaking from shock.

"I did." His voice was hoarse, and she lifted her head from his shoulder to look at him. "And we do. But I find, just at the moment, that I'm not particularly ready to talk."

"Why not?"

"Because," his hand came up to cradle her cheek, "I'd much rather do this." His head came down and his lips swept gently over hers. Her whole body stilled, waiting for what might come next. He tilted his head and his mouth touched hers again, just a passing brush, the friction sparking through her whole body. When he came back a third time, she was ready. She pressed upwards, increasing the contact. His mouth opened over hers and the tip of his tongue traced her lips until she opened for him. He tasted of coffee and heat, and the rough texture of his tongue sliding against hers made her squirm. She whimpered and he shifted suddenly, moving so quickly she had no clue what he was about until she found herself seated across his lap.

She should stop this. But, oh, she didn't want to. She slid her arms around his neck and pressed closer. She could feel the strength of his erection pressing against her bottom through both his jeans and her own. Her own panties had gone damp. Just from a kiss. She never reacted that strongly.

She pulled away. "I can't do this." She struggled for breath. "You can't. We can't."

"I know." His breathing came as raggedly as her own, but he didn't let her go. Instead, he held her in place and dropped his forehead to rest against hers. "I'm sorry. I always seem to be apologizing to you. But, damn, I've wanted to do that from the moment you opened the door Sunday morning."

She felt a flush rise up her neck and gave thanks for

the darkness. "Well, as I'm sure you could tell, the feeling was mutual. But it can't go on. Not if you hope to get elected."

"I suppose not. Although—"

She didn't wait for him to finish the thought, standing before the second syllable fully left his mouth. "Thanks for calling. I'll see you later."

"Evie, please."

"Please what? Please don't be offended that you were about to suggest maybe we could just have sex once in a while and you could otherwise pretend we barely knew each other?"

"That's not what I was going to say."

"No?" Hands on hips, she faced him down. "What, then?"

"I just meant maybe we could, I don't know, take things very slowly? Let people get used to you?"

"Let people get used to me. Give me a break. They won't get used to me and you know it. You just wanted a little free nooky before you said 'sayonara, guess this won't work out.'"

"No."

"No, you don't want nooky?" Her eyes dropped to his crotch.

"Of course I do. For crying out loud, Evie, you're a beautiful woman. What guy in his right mind wouldn't want to have sex with you? But that's not what I was suggesting. That's not who I am."

"Of course not" The younger Griffin would have had her in bed before she'd blinked, but not this one. And why did that piss her off? "You're far too upstanding a citizen to plan something so sordid."

"Evie, talk to me."

"No, thanks." She climbed into her car and drove off.

EVIE CRAWLED BACK INTO BED when she got home, but she couldn't force herself to sleep. Slut. People thought it, of course. Plenty of people believed showgirl was just a euphemism for stripper, or even prostitute, but no one actually said it to her. Had she brought shame on Patricia? She'd have to tell her aunt about the sign in the morning.

And what to do about Griff? Although, after tonight, it probably wouldn't be an issue. Most men wouldn't take kindly to being left at the starting gate. Plus, she'd no doubt confused him. She'd confused herself, after all. But she hated the idea that he thought so little of her as to believe she'd settle for being hidden away. She'd done that once, with Kenny, the first man she'd dated in Vegas, without even realizing it. He'd told her he didn't want to share her, didn't want to waste the little time they had together by going out with friends. What he'd meant was he didn't want his wife finding out about her.

So why did the knowledge that Griff would never behave in such a way, that he would reject her outright rather than have a back-alley relationship, piss her off? Maybe because coming in second to his career tasted too much like coming in second to another woman? Or maybe just because rejection stank, no matter the reason.

A couple of hours of fitful sleep did little to improve her mood. Patricia had given Evie a key to the main house, so she went over early in the morning to prepare their standard breakfast. Patricia, she'd learned, brought home the leftover muffins and scones from the café and froze them. When the freezer filled up, she created baskets for the senior center or the nurses at the hospital.

Evie selected blueberry muffins for the morning, and popped them into the microwave to defrost. She was filling the kettle for tea—she'd get the big cup of coffee she desperately needed when they made it to the store— when she heard Patricia maneuvering herself down the stairs. The first day, she'd tried to help her aunt get around in the house, but Patricia had snapped at her.

Until Patricia entered the kitchen, Evie had forgotten the previous day's argument. One look at her pinched lips and sour countenance, however, brought it all back. Evie ignored the waves of tense disapproval flooding the room and placed the muffins on a plate in the center of the table.

"Griff called last night," she said, rather than attempting small talk. "We had another incident at the store."

Patricia gasped. "What happened?"

"Nothing serious. Someone duct-taped a sign to our window." Evie swallowed hard, reluctant to admit what the sign had said. When she did, Patricia gasped again.

"Well, I never."

No, she probably never had. "Griff thought a woman probably did it. Possibly a regular customer who's offended by Benny's background or the book titles."

"One of my customers? I can't believe any of them would sink to that level. Besides, they're my friends, and I can't imagine one of my friends calling my niece a slut."

Evie suppressed a sigh. The kettle whistled, and she poured boiling water over the teabags in the large, glass teapot to steep. Placing the teapot next to the plate of muffins, she sat down and faced her aunt.

"I don't know what to do."

"We go on."

"But the vandalism...."

"Once in a while, Evangeline, you'll run across someone you simply cannot please. It's best to move along and let them sort themselves out. The person who painted my window is a criminal, and we cannot worry about the opinions of criminals."

Of course not. How clearly Patricia saw her life. If only Evie herself could make such distinctions.

EVIE REMAINED TENSE ALL DAY, waiting for some new unpleasantness, but nothing happened. People came in. They bought coffee, they bought books. Some even asked about Benny, whether he was the same man they'd seen on television. But Evie couldn't relax, and she couldn't sleep that night, either.

The next day, she got up and put on the same dress she'd worn the previous Sunday. It was the only dress she'd brought with her. Shadows lay beneath her eyes and she cursed her foolishness in not making time to buy a coffee maker. She hated feeling hazy and hungover without even having had the pleasure of drinking the night before. She'd just have to chug a gallon of tea before they left. Nothing like snoring in church to really piss people off.

And she wouldn't have time to pick up a machine today, either. She had to lug the boxes up from the garage and sort through the stuff Benny had sent home with her. She had no idea what he'd included, though it wasn't beyond him to have given her one of every single item in inventory.

Which also meant she wouldn't have time to nap, and she wouldn't get to bed early. Dammit.

She slapped on makeup, attempting to at least hide the worst of the damage, and then removed it when the cakey foundation only served to highlight the bags. *Take your time. You know how to do this.* She reapplied it with a lighter hand, then used eyeliner, mascara and shadow to draw attention to her eyes themselves rather than the bruises beneath them. Better. Now her appearance didn't give away the constant worry.

At the main house, Patricia already had the tea on, and three cranberry scones in the center of the table. Perfect. Evie had hoped her own presence would keep Griff from taking them to church, but clearly Patricia still expected him to accompany them. Indeed, she'd no sooner noted the table settings than the doorbell rang. With only the briefest of hesitations, Evie went to answer it.

"Good morning." She smiled through gritted teeth. Naturally, Griff's late nights hadn't left marks on him.

No, he looked as appealing as always. And he'd look even better, she knew from the week before, when they got to the church and he put on his dress uniform jacket.

But he didn't return her smile. And he didn't let her turn her back on him to escape into the kitchen.

"Stay," he said, laying a hand on her shoulder when she started to move away from him. "Please. I owe you an apology."

"You do?" Why was her voice so raspy? She swallowed.

"I do." He laid a hand along her cheek. "I took advantage the other night. The past few days have been hard on you, and I knew it. I shouldn't have kissed you."

"And the other?"

"Other?"

"I don't need an apology for the kiss. To ask for one would be disingenuous. You know perfectly well I wanted it as much as you did."

"Oh, I doubt that." He winked and she almost lost her train of thought.

"Seriously, Griff. I'm talking about what you said. Or would have said if I hadn't stopped you. And don't give me that nonsense about taking it slow so people could get to know me."

He nodded slowly. "You're right. I wasn't being precisely honest about my intentions. Fact is, I don't give a flip whether anyone else gets to know you. *I* want to get to know you."

"Biblically."

He laughed, and she found herself reluctantly joining in.

"Yeah, that, too. But in all ways."

"Evie! Is that Griffin?" Patricia called from the kitchen.

"Oops. Time to go." Evie led him in, avoiding dangerous waters. Over breakfast, Patricia and Griffin made small talk while Evie did her best not to fall asleep in her tea.

As usual, Candace and her family awaited them at church. This week, however, Griff slid into the pew next to Evie. Then he leaned over and tickled Billy, who sat on her other side. His shoulder slid across her breast as he did so and she shivered. It could have been an accident. Possibly.

Reverend Masters, Evie discovered once the service began, had been listening to town gossip. Or perhaps he had peered into the Nook's window late one night when none of his parishioners would see him. Either way, he'd chosen to rant about sins of the flesh, a subject Evie found no more appealing than the previous week's.

"The Devil will try to draw you in," he admonished from the pulpit. "He will seduce and tempt you, using your carnal weakness to overcome your better instincts. Do not give in! Faith is a muscle that must be exercised!"

At first, Evie's face burned with anger and humiliation as she felt the sidelong glances of the other members of the congregation. But the longer the sermon dragged on, the more the minister's words began to blend together. She felt herself dozing off. Twice, she caught herself as her chin sank toward her chest and twice she forced her eyes open and her spine straight. The third time, darkness claimed her until she felt a sharp pinch on her butt.

Startled, she sat up and whipped her head around to scowl at Griff. He, however, faced forward, ignoring her, his expression perfectly serious. Almost. A tiny twitch at the corner of his lips gave away his amusement. A forbidden giggle rose in her throat. She so did not need to burst into laughter in the middle of the minister's chastisement. But the harder she tried to suppress the laughter, the stronger the urge became.

On the verge of losing control entirely, she faked a violent coughing fit, excused herself, and practically ran down the side aisle and out of the building. In the bright fall sunlight, she let the laughter escape. Soon, she was leaning against the stair rail, panting for breath. She didn't even hear the squeak of the door as it opened behind her.

"I doubt that's the reaction the good Reverend intended," Griff intoned solemnly.

Evie hiccupped. Oh, man, she always got the hiccups when she laughed too hard. Griff grinned.

"This isn't about the sermon and you know it. You pinched my ass. In church!" She hiccupped again and Griff snickered.

"You were falling asleep. And after Masters had obviously worked so hard to write something specifically for you."

Evie hiccupped again and they both laughed. And laughed. Until Griff caught his breath and said, "We need to stop. Can't have everyone coming out here and finding us like this."

Evie sobered immediately. No, naturally Griff wouldn't want to be caught enjoying her company. Even her hiccups disappeared.

"You're right, of course."

Griff captured her chin between his thumb and forefinger and tilted her face to his. "Now what?"

"Nothing!"

"Don't give me that, Evie."

"Okay, then I was wondering whether you'd help me carry a couple of boxes up to my apartment when we got back, or whether that would endanger your reputation." *Oops. Little too bitter there.*

Griff seemed about to argue, but the church doors opened and he stepped away. His inquisitive eyes shuttered. "Of course. It would be my pleasure."

And hers. Benny must have included cases of batteries in at least one of the boxes, because Evie'd had the very devil of a time unloading them and hauling them to the corner of the garage. Perhaps he'd even stick around and watch while she sorted through whatever Benny had sent and decided what to take to Rachel's party. She wouldn't mind seeing him half as discomfited as she always ended up in his presence.

"Are you feeling all right?" Patricia asked as she joined them.

"I'm fine," Evie assured her. "Just got something caught in my throat." Like a laugh. "Shall we hit the road?" God forbid Patricia should insist upon introducing her to the minister.

But her aunt did not fret over Evie's desire to leave. She handed Griff one of her crutches and he took her arm and assisted her through the church lot to the SUV. Out of the corner of her eye, Evie saw Candace and Beth Ann talking. Both frowned, and their displeasure floated across the parking lot like the smell of burnt barbeque at a summer fair. But the display window was down and sales were up, so Evie refused to let their condemnation bother her.

At the house they settled Patricia in and Griff dutifully followed Evie out to the garage.

"Jesus," he said, hefting one of the boxes up onto his shoulder. "What the hell is in these things?"

"I have no idea. Knowing Benny, it's a Russian Assortment."

"A Russian Assortment?"

"Yeah. Someofich. I'll have to lay it all out and put batteries in whatever needs them before Rachel's party tonight."

"I didn't realize that was so soon." Griff laid the first box on the floor next to Evie's bed.

"She has tonight off."

"Ah, right." He cracked his neck. "I'll be right back with the other one."

Evie watched him as he headed back down the stairs, muscular butt and thighs visible even in his dress slacks. She should keep her eyes to herself when all too soon she'd be unpacking provocative items that could only ramp up her already over-active and under-served sex drive.

Far too soon for her peace of mind, Griff was back, the second box in his arms. He set it down next to the first, then pulled a small knife from his pocket and flipped it open. "Go on, crack them. Let's see Goody's Goodies."

"Are you daring me, Griff Barstow?"

"If that's what it takes, sure."

Evie shook her head, took his knife and slit the packing tape on the first box. She plopped down cross-legged on the floor and plucked out the first item—the ever-popular edible underwear for women, in chocolate—and passed them over to Griff.

"Well, hell. Even I know about these." He sat next to her and her skin tingled at the memory of his arm brushing her breast earlier.

"But would you wear them?" She handed him the male version.

"Depends on who asked me." His silver gaze had deepened to almost black and heat rose along her cheekbones. "Are you certain you sell this stuff? You blush awfully easily."

"No, I don't."

His mouth twisted into a mocking half-smile. "Could have fooled me."

"Shut your trap, Barstow, or you'll have to leave. I have work to do!"

"Yes, Ma'am."

Next, she unearthed a series of lotions, scrubs, and massage oils. None impressed Griff until she pulled out Friction's Friend.

"Hold out your hand," she ordered. When he did, she poured a small amount on the back, sternly warning herself not to linger over the knots and veins, the few, coarse hairs setting off the intriguing smoothness of his skin.

"Rub it in," she said, her voice slightly husky. When he had, she told him to blow on it.

"Why am I the only one working here?" he asked. He

held out his hand. "You do it."

Her eyes never leaving his, Evie leaned over, put her mouth close to his skin, pursed her lips, and exhaled.

GRIFF THOUGHT HE MIGHT JUMP out of his skin when Evie leaned over his hand. The unabashedly sensual position, with her head bent as if in supplication, sent his mind spinning in directions he'd been suppressing for years. And then her breath washed over him and every thought went out of his head. The skin where he'd rubbed the lotion heated, sending arrows of fire through every nerve straight down to his cock.

He snatched his hand away and shot to his feet. "What *is* that stuff?" He scrubbed the back of his hand on his pants, hoping to remove the cream, but to his chagrin it only heated more.

Evie's face lit with humor as she looked up at him. "Friction's Friend, remember? The more you rub, the hotter it will get. Same with blowing on it. Don't worry, the effect doesn't last long."

And what about the raging hard-on he'd acquired? How long would that last? At least his dress slacks were loose enough to hide the effect Evie and her toys had had on him. Or so he hoped.

"Do people really buy that?"

"All the time." Evie had returned her attention to the box and was pulling out items and laying them on the bed. "It's one of our most popular items."

"But why? It seems so unnecessary." All he had to do was look at a woman and he knew whether he wanted her. If he didn't, no amount of cream would help. If he did, why bother with extra incentives?

"Sex isn't about necessity. Unless you really believe it's only for having babies. Here's the thing: necessity is a roof over your head and enough calories to stave off starvation. But for myself, I prefer my own space with a nice kitchen and a soaking tub, and dinner at a white tablecloth restaurant once in a while. Completely unnecessary, as you say, but it's what I like."

"And these?" He gestured to the items on the bed. "These are soaking tubs and good restaurants? You use them?"

"Not all. But, sure, I've tried out a lot of them. Quite aside from the fact that testing products makes me a better salesperson, I enjoy them."

She'd emptied the first box and a positively alarming array of gadgets and gizmos in wild neon colors lay on the bed. How could a mere man be expected to live up to an oversized vibrator with, if he was not mistaken, a tiny, turtle-shaped clitoral stimulator?

"Knife, please?" Evie held out her hand and he dragged his attention from the glimpse inside a woman's world he'd never imagined to pass her the pocketknife. She sliced into the second box and handed it back. He carefully avoided any contact. The last thing he needed was to feel her skin against his at the moment.

The first thing she withdrew, to his relief, was a sheaf of papers. He wasn't sure he could take much more of Evie demonstrating her wares on him.

"Oh, excellent. Order forms and price lists. I was afraid I'd have to write everything out by hand. Trust Benny to know the market better than I do, even in my own home-town."

"What do you mean?"

"He's a bit of a control freak." The fondness in her tone scraped his nerves. "He can enter a zip code into his database and find not only every store in the area that carries Goodies merchandise, but also whether anyone in the neighborhood is doing home parties. He obviously checked and didn't find anyone around here."

Evie set the papers aside and reached back into the box. This time, she held up a pair of pink, fuzzy handcuffs.

"Want to take these on patrol with you, Sheriff?"

"Uh...not particularly." He grinned, though, imagining the faces of some of his deputies if he showed up with those hooked to his duty belt. The next item wiped the smile off his face. Black and almost evil-looking, it was circle with small rubber spikes all around and one larger protrusion so that it looked a bit like the symbol for Mars. At the end of the prong, however, a perpendicular spike gave the impression that someone had twisted the arrowhead of the symbol to stand straight up.

"*What* is *that*?"

Again, Evie's fair cheeks reddened. The contradiction between the woman who could passionately defend the use of creams and toys and the one who blushed attempting to explain the actual use of such products entranced him.

"Uh, that's for men. I mean, it's nice for women, too, if the guy wears it, but it's more designed to increase his pleasure than hers."

"Please tell me this doesn't sell."

She'd regained her composure. And her starch. "Everything sells. But no, that's not a top ten item."

"Thank God for small favors."

She handed him a tube of something else. "This is, though."

He practically choked as he read the name aloud. "Staze-Long?"

"Yep! Between that and the numerous offers I get in my email every day, I can only assume many men in this country have a premature ejaculation problem."

"I don't think I can take this."

She dropped her head and glanced up at him through the screen of her thick lashes. "I didn't say you could. I need it."

He dropped the tube and rubbed his hand against his leg. "That's not what I meant and you know it."

"Yeah, but you're so easy to tease. Who'd have believed that under the bad boy of Fairview High lay a closet prude? Your reputation has suffered here today,

Barstow."

"Is that a dare, Bell?"

She cocked her head. "It may be. I'll think about it."

His heart pumped harder and he felt more alive than he had since the day he'd moved home to Fairview. *You've always been addicted to danger, Bub, and it's never done you a lick of good. Stay the hell away.* But he had a sinking feeling he wouldn't be able to take his own advice.

CHAPTER 5

B Y THE TIME GRIFF LEFT her apartment, every last nerve in Evie's body was stretched tight and scraped raw. She'd maintained a cheerful, flirtatious front, but underneath she'd practically been drooling. And she didn't understand why. Handsome men lay thick on the ground in Vegas. Wealthy, well-dressed, many of them had offered her a night on the town...or more. None of them set her back the way Griff Barstow did.

She packed the items she needed for the party into her rolling suitcase and hauled it down the stairs to the garage. After hefting it into the back of her car, she checked her watch. No time for a supermarket run, so yet another day without a coffee maker. *Piss poor planning, Evie.* But she stretched her arms over her head and went to check on Patricia to be certain she didn't need anything before she left for Rachel's.

Patricia shooed her out, so Evie got directions off her computer and made her way across town to Rachel's through the gloaming. The year was almost over, dusk coming early, and Evie opened her windows to the cooling evening air. Nostalgia swamped her. A kind of homesickness that had nothing to do with location. In Vegas, for practical reasons, she lived in a massive apartment complex just off the Strip. Even families there rented, fortunes all too often dependent on the tourist-driven economy.

And once outside the urban sprawl, past the strip malls and strip clubs, the desert took hold. Ranch houses fought to stay cool in summer without the shade of the great oaks and weepers of the southeast. No sweetly-scented clinging vines softened their angular lines. Brush grew along the side of the highway and lawns could not survive, let alone thrive.

In Fairview, by contrast, crabgrass earned disapproving looks from neighbors and dandelions might even inspire a Sunday sermon on caring for that which was yours. In the semi-darkness, alone in the car with only the Allman Brothers playing on the radio for company, Evie could almost consider moving back. Not to Fairview, of course, but maybe to Memphis. Or possibly she could give Atlanta a shot. Two of the girls in her apartment complex came from there and talked about the city as if it were heaven on earth.

She pulled up in front of Rachel Jennings' small, blue-siding-covered cottage. Two garden gnomes watched her make her way up the path, her suitcase rumbling and bumping along behind her on the uneven pavement.

"Up for a party, little men?" she asked as she passed them. They didn't speak, but she imagined them gossiping about the goings-on in the house as the evening progressed. Or perhaps gnomes didn't concern themselves with the activities of humans. Perhaps they frolicked in extreme ways, abandoning their lawns and hotel commercials when no one could see. She was grinning at the idea of gnomes doing the Lambada when Rachel answered the door.

"Hiya, Evie, come on in. Can I take the bag?"

"No, no. It has wheels." She tugged the suitcase inside. To her left a small group of women stood around a table in a dining room, munching on cheese and crackers and drinking wine. To her right, a living room held a well-worn couch, a couple of chairs, and a coffee table.

"Can I put my stuff out in there?" She asked, gesturing to the living room.

"Sure! Then come on in and have a drink and let me introduce you to everyone."

Benny had sent along a letter describing the usual progress of a party, starting with the oils and lotions and then moving along to the toys. *Take a break in between. Let everyone adjust and stretch their legs,* he'd advised. *Don't put the toys out until you—and they—are ready to talk about them.* He'd also included a handbook of games many consultants played at parties, but Evie didn't see herself as the game director type. She set out the items she'd shown Griff, along with several other types of creams she thought the women might enjoy, then went to meet the others.

There were five women, not including Rachel, and only two of them looked familiar. Either the others were new to town in the years since Evie had left, or they'd changed enough that she no longer recognized them. Three had blond hair, though at least one had gotten hers at the salon.

Rachel introduced the first as Jenna, a stay-at-home mother of three who'd agreed to come to the party because she was desperate for adult companionship.

"I'll be the one who's bright red through your whole presentation," she said. "But if I have enough wine, I can probably handle it."

Evie laughed, liking her immediately.

The second woman she met was Gabby, the brunette. As it turned out, she'd gone to school with Evie, though she'd been two years younger. "I was so envious of you," she said, gesturing to her own short, round body. "You were always so glamorous. And then you went off and became a showgirl. I always imagined that was like being a movie star."

"Not hardly," Evie replied. "I wanted to be a movie star, actually. That was my grand plan when I left. But I never got out of Vegas."

The third and fourth women, Hazel and Bonnie, looked and sounded so much alike they might as well have been sisters. Both had blonde hair, slender figures, and wore tidy but not elegant clothing. Neither made any overt act of friendship, and both examined Evie as if she were some sort of oddity.

Rachel started to introduce Evie to the last woman, a tall, sepia-skinned African-American woman, but at the last minute Evie realized they'd already met.

"You're Juliette Robbins. You were in Candace's class in high school." She shook her head. "My goodness, you've really changed."

"I was rather large in those days." She gave a self-deprecating laugh. "My mother believed food was the answer to all life's problems, and until I moved out I never met a fat, sweet, or starch I didn't like."

The kids in school had been incredibly cruel to her about it, too, as Evie recalled. They waddled down the hallway after her, huffing and puffing as if just walking were a tremendous effort. And the truth was, Juliette hadn't been obese, not the way some kids were, she'd just been too fat for their school. Too fat and too dark. But it wasn't acceptable to pick on her for her skin color, so they'd laid into her about her weight instead.

Evie had watched, as she watched everything, and done nothing about it. Already an outsider because of her father's desertion and her mother's death, she couldn't afford to draw attention to herself.

"You're feeling guilty," Juliette said. "Stop right now. You didn't do a single thing. You had your own cross to bear. That's life in high school."

"I suppose. I doubt I'd be so forgiving, though."

"Oh, girl, I don't forgive and I don't forget. But I'm completely up front about my feelings. So if I say you're not among the unforgiven, you're not."

"Of course, *I* won't forgive you if you don't drink some wine and eat some of these hors d'oeuvres," Rachel put in. "I don't want to be left with all of it at the end of the night!"

"I can't drink. I just can't. I'll pass out. But I'm more than happy to help you with the food."

"Good deal. Can I get you a diet soda or something?"

"That would be fantastic."

Rachel headed into the kitchen and Evie made herself a plate of crackers, cheese, veggies, and ranch dip. A large tin of brownies, clearly homemade, rested on the end of the table, but she told herself to eat the real food first and go back for that later. She'd gotten lazy about her weight since she stopped dancing, and the pounds were slowly creeping on. She didn't mind terribly, but it wouldn't do to let the situation get out of control since she couldn't afford a new wardrobe.

After about half an hour of small talk and eating, she suggested they get started with the presentation. Rachel dragged a couple of the dining room chairs into the living room and all the women sat down and stared expectantly at her.

"I'm going to start with lotions, oils, and the like," she said. "Some are edible, some are not. Things that are edible will go on your right hand, things that are not edible will go on your left. That way you can remember which side is all *right* to taste. Got it?"

The women nodded. Bonnie's expression had shifted from curiosity to mild disgust. Too bad for her. If she didn't loosen up, she wouldn't have near the fun the other women would. Hazel, on the other hand, leaned forward with an earnest, almost studious expression.

She started with the most inoffensive of items— scented massage oils and candles for setting the mood.

"If I had someone to set a mood for, I wouldn't be looking to buy a battery-operated boyfriend," quipped Rachel.

"Oh, yes, you would," Jenna assured her. "Doug is glued to the television during the summer for baseball season and then again all fall for football. He's committed to being home for dinner as a family, but after that, he's parked on the couch with a glass of bourbon or several. I think he gave up on romance after Charlie was born."

"Charlie's their third," Rachel explained.

"Yeah. I told him sex doesn't have to mean children, but I'm not sure he believes me."

Evie laughed. "Well, we have something for you, too." She plucked a small vial off the table. "I am going to put this on everyone's left wrist. Smell it when I first put it on. Periodically, as the night goes on, I'll ask you to sniff again and you'll see how it changes."

She went around the room dabbing the liquid on each woman. "This is our pheromone essence. Pheromones are the animal scents that attract a mate. Time to remind him that you're more than a mom."

When she'd made it around the loose semi-circle the women had formed, she instructed them to test their neighbor's wrist and see how the scent differed from person to person.

"Ooooh, I want some of this," Jenna said. "I mean, even if it doesn't work, I like the way it smells on me. And it's like having someone make perfume for you alone."

"It is. And you've reminded me I forgot to pass out these order sheets so you can mark things you're interested in and see how much everything costs." She dug through the bag and found the order sheets and pens.

"Sorry about that. Home parties aren't my usual thing, so there are bound to be some glitches."

"Do you wear this pheromone oil?" Hazel asked.

"We're not allowed to wear anything scented at the store. People need to be able to smell the products on themselves."

"What about in your off time," she persisted, "do you find it actually works?"

"I honestly can't say. I can tell you I have customers who swear by it, but it may just be that it smells really good when combined with their body chemistry."

Hazel nodded and marked something on her paper.

"Speaking of things that smell good, I'm not going to go into them now, but we do have an extensive supply of products designed to attract men—or women—with a variety of tastes. For example, we have a brown sugar scrub that I can attest to. It's wonderful on dry, cracked heels and it smells, well, like brown sugar. I have a jar here, and you're all welcome to try it on your hands or elbows or something if you like, or you can just sniff it, but we might want to save that until the break so you can test it and wash it off.

"We also carry a full line of flavored massage oils. I like lemon, myself." Unbidden, the image of rubbing Griff's broad shoulders with the oil, then licking it off popped into her head. She banished it firmly.

"Now, let's say you've found a man for the night, if not for life. As I'm sure you've all figured out by this stage in life, it usually takes women longer to achieve orgasm than it does men. We take longer to heat up, as it were. So Goody's Goodies has two products to help alleviate the 'left hanging' syndrome. The first—if you can convince him to wear it—is called Staze-Long. It adds an average of fifteen minutes to half an hour to a man's staying power."

"Does it come with suggestions on how to get him to put it on without having him run off in a huff?" asked Juliette.

"Afraid not. Which is why we also sell Hot To Trot, which is for you. I need a volunteer to put it on her hand and see how it feels."

No one said a word, so finally Rachel spoke up. "Hell, hand it over here. I'll try it."

Evie put a dab of the ointment on the web between Rachel's thumb and forefinger. "It will create some distinct sensations. Let us know when you start to feel them." Rachel nodded. "OK, now, obviously, this isn't meant to go on your hand. But what it does do is get your engine revving quicker so you can get off faster."

"Ooooh," said Rachel. "It's all warm and tingly. If my hand were a clitoris, I'd be having a good time right about now."

They all cracked up.

Evie showed them a few more things, and then they took a break. The other women went to get more food and booze, while Evie packed up the lotions and took out the toys. About ten minutes later, they all congregated in the living room once again.

"Okay," Evie said, "before we get to all the fancy electronics, I have two basic dildos. This guy, I call him Howard because to me that's a kind of average, common name, is silicone. He's the most anatomically correct toy we have."

"If that's anatomically correct," Gabby spoke up, blushing, "my boyfriends have been sadly lacking."

"Mine, too," Rachel agreed, and the other women chimed in as well.

"Yeah, well, Howie here is on the large size. That's true."

"Better to *have* a big dick than to *be* one." Once again, Rachel's statement—probably combined with the wine they'd had on the break—sent them all into gales of laughter.

"Howard" was passed around.

"The other non-electronic toy Goody makes is this glass dildo." She held the item up. "I call him The Duke because he seems so tall and slim and elegant, like a historical romance hero, compared to Howie." The women giggled.

The rest of the night passed in a blur of hilarity. Even Hazel loosened up enough to join in on occasion, though Bonnie held herself aloof. At the end of the show-and-tell session, Rachel set Evie up in the kitchen so the women could order in private. Rachel waited until last.

"I hope you made some money off them," she said. "And I apologize for Hazel and Bonnie. I invited Hazel because she's a part-time dispatcher at the sheriff's office so I know her pretty well. She's always curious about everything, even if she can come off a bit conservative. Really it's just that she's shy. She asked if she could invite Bonnie along and I agreed because I wanted to be sure there were enough people here so you could make some cash."

"They were fine. And don't worry about the money. It was great being with people who see this stuff for the fun it is and don't freak out about it being unseemly." She winced. "Ooops. Sorry. Didn't mean to whine."

"Oh, that's not whining! But I don't think as many people disapprove as you might imagine. It's just that the ones who do make a whole lot more noise. That's always the way it is. I mean, think about your average political debate. The people who are *for* something are never as impassioned as those against it."

"I suppose." She and Rachel went over Rachel's order, and Evie gave her a hostess discount. "Can I help you tidy up?" she asked when she'd put her paperwork away.

"No, no, this won't take long at all. You get on home. It's ten o'clock already and you've got to be up a lot earlier than I do."

Evie drove home slowly. The evening had surprised her. She would be placing a far larger order from Benny than she'd imagined. All of the women had bought at least oils, and three of them had chosen vibrators as well. Even shy Gabby had bought a small, bullet-shaped vibrator. Both Juliette and Rachel had gone for bigger, more advanced models. Jenna chosen various oils and lotions, and both Hazel and Bonnie had purchased bath scrub. Hazel had asked a bunch of questions, however, and Evie wondered wehther she might not order something more risqué from the website later, when she didn't have to face anyone.

Back in her apartment, she logged into the system Benny had set up for her to order everything. The items would be drop-shipped from his warehouse to the women individually in unmarked boxes. Evie herself would get a check for forty percent of the retail price of the items she'd sold. She'd also make money, though only a small amount, if any of the women ordered from the Goody's website in the future.

She could buy a coffee maker. Hell, she could buy a nice coffee maker. Assuming she had time one of these days. She fell into bed, praying nothing happened that would force her to get up before her alarm went off at seven.

FATE—AND THE TOWN VANDALS—cooperated, and Evie felt considerably refreshed the next morning. Patricia didn't ask her about the party at breakfast, and Evie didn't volunteer anything. If her aunt wanted to ignore what she did for a living, so be it.

Unfortunately, Beth Ann wasn't so cooperative. And she waited, Evie could almost swear, until Griff had bought his morning coffee and was leaning on the counter in the bookstore talking to Patricia to stick her head in and ask how the evening had gone.

"How did you know about that?" Evie asked, then silently cursed her own defensiveness.

"Oh, dear," Beth Ann's laugh trilled through the café and bookstore, drawing attention. "You forget what a small town this is. If you're going to sell sex toys, you have to expect people to find out. Hazel mentioned she was going to a Goody party. Who else could be giving such a thing?" She turned to ask this question of Griff, who frowned.

"Well, I guess if Hazel was attending the party, she might be giving the next one."

Evie melted just a little. He hadn't stood up for her, not precisely, but he had pointed out that she wouldn't be in business if other people didn't like the products she was selling.

Beth Ann stiffened. "I highly doubt Hazel needs to

supplement her income in such a fashion."

"I hope we pay her enough so she doesn't need to supplement her income at all," Griff replied, with a conciliatory grin. Beth Ann smiled back at him, and the trickle of warmth Evie had felt at his support dried up. Of course he concerned himself with staying on Beth Ann's good side. He was a politician, after all, and Beth Ann voted in his district. Which, come to think of it, Evie needed to consider. She probably wouldn't be back in Vegas before election day.

She'd met Griff's competition, a deputy by the name of Clark Devane, a few days earlier, when he'd stopped in to pick up the latest legal thriller. Ginger-haired and freckled, he looked far younger than his age, which Patricia confided to be in the late forties. He had a boisterous laugh that both Evie and Patricia had responded to. Although Griff was popular, Devane seemed eminently likable and Evie suspected the race would be a tight one.

Beth Ann was called back to the café side. When she left, Evie turned to Griff, determined to dispel the adversarial mood.

"So what do you like to read?" she asked.

He blinked. "Uh. I don't really read all that much."

"Oh, you should. Shouldn't he, Patricia?"

"I'm sure it would relax you after a long day," Patricia agreed.

"I'm more of a TV and beer kind of guy when I'm done with work," he said.

"Oh, that won't do at all," Evie teased. "No, we'll find something for you to enjoy. Perhaps a nice romance?" She gestured to the romance section where two women browsed. Both looked over, and the younger one tittered.

"Um, I don't really think that's my kind of thing."

"Well, what do you like to watch on television?"

He fidgeted. "Sports. Baseball. Basketball. Mixed martial arts."

"There's a romance series about extreme fighters," one of the women offered helpfully. Evie had to smother a giggle at the hint of panic that crossed Griff's face.

"I'll, uh, keep that in mind. I'd better get going. We can talk about books some other time." He waved good-bye to everyone and escaped.

Patricia laughed aloud when he had gone. "Oh, dear," she said, gasping, "I haven't seen that poor boy so uncomfortable since I caught him and Candace smoking when they were teenagers."

The four women shared companionable grins, which set Evie's mind—never fully relaxed—to considering how to make the store more of a meeting spot. Her aunt's idea of a book club was a fine one, but too limited. Somehow, these women, who so readily grouped together to tease their would-be sheriff, had to be convinced that The Book Nook and The Nook Café were the best place to spend their free time, and their money.

CHAPTER 6

THE WEEK SPED BY AS Evie concentrated on creating and maintaining a flow of people through the store. The days developed a pattern: busy mornings, when café customers—including Griff—dropped in to chat, slow mid-day periods that gave Evie and Patricia a chance to stock shelves and reorganize the store, and a brief, late-afternoon rush of after-work customers.

Several people asked about Benny's visit, and by Thursday, Evie had convinced Patricia to move his talk into the café, where they could host a larger crowd and make money on drinks as well as books. She'd also bought a coffee pot, which—for a mere $19.99—improved her life immeasurably.

And then, Saturday afternoon at four-twenty, Benny arrived.

"Hello, ladies!" he called out as he entered the store. "It's goody time!"

Evie shook her head, but slipped around the corner to hug him nonetheless. "Benny, this is—"

"Well, you just have to be my Evie's Aunt Patricia. I can see the resemblance."

"Oh, no, we look nothing alike." But Evie could swear Patricia batted her lashes just a little.

"Where am I taking you lovely ladies to dinner this evening?"

"Benny, you don't have to take us out. It's enough

you flew down to give your talk."

"Now, sweetheart, no arguing. I came because I wanted to; I simply had to see the town that produced one of my favorite people in the whole world." Patricia looked back and forth between them and Evie could almost see the wheels turning in her head. Benny's professed admiration for Evie and their obvious closeness clashed with the flamboyant air and extravagant mannerisms that often led people to assume he was gay.

"But if this town, or one very near it, doesn't have a decent steakhouse, I may turn right around and go home."

"Cabot House does a very nice steak," Patricia said. "But you don't have to drag me along with you. You young folks go enjoy yourselves."

Young folks? Luckily, Benny replied before Evie could call her aunt on her obvious matchmaking.

"Don't be silly! You've generously allowed me to stay in your garage apartment. The least I can do is treat you to dinner. And a nice bottle of wine. I presume they have one of those at this Cabot House as well?"

"Well, yes, they do have an excellent wine cellar."

"Perfect! It's all settled then. I'll wander around your fair burg until you close up here. Evie said six o'clock?"

"Yes."

"I'll be back here by then, then. All I need is a quick shower and I'll be right as rain and ready for dinner!"

"My, my," Patricia remarked when the door closed behind Benny, "he is a bit overwhelming, isn't he?"

"He can be. And the less comfortable he is in a situation, the more overwhelming he becomes. When I first met him, he'd only just moved to Vegas and was throwing his money around like crazy, trying to be accepted. He's actually slowed down since then, if you can believe it. Though this is obviously not his usual milieu, so he's a trifle frantic."

Patricia smiled. "Thus the steakhouse, which is in his comfort zone?"

"Got it in one." Again Evie found herself wondering how a woman as smart as her aunt could have found herself in such a tenuous financial position. But it was the wrong time to ask. Instead, she busied herself re-shelving books people had taken out and left in the café or in the wrong spots on the shelves.

Benny followed them back to the house in his rental car. He'd flown into Knoxville where he'd managed, Evie noticed with some amusement, to find a Mercedes to rent. God forbid he should drive anything but a luxury car, even on a short jaunt to a small town.

When they arrived at Patricia's, Benny dragged a giant suitcase and a small overnight bag out of the trunk.

"Celia gave me this to bring with me," he said, holding up the suitcase. "She wanted to send even more, but I told her I wasn't a pack mule. And besides, you aren't staying so long you'll need your entire wardrobe, right?"

Evie shook off an odd pang at the thought of leaving. No matter how well she and her aunt might be getting along, Fairview was no longer her home.

"Absolutely. Though I have to admit, it will be nice to have more than one dress. I've been wishing I packed a few more nice things."

"Really?" Benny set the case down on the floor and looked around the apartment. Then he turned back to Evie and wiggled his eyebrows. "Who for?"

"Nobody! Get your mind out of the gutter. Patricia attends church every Sunday, and I only have one appropriate outfit."

"I had no idea you were religious. You worked Sundays for me."

"I know. I'm not. To be honest, I feel a bit hypocritical, but it's important to Patricia. I can put up with it for a couple of months."

Benny gave an exaggerated shudder. "I hope you don't expect me to come with you. Silver isn't exactly a nice, Christian name. Especially when it used to be Silverstein."

"No, I don't. In fact, I'm counting on your presence to allow me a pass this week, before they all start talking about poor Evangeline who can't afford a second dress on her hooker's earnings."

He burst into laughter. "They think because you live in Vegas you're a prostitute?"

"The term 'showgirl' seems to carry all sorts of prurient connotations here."

"Oh, the glamour." He snorted. "If they only knew."

"Right?"

Evie selected one of the outfits Celia had sent—black linen pants and a pale blue silk shirt—and took it down to the main house to change. She'd moved a few things over that morning since she was giving up her apartment to Benny while he was in town.

BENNY INSISTED ON DRIVING, THOUGH he didn't know his way around town yet, and he carefully helped Patricia in and out of the big sedan. If such manners in a man who'd made his fortune selling sex toys surprised her, Evie's aunt gave no sign. He, too, had changed clothes while Evie making herself presentable, and now wore a blue linen dress shirt, a navy jacket, and khaki slacks. His wavy hair had been tamed and he appeared far more put together than Evie remembered seeing him in the years they'd been friends.

When Patricia directed them up a long drive lined with elms to a grand old Victorian building, Evie sat up in surprise.

"This is Cabot House? But it used to be the Four Winds Club!"

"What's that?" Benny asked. "Some kind of country club?"

A giggle bubbled up in Evie's throat. "We're not a country club town. But it was the closest thing we had. They had dinner dances, weddings, all kinds of things there. And in my senior year my friend Isabelle Edwards and I scandalized the place. Neither of us had prom dates, you see—"

"You didn't? How is such a thing possible?" Even as he asked, Benny was slipping from the car. He ran around the front and opened the door for Patricia.

"Oh, don't assume we were heartbroken," Evie assured him, climbing out herself. "Neither of us were interested in boys at the time." Most boys, anyway. And by then, Griff had been long gone. "But this was a popular place for kids to bring their prom dates before the dance. Izzy and I came together. And then we didn't leave. We stayed and danced together all night to the swing band that played here on Saturday nights."

"And that horrified people why? I mean, I could understand if two boys did it, but girls dance together all the time."

"Oh, it wasn't the dancing," Patricia said. "Both Evangeline and Isabelle loved to dance. It was skipping prom. Date or no date, everyone goes to prom; the school's small and the sophomores, juniors, and seniors all go together. A couple of the class parents who'd been involved in organizing it took the whole thing rather personally." Patricia sniffed. "Some people lead excessively narrow lives."

"I see." Benny squeezed his lips together, but the laugh lines forming at the corners of his eyes gave away his amusement.

They made their way up the front steps slowly in deference to Patricia's crutches. Before Benny could reach for the door, it was flung open from inside and a lithe, pixie-featured woman with flaming red hair popped out.

"Evie! I couldn't believe it when Tammy said you guys had called in a reservation! I've been out of town all week, so I couldn't get into the shop to see you!"

"Izzy? What on earth are you doing here?"

"Well—" Izzy executed a perfect pirouette, dropped into a curtsey, and doffed an imaginary hat. "You see before you, Isabelle Cabot, owner and proprietor of Cabot House."

"You?" Questions crowded through Evie's mind and clogged her tongue. Only one managed to make its way out. "But I thought you were going to school for ballet?"

"Oh, sugar, I am far to fat to be a prima ballerina, and you know I was never one to settle for the chorus."

"Fat? Are you nuts?" Benny spoke right over Evie, who'd just opened her mouth to ask the same thing. She noticed he avoided the expletive he would normally have used before "nuts." In deference to Patricia? Or to Izzy? He'd certainly had no problem using such language around her or Celia.

Izzy grinned. "Not for a normal person. But for a ballerina, yeah. And my Gramma makes apple pie to die for. I wasn't about to give up desserts for my art. Sorry, a woman has to have some limits." She studied him. "You must be Benny. The town's all abuzz about your arrival."

"At your service," Benny said with a courtly bow. He really was on his best behavior.

"Well, y'all come on in. You can try Gramma's apple pie yourself. Of course, it's not quite the same now that we're making it, even though it's still from her recipe. It doesn't have her special magic, but it's pretty darned good."

"I know what I'm having for dessert," Benny joked as Izzy led them all into an exquisitely renovated anteroom. An old-fashioned leather-topped desk dominated the space, with a computer monitor squatting atop it like an alien creature from the future.

"I am desperate to find someone to make me one of those steampunk computer enclosures," Izzy said. "Then this room will be perfect."

"You've done an amazing job, though," Evie assured her as they moved through the dark, wood-paneled bar and paused on the threshold of the dining room, allowing the full effect to sink in. Chandeliers hung from the twelve-foot ceiling and candles lit every table with a warm glow. "This place has had a lot more than just a coat of paint!"

"George—my husband—was an architect and all-around building genius." Izzy smiled sadly. "Cabot House was his final project. He died of leukemia two years ago."

"Oh, no!" Evie put an arm over her friend's shoulders. "I am so sorry."

Izzy shrugged and smiled again. "It's okay. We knew it was coming. And he got to see our grand opening and the beginnings of Cabot House's success before he died." She started to lead them to a table, when a voice Evie was coming to recognize all too well stopped them.

"Evie? Patricia?" Griff placed a hand on Evie's shoulder. "What are you guys doing here?"

Evie turned to find both him and Hazel standing behind them.

"What does one usually do in a restaurant?" she asked rather more sharply than she intended. "We're having dinner."

Griff raised his left eyebrow. "I guess it just came as a surprise—I've never seen Patricia here."

"Well they have *company*, Griff," Izzy said. "And this is the hottest place going to bring out-of-town visitors." She widened her green eyes in a way that set every one of Evie's suspicions alight. "Hey! You guys should all sit together! Benny's never been to Fairview, and Hazel's the town's resident historian. She can tell you anything and everything about the place!"

"Oh, I don't think—"

"What a wonderful idea," Patricia said. "As long as you two don't mind?"

"Not at all," Griff replied. Hazel, Evie noticed, didn't say a word. Because having her date interrupted upset her, or because she just didn't talk much by nature? She'd kept fairly quiet at the party, as well. But she hadn't given the impression she was dating anyone, so why was she here with Griff? And how could he be dating Hazel and kiss Evie the way he had? Maybe it was Hazel, not his career, he wanted to keep Evie hidden from.

Izzy led them to a table but while the others sat Evie excused herself, asking her friend to show her to the ladies' room.

"What do you think you're doing?" she muttered once they were out of earshot. "Could you *be* any less subtle? 'You guys should all sit together!' How long were you going to keep us standing there in the doorway if Hazel and Griff didn't show up on time for their reservation?"

"Oh puh-lease. As it happens, they didn't have a reservation. Griff eats here regularly. And, yeah, I took advantage of their arrival. Girl, no one else around here may remember you as a kid, but I do. You mooned after Griff Barstow practically from the minute you hit town."

"That was years ago! For heaven's sake, Izzy! I don't even know the man."

"That's not what I hear. Word is you two have been seen together on several occasions."

Evie froze. "He can't… Griff has an election to win. If you care about him at all, you'll squash any rumors on that subject you hear in the future. And you won't play any games like 'table switch', either."

Izzy cocked her head to the side. "You're not that important, Evie. You're not going to scuttle his entire campaign just by dating him."

"I am not dating him. Okay?"

"Whatever you say, sugar. Now, you go ahead into the restroom. I have more guests to greet."

Evie glanced back over her shoulder and saw Patricia watching her. She stepped into the ladies' room and peered at herself in the ornate, gilt-framed mirror. Her eyes were tired and her hair was flat. Even her skin had lost its color. The humid air of Tennessee should have helped, but it apparently had none of the restorative properties she remembered.

With a sigh, she headed back out to deal with Griff, Hazel, Benny, and Patricia. What a combination. Hazel was telling Benny the story of Fairview's founding. Evie'd learned it in school, so she sat back and tried to relax.

A waiter carrying a large basket of rolls came over and placed one at each of their places, followed almost immediately by another who took their drink orders. Benny ordered a Grey Goose martini up with olives and Hazel ordered a Chardonnay, but Patricia, Griff, and Evie stuck to iced tea.

For a few minutes, they studied their menus. Once the waiter had returned and taken their food orders, Benny addressed Griff. "So you're the sheriff. That an elected position here?"

"It is."

"Does that mean you've lived here your whole life?"

Griff chuckled. "Guess you've spent some time in small towns. Yeah, I was born here. Went away for a few years, but folks here have long memories."

"Griffin was in the Army," Patricia said.

"He's a hero," Hazel agreed.

"Don't listen to them," Griff demurred. "Hazel's my campaign manager. She has to shower me with compliments any time we're in public."

Army? Was that where he disappeared to after high school? How could a boy so wild and free possibly conform to the military? And Hazel was his campaign manager? So maybe tonight's dinner wasn't a date? Evie shut down the thought, reminding herself that Griff's private life was none of her concern, and tuned back into the conversation.

"If you grew up here, you knew Evie when she was a child."

"Sort of. I'm older than she is. I dated her cousin, Candace."

"Cousin? I didn't—" Suddenly, Benny seemed to

realize he'd said something wrong, and rushed along. "Well, that's fascinating. I am dying to know what Evie was like when she was little. She always seems to me the kind of person who popped out as a little adult."

Damn, damn, damn. Evie didn't talk about Candace. There wasn't any point. Benny would only have wondered why Candace wasn't taking care of her mother herself and since the situation irked Evie enough, she had no desire to have him questioning her about it.

Griff gave her a questioning glance, but she ignored him. "I keep telling you, Benny, I was a kid like any other."

"Oh, no, never like others," Hazel said. "Evangeline was always dancing," she explained to Benny. "I was a few years older, like Griff and Candace, but even I remember that when she came to town after her poor mother's death, she was already an accomplished dancer, and she never stopped practicing. I admit, I really envied her talent. I thought for sure both she and Izzy would get to tour the world as dancers. I didn't envy the hours they had to put in, though, so I figured I'd be better off as an armchair traveler." She smiled.

Evie waved the words off. "Oh, please, it wasn't that bad. Izzy put in way more time and effort than I did!" Luckily the waiter arrived with their dinners so she could change the subject. "Oh, my, this looks delicious." And it did. The salmon fillet she'd ordered had been seared before roasting, giving it a crispy brown crust, and a spill of white wine and Dijon mustard sauce had been artfully drizzled over the top to pool at the end. It was accompanied by broccoli rabe that smelled of sautéed garlic, and thickly cut herbed roasted potatoes.

Everything else looked equally good; even Benny's steak, which Evie normally didn't find at all appealing, had a thick charred crust and a bright red interior. From the appreciative sound Benny made when he cut into it, she gathered he, too, approved. For some time, no one spoke as they all devoured their dinners.

At last, Griff broke the silence. He leaned back from an utterly clean plate and directed his attention to Benny.

"So where are you staying while you're here in town?"

"Evie has been kind enough to give up her apartment."

"Really?" Griff cocked an eyebrow at Evie. "So you're staying in your old bedroom for the weekend?"

A sudden, shocking memory of Candace climbing out that same bedroom window while Griff waited in the moonlight slipped through Evie's mind, evoking long-forgotten heat and jealousy. She'd watched them leave those nights, wishing she dared follow suit, if not to join a lover, at least to run free in the darkness. She only hoped the old feelings didn't show on her face.

"Things do change, you know, Griffin," Patricia said. "That's the boys' room now. I hardly think Evangeline would be comfortable in a twin bed surrounded by trucks and trains. She is sleeping on the pull-out in the living room, which may be old, but at least it's a queen."

Griff's sharp, gray eyes studied her. Did he wonder why she and Benny couldn't share the apartment? Had he assumed they were dating, or at least sleeping together? And why, above all things, why should it matter?

"What time's your talk tomorrow, Benny?" Hazel asked.

"Four o'clock. You must come."

"Oh, no." Hazel blushed. "I'm not a businesswoman. I just work part time at the sheriff's office."

"And you're Griff's campaign manager," Benny reminded her. "Believe me, you above all people are selling a product."

"I never thought of it that way."

"Neither did I," Griff muttered.

"Oh, but you must." Evie could almost see Benny rubbing his hands together under the table. "Public figures are no different from any other commodity. If you're talking about movie stars, people pay for them by buying tickets. With politicians, it's contributions to campaigns and, ultimately, with their votes."

"That's awfully cynical."

"Realistic."

"Benny, don't start. You're going to talk marketing all day tomorrow. Let's leave it alone tonight, okay?"

"Of course." He smiled his most charming smile.

"How did you decide to…um…do what you do for a living?" Hazel asked Benny.

"Sell sex toys? Well, that was just business. I started by taking cues from my mother and grandmother. My grandmother, for whom Goody's Goodies is named, sold Tupperware in the fifties and sixties. My grandfather died young, and Tupperware and life insurance were what she and my mother lived on for years. My mother sold Tupperware, too, and Avon. I grew up understanding the direct-marketing method of sales and seeing it in action. Both my mother and grandmother were big proponents of selling to women, and they made sure I understood that no matter who *made* the money in a household, it was usually women who decided how it got spent. Women bought for children, for their husbands, for themselves.

"But the usual goods women were interested in already had a ton of direct sales marketers. Jewelry, cosmetics, kitchenware, even kids' clothes and toys all had people going door to door and doing parties. I wish I could tell you I came up with the sex toy idea out of thin air in an act of pure genius, but I didn't. I was at a comedy club in New York City and there was a bachelorette party there. They were drinking pink drinks and waving dildos around. The guy I'd gone to the club with got all excited, thinking they represented prime pick-up possibilities, but all I could think about was where they'd gotten those dildos and whether anyone had considered doing home parties for sex toys. Wouldn't women rather have the goods shown to them in private than have to walk into a store? I barely even noticed the comedian on stage because of all the possibilities filling my head.

"The guy I went to the club with did, indeed, pick up one of the girls at the party. But by the time they got married two years later, I'd already gotten Goody's Goodies up and running. In the beginning, I was just a retailer of other people's goods, but I found investors so I could manufacture my own stuff. It's the only way to make a profit. Next thing I knew, I was Benny Silver, the Sex Toy King."

"You named the company after your *grandmother*?"

"Yep." He grinned at Hazel. "Her name was Gertrude, but the kids couldn't say that, so instead of Gramma Gertrude, we ended up with Goody."

"Doesn't she *mind*?"

"Not really. She gets a kick out of it."

Patricia shook her head. "That's quite a story."

Benny shrugged. "Everyone's got one. Some are just a little more extreme than others."

<h1 style="text-align:center">CHAPTER 7</h1>

THE FOLLOWING MORNING, EVIE WAS up with the sun, and not just because the pull-out sofa had a mattress a hundred years old and half an inch thick. No, nerves twanged in her belly as she considered how her neighbors might react when they finally met the infamous "Sex Toy King" in person. She pulled on a pair of clean jeans and a peasant-style blouse she'd brought over the night before, brushed her teeth, and pulled her maddening hair back into a high ponytail.

Then, at the last minute, she reached into the little makeup bag she'd used for her toothbrush and pulled out some eyeliner, blush, and mascara. She had to look professional, after all. Finally satisfied with her appearance, she exited the bathroom just as the doorbell rang.

"I'll get it," she called to her aunt, who had already begun breakfast preparations. Her heart gave a queer little thump and she firmly admonished it to behave, then opened the door for Griff.

His storm-silver eyes swept over her body, taking in everything in a single, comprehensive stroke she felt all the way to the bone. Her nipples tightened in response, and she turned her back so he wouldn't realize his effect on her.

"Come on in, Patricia's getting breakfast."

"You're not dressed for church."

"I'm taking the day off. Giving Benny the ten-cent tour of Fairview."

"You guys are good friends, huh?" Griff's hand on her shoulder stopped Evie when she would have entered the kitchen. She turned to face him.

"Yes. Benny's like a brother to me."

"So, not friends with benefits?"

A blush crawled up her neck. "Not that it's any of your business, but no."

"Oh, but it is my business, Evie." Without letting go of her arm, Griff stepped forward, all the way into her space. She hadn't put shoes on yet, and without her usual heels the position forced her to look up at him, leaving her both vulnerable and annoyed. Her heart fluttered again, and she quelled its foolish dance.

"What on earth makes you think my personal life is your business?"

"Oh, sugar," his voice, low and raspy, spread over her nerves like peppered honey, soothing and exciting at the same time. "You really don't expect me to answer that, do you?"

She had to stop toying with him, toying with both of them. She knew it, but she couldn't help herself. The heat of his body so close to hers sent a visceral memory of his kiss burning through her. She couldn't date him. She couldn't. Even if he weren't trying to win over the favor of a bunch of prudes, she didn't have any desire to get involved with a man in Fairview.

But while the sensible, practical side of her brain shrieked its protests, her instincts took matters into their own hands and she leaned even closer to him, so close that only a breath separated them.

"Christ," he muttered. Then, "You asked for it." His head dipped, his lips touched hers, and the heat that had been simmering between them burst into a raging conflagration. Her arms went around his neck, which brought her to her toes. One of his hands slid behind her head to hold her in position for his tongue, which tasted, tempted, then invaded. The other arm wrapped around her hips, pulling her against the broad ridge of his erection. Through his dress pants, through her jeans, she felt the throb and its answer in her own blood.

The moment ended as suddenly as it began when Patricia called out to them from the kitchen. Mere inches and a swinging door separated them from her, and her voice had the sudden cooling power of a block of dry ice. Evie could almost feel the mist pouring off her body as she froze. She pushed Griff away, then—before he could pull her back—stepped into the kitchen.

"Here we are," she said with as much cheer as she could muster. "We were just talking about dinner last night and how much fun it was."

"Indeed." Griff had his hands on the back of one of the chairs and was leaning forward slightly. The attempt to hide his erection made Evie grin. A quick, hot interlude, and she didn't have to go to church. Things were definitely looking up. Oh, sure, she'd have to deal with Griff later on, but for the moment life was pretty good.

Griff and Patricia were barely out of the driveway, Evie still standing on the step and waving, when the door to the garage apartment opened and Benny appeared.

"Tell me you weren't standing up there watching from the window."

His eyes sparkled and he answered in his most pious tone. "I don't like to lie."

"Why didn't you come down?"

"I don't think your sheriff likes me."

"He's not my sheriff." But the treacherous heat rose in her cheeks. "And I am sure he likes you just fine. Everyone does. It's a talent."

"Ah, but not everyone wants my Evangeline for their own."

"I'm not yours, Benny, and Griff doesn't feel that way."

"Evie, honey, you know I love you but I am calling

bullshit on that one. I've seen the way the man looks at you."

"Can I offer you a scone and some tea?" Evie asked, turning away so he couldn't see the blush that continued to deepen at the memory of the morning's encounter with Griff. "Or we can go get a full breakfast at the diner."

"After dinner last night, a scone will be just fine. But I'm going to need coffee."

"Yeah, that's a problem. Patricia only drinks tea, and there's a coffeepot in the apartment but it doesn't make anything fancy like espresso or cappuccino. Normally, we could go to the café attached to the bookstore, but nothing except the diner is open before noon on Sunday. We can make the run up to Greeneville and get some. It's not far, and they'll have a Starbucks or something similar."

"Sounds like a plan."

Evie got Benny a scone from the freezer and zapped it in the microwave to warm up. She thought he might insist on taking his Mercedes, but he seemed content to let her do the driving, wedging himself into her Civic with only a tiny, theatrical groan.

They drove out of town for caffeine first, and Evie indulged herself a cappuccino. On the way back in, she pointed out a few sights, but Benny was not to be sidetracked from the conversation he'd begun at the house.

"So how come you and the sheriff aren't an item?" he asked as they turned onto Main Street. "And don't tell me you're not interested, because I know better. I've seen you turn down guys you're not interested in, including, if you remember, my own fabulous self. This is different."

"Not really. Yeah, I admit, the guy's hot, okay?" Evie took her eyes off the road for a minute to glare at Benny. "But he's straight-laced as they come and running for election. Plus, I'm only here for a couple of months and

I don't do flings."

"Fling, schming. Take the guy out for a test drive."

"What's the point of a test drive if you know you can't afford the ride?"

"Oh, come on, Evie. Have a little fun."

"Right. And confirm everyone's poor opinion of me. It's common knowledge I'm not planning on staying, and around here you don't test drive unless you're serious about buying."

Benny humphed. "As far as I can tell, all you do is work. Not that I'm complaining, since your work brings me money. I noticed you had a party."

"I did. It was actually…fun."

"See? And where there's one, there are more. So I really doubt you'd get your sheriff in as much trouble as you believe by dating him."

"So says you." As they continued their drive, Evie pointed out various points of interest while and explained about the promotion she'd done for his talk and the resulting vandalism.

"Hmmm," he said. "You do realize that both incidents could have been done by a single, small-minded individual."

"My mind does. But it feels as if half the town is against me. Especially on Sundays when I have to go listen to Reverend Masters preach about sins of the flesh."

Benny shrugged. "So don't go. Hell, switch religions. When I told my rabbi about Goody's Goodies, I explained that it was a mitzvah to help people find joy in life."

"Oh, yeah, that would really improve my popularity in town."

They drove in silence for a while, Benny perking up with questions about things they passed. "So Greeneville's the nearest city? Or, big town—I don't really think it counts as a city if it doesn't even have a Starbucks."

"Well, yeah. Johnson City is probably the closest actual city. Even that…well, you'd probably only consider the big three here cities—Nashville, Knoxville, Chattanooga."

Benny laughed. "Yeah. I noticed that when I flew in." He studied her. "Have I ever told you about the first time I saw you?"

"I always assumed you'd come to a show."

"No. I'd been losing money at the poker tables, so I took a break and hit the buffet. I sat near the back of the restaurant and saw you in a booth in the corner. You had that lion's mane of hair up in a ponytail, one foot on the bench with your knee propping up your chin, and you were reading a book. You were wearing ragged jeans— your knee came through a hole—and a gray tee shirt. You looked at once utterly alone and completely at home. And yet it was obvious you weren't a native. Not to Vegas, not to any big city."

"You're saying you don't want me back?" Fear clutched at her. If Benny considered her too small town, if she couldn't go back to work at Goody's Goodies, what would she do? All well and good to consider moving away in the abstract, but to be forced into it—

"Don't be ridiculous. Of course I want you back. I'm just trying to explain something here."

"Oh. Okay." Even forced her fingers to loosen their grip on the steering wheel.

"Big cities mark their occupants. I can't explain how. Maybe it's as simple as it takes one to know one. I grew up in a city—or at least right outside one—and when I looked at you that day I registered difference, not similarity.

"In my opinion, it's part of what makes you so good in the store. Kai's good with people, too, but it's because with her dog collars and multiple piercings, they figure there's nothing she hasn't tried. But you…no. You come across as…quiet, for want of a better word. And they think if you're selling toys, there must not be anything wrong with them." He saluted her with his coffee cup. "Like this. People look at you and see a woman who grew up in a town without a Starbucks."

"God, Benny, you're such a snob. Beth Ann's coffee at the Nook is way better than Starbucks, even if she doesn't make frappuccinos and crap like that."

"I'll admit her scones are far better than Starbucks. I could get addicted to those."

"See? Not everything is better in the big city."

"Are you listening to yourself, Sweets? Because I'm not sure it's me who needs convincing."

AN HOUR LATER, EVIE PULLED up outside the Nook and parked. As she unlocked the door to the store, Benny gestured to the display window.

"What do you have planned next?"

"I don't know. I plan to leave that up for at least a week as word of whatever we talk about this afternoon percolates through town. After that…you have any suggestions?"

"Maybe." He followed her inside. "We can talk about it later."

They started moving the café tables to the side and arranging the chairs in the center. Evie dug a tripod display out of the closet and set it up with a large pad of paper on it for Benny to use during his presentation. She'd just pulled a folding chair from the closet and was bringing it out to set up when Benny spoke.

"So how bad shape is the store in?"

Evie froze, then set the chair down with excessive care. "What do you mean?"

"Don't kid a kidder. I know retail and I know you. Bookstores in general are fighting for survival and *I* can tell how worried you are, even if your aunt can't. You called me down here to generate interest, even knowing full well that people would be pissed off at the whole sex toy thing. That couldn't have been easy for you."

Evie's throat tightened. "What good are all the damn marketing and business classes if I can't help her?"

"You will. You've only been here a couple of weeks and you've already got people talking."

"Yeah, about Patricia's crazy, sex-toy-selling, showgirl niece. Not about how much they love to read and how they need to spend more time in the bookstore and more money buying novels."

"Give them some credit. You surprised them. Even shocked them. Takes people a while to adjust. They'll get there. You already seem to have made some friends. Hazel, the sheriff. That's all it takes. Especially with folks like that, who are integral to the community. And there's your friend Izzy, too. I'd say you're fitting in nicely here. That's the first step to injecting new life into any local business and you know it."

"It's not all about making friends, Benny."

"You have everything else you need, too. I have faith in you."

Impulsively, Evie flung her arms around him. "What would I do without you?"

"If you're very lucky, you'll never find out."

Once the café was set up, Evie hung a sign in the window: *Open at 3pm today! Book signing and seminar at 4pm!* Then she and Benny locked the door and headed back to Patricia's.

BACK AT THE HOUSE, EVIE was somehow unsurprised to find Griff's truck in the driveway. Inside, they found him taking tea with her aunt, still dressed in his Sunday best.

"All ready for the hordes?" he asked, rising at their entrance.

"I hardly think we'll have hordes," Evie scoffed.

"I wouldn't be so sure," Patricia said. "Plenty of people came up after church and told me they'd be coming by." She focused on Benny. "Apparently, you're quite the celebrity." The *even if I've never heard of you* remained unspoken.

Benny shrugged. "Fame is fleeting and fickle."

Evie suppressed a laugh. If anyone enjoyed celebrity more than Benny, she couldn't imagine who it might be. A professional athlete, perhaps.

"Who's taking care of café sales this afternoon?" Griff asked. "I heard Beth Ann wishing you luck."

"I'll handle it," Evie and Patricia said in unison.

"Don't be ridiculous. Evie, you'll be introducing Benny and probably answering questions. And Patricia, you can't be running back and forth serving coffee at one end of the counter and pastries at the other. You sell books. I'll do the café."

Evie's jaw dropped. When she regained control of her shock, she reminded him of the upcoming election. "Aren't you concerned that people will view your attendance, your *assistance* as an endorsement?"

He had the all-out brass balls to wink at her. "You forget, sugar, people in Fairview *like* me. They'll see it as doing a favor for Patricia."

"Which it is," Patricia noted.

"While in fact," Griff continued, with just a glance and half-smile acknowledging Patricia, "you piqued my interest, Mr. Silver, when you called me a product."

"Sorry about that."

"No, you're not." He grinned and Evie's breath stuck in her throat. God, he was beautiful. *Not for you, Evangeline. Never for you.*

"You were right. If you're a politician, you're a commodity. A brand. And you have to decide what you want associated with that brand. Me, I don't mind having any project the people in Fairview come up with linked to my brand."

"And your campaign manager? Is she coming this afternoon?"

"Hazel? Yup. She'll be there. Said she wouldn't miss it for the world." Griff stared at Benny and something passed between them, some secret language of men that Evie could recognize but not interpret.

"With all these people coming, where will they all sit? We only have about twenty chairs in the café, including the four folding ones I keep in the closet to go outside during the spring and summer."

"I've been thinking about that," said Griff. "My dad has eight folding chairs in the basement. My mom used them for bridge night, then he kept them for poker night after she passed. If Benny can bring you to the store, Evie and I can go grab the chairs from my place and get them set up."

"Oh, Griffin, that would be wonderful."

"Hey, not enough seating is a high class problem to have, but it's still a problem."

"Indeed. What do you say, Mr. Silver? Can I impose on you for a ride?"

"Only if you'll remember to call me Benny."

"Benny."

Evie could swear her aunt blushed. Would wonders never cease?

"All right, then. Off with the two of you, and we'll see you at the store." Again, that odd undercurrent of masculine communication before Griff slid a hand to the base of her spine to guide her out. The simple gesture set her nerves alight and once again she recited what was becoming her mantra: *Not for you. Never for you.*

They drove out to his father's place in silence. When they were inside, however, she saw the empty glasses on the coffee table and the shoes kicked off next to the television, and realized Griff had been living there.

"Were you staying with him before the heart attack?" she asked as Griff led the way down to the basement. In her memories, Griff and his dad had always been at odds.

"Nah." He easily lifted a stack of chairs and headed back up the stairs, leaving Evie to grab only the final two and follow. "But when he got sick and then decided on an extended vacation, keeping two places seemed silly. When he comes back, I'll find another apartment."

"Why not a house?" No reason his dreams should be hers, of course, but Evie couldn't imagine choosing to rent an apartment if she planned to stay in a town full of houses.

"Houses are for families."

"And you don't want a family?" *Dangerous waters, Evie.*

But Griff only shrugged. "Eventually. I like kids. Always assumed I'd have a few of my own. But I figure a woman has the right to have some say in the house she's going to live in. So I'll find her first, then the house."

"But that's somewhere down the line?" Kids. One more strike against her. Not that it mattered, since she wasn't even in the game.

"Maybe." He slanted her an impenetrable look.

They loaded the chairs into the back of the SUV, and Griff opened the passenger door for her. The old-fashioned courtesy made her grin inwardly. Who would have believed Griffin Barstow would grow up with such good manners?

"Are you nervous?" Griff asked as they drove toward the store.

"I'm not sure." Evie sucked in a deep breath, let it out slowly. She *was* nervous. "Benny could sell ice cream to Eskimos, but partly he does it by trying new things all the time. They don't always work. If there are a ton of people there and they try his methods and they don't pan out, I don't want them to blame Patricia."

Griff took one hand off the wheel and laid it on her shoulder. "Are you always so invested, or is it because it's Patricia?"

"Of course it's because of Patricia. I owe her everything. I could have ended up in the foster care system when my mother died."

"Your dad's family couldn't take you?"

"I doubt they even knew I existed. I only met my father a few times that I remember. He and my mom really did love each other, despite what people might say, but there was no room in his life for a kid. He was a rodeo rider, so he was only around when he came through on the circuit, and one day he stopped showing up even when the rodeo was in town. When my mom died, her friend Amelie called Patricia, and Uncle Harry came to get me."

"So putting your life on hold to help Patricia with her health and improve her sales is all about duty? Not about love?"

He said the word so easily, as if it weren't fraught with a million dangerous complications. For a moment, Evie's stomach dropped and she couldn't even speak. At last, she swallowed and asked, "What do you mean?"

"It's pretty straightforward. Do you love your aunt, or are you just helping her because she helped you?"

"Of course I love her! She raised me. But those two things—love and obligation—can't be separated. They're all tied together."

They pulled up to the curb. Saved by the proverbial bell. But Griff wasn't done. "You should tell her," he said as Evie jumped from the truck.

Griff hoisted the stack of chairs from the back and Evie let him into the shop. She gritted her teeth against the question the whole time they were unfolding the seats and rearranging the café to accommodate them, but finally she couldn't resist.

"I should tell her what?"

"Hmm?"

"What do you think I need to tell Patricia.?"

Instead of answering directly, he said, "She's afraid of losing you again. She believes the minute her cast comes off, you'll take yourself back to Vegas and she won't hear from you."

"Don't be ridiculous. She's made it abundantly clear she thinks I'm back to stay, regardless of what I say."

"It's her way of saying she's happy to have you back. She insisted Candace call you, you know, even after Candace said she'd hire an assistant to help out."

Evie's head spun. She reached for a chair and sat heavily. "Candace offered to hire someone?"

"Of course. You thought she'd deserted her own mother? They have their differences, but Candace would never leave Patricia to fend for herself." He sat next to her. "You did."

"How was I to know any different? We're not the world's most communicative family. Candace called, said Patricia needed me, and I came. I didn't ask for all the gory details, and given the state of Patricia's finances—" she caught herself.

"You figured they couldn't afford anyone else. Well, you have a clearer picture of Patricia's situation than I do, but I can tell you Candace is doing just fine. Patricia asked for you because she *wanted* you, not because there was no one else."

Evie massaged her temples, where a headache was taking up residence.

"Is it so awful to have someone care about you?"

"Of course not! It's just…complicated."

"Life is complicated, sweetheart." Griff's voice had gone low and husky, and it sent a warm shiver through her. "And family's the most complicated part of life.

"Speaking of which—" he nodded toward the window and Evie saw Benny's rental Mercedes pulling up to the curb.

"Showtime." Griff winked, then rose and reached out to help her up. She rested her fingers in his, for once not fighting the tingle that spread outward from where they touched.

Benny held the door open for Patricia, who swung in on her crutches as if she'd been born with them. Could she really be concerned that once she was well, Evie would leave her?

But you are *leaving.* How to explain that leaving

Fairview didn't mean abandoning her aunt? Now that Patricia understood why she hadn't come home for Harry's funeral and now that Evie's career was out in the open, things wouldn't be so strained. They could keep in touch much more easily. Assuming Patricia wanted to.

"Now, Griffin, I hope your math skills are up to snuff," Patricia said as she led Griff behind the bakery counter. "We don't have fancy electronic registers, so you'll have to calculate the change in your head."

"I think I can manage that," he said, a small smile playing about his mouth. Evie felt her own lips twitch in response. He treated Patricia like a member of his own family.

"Beth Ann's cousin complained about the register constantly when she worked in the Nook." Patricia sniffed. "Honestly, I don't know what they're teaching children in school."

The door opened again and Evie turned to explain they weren't yet open, only to be faced with an unsmiling Candace. For a moment, simple shock robbed her of speech, and even when she regained her voice, all she could think of to say was, "I didn't expect to see you today." Which, even to her own ears, sounded less than gracious.

"It's my mother's first author event at the store. Of course I would come to support her."

"You must be Candace." Benny stepped in, diffusing the tension. "I've heard so much about you, I've been just dying to meet you. I'm Benny Silver." He held out a hand and after only the slightest hesitation, Candace took it.

"Nice to meet you, I'm sure," she said.

"No you're not." Benny laughed. "Nobody's ever *sure* they're glad to meet the Sex Toy King, but I promise I am completely harmless."

Candace blushed and Evie grinned. Benny was so…not southern.

The door opened again, admitting Rachel and Hazel.

"Thought we'd come by early and see if we could help out," Rachel said.

"You might as well open officially, Patricia," said Griff. "Every woman in town will be stopping in early, I have the feeling." He introduced Rachel to Benny while Evie, under Patricia's direction, put the coffee on and laid the pastries out in the cases.

GRIFF WATCHED WITH A MIX of amusement and pleasure as people crowded into the store. Patricia, seated behind the register on the bookstore side, was doing little business, but he was serving up coffee and treats like mad.

Social hour in Fairview with Benny Silver, the Sex Toy King, glad-handing the residents like a politician. In a million years, Griff couldn't have imagined such a scene. Clark Devane was notably absent. Was he on duty, or had he decided the event would hurt his election chances?

Eventually, everyone settled down and Benny began his presentation.

"Sex sells," he said loudly, quieting the last, lingering buzz of conversation. "That's the biggest complaint I hear when I try to talk to businesspeople. 'Oh, Benny, what would you know? You've got a product people already want.' But that's garbage. Nobody goes into business to sell a product people *don't* want. That would be *insane.*"

A few slight nods in the audience.

"So the trick is twofold: how do you make them want to buy that product from *you*, and how do you introduce your product to new customers who might otherwise not think of buying it?"

He surveyed his audience. "I assume most of you are here because you either own businesses or are involved in running them."

Nope, Griff thought. *Most of them are just curious.*

Sex does sell.

"So why doesn't one of you introduce yourself and tell me what kind of business you have?"

Norm Bennet spoke up. "I'm Norm. I run a pet store."

"Nice to meet you, Norm. By 'pet store,' do you mean you sell animals?"

"No, no. Toys, food, treats, beds, that sort of thing."

"Excellent. And what's your biggest obstacle, would you say?"

"The chain stores and the Internet can sell things so much cheaper than I can."

"Right now, that's probably the biggest issue for any small business. You cannot compete on price, so you have to find another way. And when it comes to retail, there are really only two variables: price and service. Anything from selection to store hours falls under 'service.' So tell me, what can you do to increase your service?"

"I thought *you* were going to tell *me*."

That brought a laugh from the audience. How many had come just to watch Benny—and by extension Evie—fail? Griff's muscles tensed as he waited for Benny to answer.

"Do you keep track of all your customers' animals, their birthdays, their preferences and needs?"

"I know what my regulars like."

"Sure, but that's not enough. The object is to increase your customer base to beyond where you can keep all that stuff in your head. When I was growing up, we had a mutt. He was enormous—definitely at least partially mastiff—with a ton of food allergies. All he could eat was salmon and potato food and salmon and potato treats. Every year, we'd end up giving away, or throwing away, treats people bought for him. We'd also end up donating toys people gave us because even though he was a huge dog, he only liked very small, soft toys.

"Now, if you keep track of all that stuff for the pets

here in town, whenever someone wants to buy a pet present—which are great not only for birthdays and Christmas, but for housewarmings and the like—they will know to come in and ask you what's appropriate, what won't get thrown out or donated. It may take a while, but that level of service will gain you customers.

"Which brings me to one of the most under-utilized tools in the retail arsenal: registries. How many of you have registries available to your customers?"

Martin Waters, seated up front, shifted uncomfortably, then spoke. "I read your book last week. Started thinking about how I could use that idea to sell hardware."

"And?"

"I was thinking about 'honey-do' lists."

"Perfect!" Benny crowed. "Some apologies just require flowers—others require retiling the bathroom."

The entire audience laughed at that one. Reflexively, Griff looked at Evie. She was smiling, nodding slightly, even bouncing on her toes. In her element. This, then, was her thing: solving problems for businesses, helping them succeed. And judging by the crowd she'd enticed into Patricia's shop, she was good at it. How pissed she must have been at him, at Candace, for insulting her ideas and decisions.

"The great thing about a 'honey-do' registry," Benny continued, "is that it brings in customers who normally don't hit your store. Or at least I am assuming they don't."

"That's right," Martin agreed.

"So now that they're in the door, what are you going to do to keep them? Not to be crass, but how do you monetize them?"

"I, uh, hadn't thought that far."

"No problem. We'll figure it out right now. Evie?" As if she'd been expecting the summons, Evie stepped forward.

"Most of you know Evie Bell, and you're here

because her marketing ideas brought you—her window, her invitation to me to come and speak. You may *not* know that's what Evie does for me when she's not here helping her aunt. I have ideas, but she has the business and marketing degrees to help me refine them and track their success or failure."

Now Evie was blushing and Griff fought dueling emotions. He wanted to cheer for Benny for standing up for Evie, but felt lower than a slug for not doing it himself. Not that he could have, since she'd never bothered to tell him about her degrees. Hot shame flooded him again as he remembered how shocked he'd been when she revealed her job and how hurt she'd been as she walked out before he could even formulate a response.

The damn job shouldn't have mattered. Not even if she were doing nothing more than selling toys. He should have been able to get beyond that.

As she spoke, her voice soft but carrying, Griff found himself shaking with a fierce, almost angry pride in her.

"The easiest change to make," she said, "the one that won't cost you anything, is to concentrate the items you already carry that might appeal to women around the area where customers have to go to create the registry. Also anything they can pick up while they're in the store to get their lists accomplished, like drywall patch kits or those flap things you use to fix a running toilet. Things that make people go 'wait, there's a simple kit to fix that? What have I been waiting for?'"

The conversation continued, but Griff lost track of it as he watched the faces of the crowd as they became absorbed into Evie's enthusiasm. He shifted position behind the counter so he could see her face, too. It was alive, shining in a way he'd never seen, not even at dinner when he could have sworn she was completely relaxed.

She looked up from scribbling something on the giant pad she and Benny were using to take notes, and for a second her gaze caught his. A shock so powerful it practically buckled his knees traveled through him.

Good God, what was that? She'd obviously felt something too, as her speech faltered for a minute. Then she seemed to shake it off and jumped right back into the presentation.

"She's doing great, isn't she?" While he hadn't been paying attention, Izzy had slid up next to him behind the counter. "I should see whether she has any ideas for Cabot House."

"Is everything okay?" Was he so out of touch that every business in this town was failing and he knew nothing about it?

"Everything's fine, touch wood." She tapped her fingers lightly on the counter. "But they can always get better."

They certainly could. Hadn't he just the other night bemoaned the pitiful state of his life? He'd lay money that Evie could fix that right up. But then she'd go back to Vegas, and damned if that might not leave him in even worse shape. When they'd first met, he'd figured a few dates, a short-term affair would be perfect. But now…now he was beginning to see the truth of the old song. A taste of honey might, indeed, be worse than none at all.

Was she completely dedicated to going back? She clearly had problems with Fairview, but maybe after today, people would treat her better.

Of course, she might not want to date *him*, even if she *did* stay.

He watched her, the easy way she moved, the confident set of her shoulders, the enthusiastic way she waved her hands as she described various methods of attracting and keeping customers. How could he have encouraged Jimmy Waters to ask her out? It must have been a bout of temporary insanity. If she stayed, she was his.

If. The next step, then, was to find out her plans.

And, if necessary, to change them.

BY THE TIME THE PRESENTATION ended, Evie's throat hurt. She felt as if she'd done far more talking than Benny had. Oh, right, she *had*.

It took almost an hour to get everyone out the door and another to clean up the mess and ready the café for the Monday morning regulars. Despite the work, Evie's heart sang. They'd sold every one of Benny's books, with several people buying copies for friends or family out of town.

Hazel, Rachel, and Candace all stuck around to help straighten up, and once everything was back where it belonged, Benny offered to take them all out to dinner.

"Don't be ridiculous," Patricia said. "You just did that last night! I should be feeding you! Besides, you came all this way just to help me out."

"Hey, hey, no fighting, folks," Griff interrupted with a smile. "Tell you what. We'll go to Celeste's. I'll buy. The food's good but not expensive. That way no one has to feel guilty. Patricia, you know my parents didn't raise me to let a woman pay. It may be sexist and old-fashioned, but there it is."

"Sounds good to me," said Benny, and it was settled.

They piled out of the store and somehow Evie found herself alone with Griff in his SUV once more.

"Pretty amazing night," he said as they pulled onto the highway for the fifteen-minute drive to Mama Celeste's Ristorante. "People are going to be talking about it for a while."

"Benny's good."

"So are you. Why didn't you tell anyone you were going to school?"

Why hadn't she? By the time she'd started taking classes, she was already working for Benny and her relationship with Patricia had deteriorated because of her inability to come home for Harry's funeral. Later, she'd been too afraid of what her aunt would think of her career. She hadn't wanted her aunt to shut her out completely, so she'd put off calling, depending on the occasional card and whatnot to keep the relationship limping along.

But there was more to it than that.

"Business, marketing, computers…the whole package was the first thing I'd ever tried I wasn't sure I could succeed at. I was already working at a sex toy shop. What if I failed to get the degree? Patricia would be so disappointed."

"But you didn't fail."

"No, I didn't." A little glow of pride filled her. Some of those courses, especially the statistics ones, had damn near killed her. But she'd beaten her head against the walls of numbers until the concepts made sense.

Griff took her hand and the little warm glow shot into flame.

"When Benny introduced you, I wanted to shout, 'Take that, you sanctimonious prigs!'"

A giggle bubbled up from her stomach. "That would certainly have made a splash."

She laughed, but he remained serious.

"Here's the thing, Evie. I was one of those prigs, and I need to apologize for that."

"You were not."

"I was. I judged you—well, not exactly judged, but I didn't look beyond your profession, and I didn't even really know what that was."

"It's okay."

"No, it's not. Look at my history. If anyone should know there's more to a person than what's on the surface, it's me. So I apologize."

Evie didn't know what to say.

"Just tell me you accept the apology. Don't overthink it."

"Okay, then, I accept your apology."

"Good. See how easy that was?"

He said nothing else, but when they pulled up at Celeste's, he was still holding her hand, and he released it only when forced to in order to park.

Dinner was a fairly rowdy affair. The presentation's success had put them all in a good mood. Even Candace unwound, contributing several ridiculous stories when they got on the topic of office shenanigans.

"You should have heard Rachel when she came into the station the morning you arrived," Hazel said to Evie. "When she pulled you over and you had those boxes of Goodies in the back of your car, she couldn't believe her eyes."

"Geeze, did you tell the world?" Evie teased.

"Nope! Just Hazel. I figured I could con her into coming if you were going to do parties."

Benny tsked. "You should become a consultant yourself. Then you could have as many parties as you like."

"Oh, no!" Rachel turned pink. "I'm not good in front of an audience. I'll leave that to Evie, who proved today she can more than handle it." She raised a glass in Evie's direction and the others—even Candace—followed suit.

Evie's cheeks burned and she wanted to crawl under the table. "Thanks, you guys. But I couldn't have managed without you all. And now...I have no idea what to do next. Benny's a hard act to follow."

"Impossible," Benny said smugly, and they all laughed.

Evie rode home with Benny and Patricia in the Mercedes. It made sense, but she missed Griff's conversation and the warmth of his hand on hers. Back at the house, they spent some time strategizing for the Nook's future before Benny excused himself to head up to the apartment.

"I'll miss you," Evie said, walking him out. "I really can't thank you enough for coming, for the support, for everything."

"I wouldn't have missed it for the world. In fact, give

me a few weeks and maybe I'll be back."

"To Fairview?" Suddenly walking and talking at the same time seemed beyond her, so she stopped. "Why?"

In the darkness, she saw him shrug. "Why not? It's a nice town, and if you implement any of the things we've talked about, I'll be interested to see how they work. Plus, I'd like to be on hand when you're forced to admit this place isn't so bad."

"I can do that right now. Doesn't mean I want to spend the rest of my life here."

"You will," he predicted with exaggerated gloom. "I might as well start training Kai to take over the store right now."

"Oh, please. Besides, she's more than ready and you know it."

"She's not you." He let out a theatrical sigh. "But seriously, Evie. I know you feel like you owe me something, but I don't want you coming back to Vegas just for me or the store. Kai *is* ready. If you decide to stay here, we'll be fine."

"I'll keep that in mind, but I'm not staying."

"Uh-huh." He waved and let himself into the apartment.

THE NEXT MORNING, BENNY LEFT early so he could catch his flight home. Patricia sent him off with half a dozen scones and muffins and an invitation to return anytime.

Business was brisk over the next couple of days, with several people stopping in because they'd heard reports about the presentation. Evie took names and numbers of those who wanted to be notified when more copies of Benny's books came in, while Patricia began organizing the store's next event: the kickoff of The Good Yarn club.

The idea had been born on the way home from Celeste's. Many of Patricia's friends knitted or crocheted or the like, but Fairview was too small to have its own yarn shop. They bought supplies on the internet or in Greeneville or other nearby towns. Sometimes they'd get together for a stitch'n'bitch, but finding a house where they wouldn't be disturbed had proven difficult. So Patricia planned to start holding A Good Yarn meetings every other Thursday evening after hours. She hoped to be able to convince some of the relatively nearby specialty stores to hold trunk shows with their favorite products at every few meetings and she was stocking up on new pattern books with quick, cute projects.

Busy as they were, Evie still noticed that Griff didn't come in, not even for his usual morning coffee.

On Wednesday after the morning café rush, Beth Ann sauntered over and gave Evie the answer she hadn't dared ask for.

"I wonder where Griff's been," she said, sliding a speculative glance in Evie's direction. "He usually comes in every morning, even when he's working swing like he is now."

Evie deliberately let the silence stretch out before replying. "I never thought about sheriffs working shifts."

"Maybe they don't in Las Vegas," Beth Ann said. "But here, our sheriffs work alongside their men. The guys have to do overnights, so Griff does, too."

"They probably do in Vegas, too. I just don't know anyone in law enforcement there."

"Gina says he's spending a good deal of time up-county," Patricia put in. "I guess Clark Devane's been campaigning pretty hard in the outlying areas where they don't know Griff the way we do."

"Will the fact that he's Bertram's son help him? I mean, that man was sheriff for like, a hundred years."

"Hardly *that* long," said Patricia. "But yes, the name recognition will help. Unfortunately, much of the voting public in this county doesn't know anything of Griff beyond his hell-raising high school years. He drives Hazel mad because he won't let her make campaign posters with pictures of him in his Army uniform."

Evie shivered. Griff in an Army uniform. Every woman in the county would line up to vote for him.

"Maybe Evie could convince him to change his mind," said Beth Ann. "You're the marketing expert. Tell him why it would be a good idea."

"I'm certain he knows all the reasons. I'd never try to convince a person to do something that feels wrong to them."

"Didn't stop you bossing *me* around." But Patricia's words held no heat.

"As if I could." Evie laughed.

"I still think you should talk to him about it," said Beth Ann. "When are you seeing him again?"

Well, that's direct. Even Patricia's eyes widened.

Evie shrugged. "Whenever he comes in. I'm not his keeper."

"Your friend recommended that even if I don't want a full-fledged children's section, I should have some gift-type books." God bless Patricia and her blunt refusal to tolerate gossip. "We should probably think about where to put them."

"Definitely," Evie agreed. "Plus, I think we should enlarge the Young Adult section. Most of what you have now are classics, which are great, but people will buy books for their kids even when they won't for themselves. And a lot of the titles out now cross over with adult reading as well."

"The things my niece reads are too scary for me," Beth Ann said with a shudder. "The end of the world, zombies, vampires…I don't know how she sleeps at night. I could barely manage the last of the Harry Potter books myself, they were so violent."

The conversation shifted to the far safer topic of the reading habits of teens, but Evie couldn't quite banish Griff from her thoughts.

CHAPTER 8

GRIFF CRUISED THROUGH THE TOWN, up and down street after street of silent, sleeping houses. He should go home. He knew it. But he was wired in a way he hadn't been since leaving Iraq, and if he closed his eyes all he would see would be Lila Renner's blood.

It was closing in on two in the morning. Even on a Saturday night, most people didn't stay up so late. He could have remained at the station, but that had been too busy. So he drove, hoping for signs of life and happiness in his town. Rather than making his way home, he turned toward Patricia's place. At least for part of her life, Evie had been a night owl. If he could see lights on in the garage apartment, maybe he wouldn't feel so damned alone.

Indeed, a light did shine from the apartment window. But more surprisingly, his headlights caught a figure seated in the gently swaying porch swing. He pulled into the driveway, parked, and slid out. He had no idea what he would say, but the desire to be with Evie, to touch her, was too strong to ignore.

He joined her on the swing and for a long moment neither of them spoke.

"The stars look different here than they do in Vegas," she said at last. "It's like they're closer."

"Do you like living there?"

She didn't answer right away and his heart gave a hard thump. If she didn't, might she be convinced to stay?

"I'm not sure how to answer that. As a city, as a permanent place to live, no. It's too frantic, too transient. But my friends are there, my job. I like the life I've made for myself."

"How did you start working for Benny?"

"I knew him from around the casino. After my surgery I couldn't dance. For months, I could barely walk the three flights of stairs to my apartment. Benny offered me a job and I took it. I found I liked sales, liked helping people find things they'd enjoy. And I liked business."

"The surgery... I've known plenty of people who had their appendixes out. It wasn't as straightforward as you made it sound when you told your aunt, was it?"

"No." She shrugged and bent her head, the long fall of her hair hiding her face. "I was stupid. I ignored the pain for too long. But I didn't have insurance, and the walk-in clinic seemed like a waste of money for a glorified stomach ache. By the time I went in, I had to call 911. I was in too much pain to wait for a friend to drive me. It turned out that I had a massive infection because my appendix had actually been leaking for about a week. They couldn't figure out the exact problem from x-rays or CAT scans, so the surgery ended up being exploratory. They cut me from stem to stern. Even without the weakness, that would have put an end to my career. You can't wear revealing costumes with a scar that starts above your belly button."

And she hadn't told her family. She'd suffered their anger over the fact that she hadn't come home for Harry's funeral rather than further worry her aunt.

"How long were you in the hospital?"

Evie drew her knees up under her chin and wrapped her arms around her calves in a classic defensive posture. Suddenly, he didn't want to hear her answer.

"Twelve days. Abdominal infections are trickier for women than they are for men. They ended up having to do a hysterectomy."

"Jesus." Unable to stop himself, Griff slid an arm around her and pulled her close, resting his cheek on the top of her head. "Who stayed with you?"

"Celia came by almost every day. And Benny visited a lot. The other dancers took turns coming to see me, too. I wasn't alone."

But it wasn't the same as knowing, when you closed your eyes, that someone would be there when you woke up. Griff remembered that all too well.

Evie shook off the somber mood, dropping her knees and tucking her hair back behind her ears. *Ready to face the world again.*

"And then I got out and Benny hired me and I finished school and my whole life changed." She looked up at him, her eyes gleaming in the darkness. "So that's my incredibly pathetic story. Want to give me your life in five minutes or less?"

Not really. But fair was fair. "Well, let's see. The summer I graduated high school, I wrecked my bike. I was high, and drove it through the plate glass window at a convenience store. My father gave me two choices: two years in jail or four in the military. I was crazy but not stupid—the military might be unpleasant, but it didn't touch spending two years in a cell. He made some deals and in July of 2001 I joined the Army."

Evie sucked in a breath.

"Yeah. So you can see why I am a little uncomfortable when people call me a 'hero.' I didn't have a heroic bone in my body. Of course, by the time my original four were up, we were at war and no one was allowed to leave anyway, so I re-upped. Stayed in until 2010 when I was injured and sent back to the States. Once I was fit for duty again, I joined the sheriff's department. And the rest you know."

"You were injured?"

"Not seriously. Not the way others were."

"Seriously enough if they sent you home."

Talk about uncomfortable conversations. But if he

had his way, she'd find out soon enough. So better for her to be prepared. The sight of his scars had sent more than one woman screaming.

"It was messy. I got burned over about twenty percent of my body when an IED exploded near us. Burns require too much care to be handled in the field, so I was shipped to a hospital in Germany and then back to the States for rehab. I didn't lose a limb or anything."

"And do you like it here? Was it hard to come back to the people who remembered you as a wild kid?"

"A bit. My old life seemed so far away to me that it was hard to adjust to the fact that ten years is nothing to these folks. But they took me back, gave me another chance, and it's worked out."

"And the job? You enjoy it?"

Blood. "Most of the time."

"But not tonight." She took his hand, stroking the back gently with her thumb. "You want to talk about it?"

Not hardly. But he found himself speaking anyway. "There was a 911 call. Lila Renner's sister-in-law called. Lila had locked herself into the bathroom with her nine-week-old daughter. Her husband's a long-haul trucker and he'd asked his sister to keep an eye on them while he was gone. But Lila started shrieking when Mary got there, said she'd never hurt her baby and how dare Frank send Mary to spy on her, then locked herself in. The kid was howling and Mary was scared."

"What did you do?"

"Clark took the original call, but things were out of control, so he called me to assist. We couldn't get Lila to talk to us and we couldn't break down the door because the bathroom was too small—we almost certainly would have hurt both Lila and the baby—so we took the door off its hinges. It was…bad."

The baby's wails, the smell of death, the blood everywhere. He shook himself, shoving the memory away.

"The baby?"

"She's fine. But Lila…she'd cut herself up. Arms, legs…there were scabs and scars, too. She's probably been doing it a long time. We had an ambulance standing by, but she was DOA at the hospital. The last thing she said to me was 'tell Frank I didn't hurt Rosie.'"

"Oh my God."

"Yeah. Banner night for Fairview."

She didn't reply and Griff was just getting ready to apologize for dumping his problems on her when she rose and tugged on his hand.

"Come on," she said. "I know just what you need."

AS SHE LED GRIFF UP the stairs to her apartment, Evie could feel the tension radiating from him. Her own heart pounded and she had trouble regulating her breath. She'd known the minute he'd shown up at the house that something was wrong but she'd never imagined anything like the situation he'd described. He might not consider himself heroic, but she would bet the Renner family would disagree.

Inside the apartment, she pulled the suitcase she'd taken to Rachel's party out of the closet and told Griff to take off his shirt and lie down on the bed.

"Uh…Evie…"

She looked up to find him standing in the doorway like a petrified rabbit. Oops. She'd clearly given him the wrong impression. Time to lighten the mood a little. Putting her hands on her hips, she adopted a cocky stance.

"Get your mind out of the gutter, Barstow, and do as you're told."

His lips twitched and a slow smile spread across his features. Damn, but the man was gorgeous. If he weren't so much in need of comfort, and if she didn't know it would be such a mammoth, life-destroying mistake, she'd probably change her mind and jump him.

"Yes, Ma'am," he said. As he reached for the top

button of his shirt, Evie transferred her attention back to the suitcase. *Not for you.* Which made what she was planning extra torturous. But he needed it.

Eventually she found what she was looking for: the small bottle of Dark Knight massage oil. It was a blend of scents she found both relaxing and masculine—sandalwood, mostly, with hints of tobacco and musk.

Bracing herself, she turned to see whether Griff had obeyed her orders. He had, but not in the way she had intended. She'd forgotten to tell him to lie face down, and he relaxed against her pillows, arms crossed beneath his head, watching her warily.

For a moment, she was too fascinated by the biceps bunching in his arms to realize what had him on edge. She'd known, of course, that he was built, but she'd never realized just how muscular he was beneath the standard uniform he wore most every day.

And then her eye caught the scars and she had to stop herself from gasping aloud. He'd told her about the burns, but to see the marks they'd left on his body…it tore at her. But he wouldn't want pity, and he'd see compassion as pity, almost certainly.

Still, she couldn't resist setting the bottle of oil on the bedside table and tentatively reaching out to lay her hands on him. The shiny, mottled tissue formed a rough triangle starting just beneath his left nipple and extending right across his torso in a sweeping, widening curve down to his right hip where it disappeared behind his back.

"Ugly, isn't it."

"It must have hurt so much." She ran her hands across his chest, feeling the contrast between the hair-roughened skin and smooth, almost slick scar tissue.

His abdominal muscles bunched. "Don't."

She snatched back her hands. "Sorry. I didn't mean to—"

"Not that. You can touch me any time, any way." He sat up in one swift motion, his hands cupping her face.

"It's this." His thumb brushed beneath her eye, sweeping away a tear she hadn't even realized had escaped. "No crying. I promise you, they knocked me out for weeks. I didn't feel a thing."

She didn't believe him, but she let it go. "The scars extend to your back?"

"Yeah." He grimaced. "Even uglier on that side."

"Do they hurt?" She reached for the nightstand and held up the bottle of oil in question.

His silver-gray eyes turned dark. "Sweetheart, didn't I just tell you you could touch me any way you wanted to?"

"I just wanted to be sure…"

"I have to wear cotton undershirts under pretty much anything, but other than that, I don't really notice much difference between the scarred part and the rest." He lay down, rolling onto his stomach and presenting his back to her.

As he had said, the damage was worse, and Evie had to blink back the quick rush of tears when she saw the massive swath of puckered, destroyed skin. Wrapping around from where she'd seen it disappearing, it continued to widen until, just past his spine, it ended abruptly. At that point, it extended all the way from his neck down to disappear into the waistband of his jeans.

How had they even laid him down in the hospital?

Swallowing hard, she poured a little of the oil into one cupped hand, then put the bottle back on the nightstand. She rubbed her hands together to warm the oil and release the scent, which set her slightly at ease. This she could do. She'd even taken a massage class. Many dancers did. They all ended up sore, and helping each other was a whole lot cheaper than getting professional masseurs.

But her hands still shook slightly as she laid them against his back and slowly slicked the oil over his skin. She began the massage at his left shoulder, digging into the tight muscles and ignoring her own immediate physical response to the feel of him beneath her hands. Despite the scars, he was by far the most attractive man she'd ever known. But she was determined to do the right thing by not complicating his life. Although some of Fairview had accepted her, he needed more. He needed a woman who could actively boost his profile, who would win over those he'd alienated as a kid. And who could give him the family he wanted.

So she concentrated on relaxing him and tried not to laugh at her own fantasies when his breathing eventually deepened and he let out a slight snore.

Oooh, baby, you're one exciting woman. Still, she'd achieved her goal, and she couldn't help feeling glad. He'd been in such bad shape when he showed up at the house.

As quietly as possible, she changed into a pair of shorts and a tee shirt, brushed her teeth, pulled a spare blanket out of the closet and curled up on the far-too-short love seat. No way did she trust herself to share a bed with Griff. As it was, it took her forever to fall asleep, simply knowing he was mere feet away.

WHEN GRIFF WOKE UP, HIS foggy brain took a few minutes to figure out where he was. The sun had not yet risen, and in the dark of the room he could see the numbers glowing from an unfamiliar digital clock beside the bed. 5:04.

Damn, he was at Evie's. In her bed. He sat up, eyes wide, searching the darkness. There she was, curled into a fetal position, asleep on the loveseat. That had to be horribly uncomfortable, as tall as she was. Why hadn't she just slept on the bed? True, he'd been sprawled out when he awoke. He could be a bit of a bed hog and hers was just a queen, not a king like he was used to, but he would have moved.

Of course, that would have meant she'd have had to rouse him, and he was pretty sure if she'd done that they'd both have been up considerably later. How in the hell had he fallen asleep with her hands on him anyway? It was embarrassing. *Good one, Casanova.* One minute he'd been thinking about how he should turn over and pull her down to join him, and the next he'd been out.

He slipped from the bed and pulled on his undershirt, leaving the uniform shirt hanging off the footboard where he'd laid it the night before, and moved over to squat next to the couch. Gently, he brushed a few stray hairs away from her face. In sleep, she looked even younger, completely innocent without her usual guards and the caution he always saw in her eyes. Dark eyelashes barely hid the purple circles that had been forming beneath her eyes since her arrival in Fairview. The vandalism of the store was responsible for some of them, but he had a feeling there was more to her sleepless nights than concern for the windows at the store.

How bad a financial bind was Patricia really in? He'd been so shocked by the pain in Evie's voice when she'd let slip her belief that Patricia had only asked for her help because she couldn't afford anyone else that he hadn't reacted to the monetary aspect.

He considered Evie's sleeping form. Could he move her to the bed without waking her?

He folded the blanket back out of the way and slid one arm beneath her bent knees, then waited while she shifted position slightly and settled back to sleep. Then he slipped the other beneath her back and lifted her to him. This time, he thought she really might wake. But she simply muttered unintelligibly and buried her head into the side of his neck. He laid her down on the bed, then gave in to temptation and lay down next to her. He pulled her into his arms so that her head rested in the curve of his shoulder and allowed himself to imagine a different ending to the night before.

Evie's hand crept to his chest and she snuggled into him, making his blood pressure and temperature rise.

He'd been a complete clod with her right from the beginning. She was so much more fragile than she appeared. Her emotions ran so much deeper. That conversation about Patricia had merely shown him a side to her he hadn't previously considered. Like everyone else in town, he'd looked at her and seen a woman who'd chosen to be a showgirl and then to sell sex toys. He hadn't even considered the child he'd known all those years before, and how it must have felt to her to have been ignored by her own father and left to the care of her aunt and uncle.

And Candace. Both he and Candace had laughed at Evie when they were kids. How she followed all the rules and always did as she was told. He hadn't been mean to her or anything—he'd felt sorry for her, having lost his own mother—but he certainly hadn't gone out of his way to temper Candace's occasional cruelty. Fuck, he was an asshole. No wonder Evie didn't want to go out with him.

He stroked her hair, loving the way she reacted even in sleep, curling closer, burying herself in him. Things were going to change. Clark Devane would quit the race, he was sure of it, and that meant Evie would have to come up with some new excuse if she wanted to keep him at arm's length. And then he'd find a way around that excuse, too. Because the one advantage to being an asshole was that assholes never gave up.

WHEN HER ALARM WENT OFF, Evie slapped out instinctively for the clock and shut it off before she realized she shouldn't have been able to. She should have been on the couch. At least, that's where she'd been the last time she remembered anything. On the couch, watching Griff breathe. He must have moved her after she fell asleep.

The act felt oddly more intimate even than the massage she had given him. Perhaps it was the vulnerability being asleep and having another person in complete control. Aside from the day she woke up in the hospital, when the last thing she remembered was counting backward before surgery, she had never allowed anyone that kind of liberty.

And he'd allowed it to her, as well, falling asleep in her bed, under her hands. Her heart squeezed, and she threw off the covers he'd drawn over her.

Still half-asleep, she staggered to the closet and poked through it for an outfit suitable for church. For church on the day a member of the community had died. Not that Lila Renner had been a friend—she'd never met the woman—but it still seemed hardly appropriate to wear one of the cheerful cotton sundresses she usually relied on for dressier occasions. Celia hadn't packed much, but there was one pair of navy slacks she could wear with a white shirt and look reasonably sober.

Of course Celia, who quite happily spent most of her days in sweatpants tapping away on her laptop until she had to leave for the theater, hadn't taken much care with the packing. Both the pants and the blouse would have to be ironed. Evie laid them on the bed, made herself a cup of coffee, and pulled the iron and board her aunt had given her from the back of the closet.

When most of the wrinkles had been subdued, Evie cleaned herself up, put on makeup to hide the ever-deepening circles beneath her eyes, and headed over to Patricia's.

Her aunt, of course, was already up and fussing about in the kitchen. Did the woman never sleep? In the living room, Evie hesitated. Should she tell her aunt about Lila Renner? And if so, how? It was Sunday, which meant Griff would show up to take them to church. Maybe it was better to let him break the news. After all, he actually knew the people involved.

Bracing herself, she pasted on a smile and entered the kitchen. Patricia was standing at the refrigerator, the freezer door open.

"I can't decide whether I want blueberry or cranberry this morning."

"Pull out one of each, and I'll split them with you."

"Oh, that's a good idea. And we'll do one of each for Griffin. He can eat one and take one home with him." She lifted the pastries from the freezer and laid them on the counter. "The boy needs his energy."

The teakettle went off before Evie could react to that semi-suggestive statement, and Patricia set the cups on the table while Evie dealt with the frozen scones.

She had no sooner set them in the microwave than she heard the doorbell. *Griff.* Every muscle tensed, but she refused to rush, concentrating on getting plates from the cupboard and putting the warm scones on them and onto the table. When she had her breathing under control, she answered the door. When Griff moved to touch her, however, she danced out of his way and hurried back into the kitchen.

Griff followed her, but when he bent to buss Patricia on the cheek rather than greeting him cheerfully, she scolded him

"If you are going to be sneaking around with my niece, Griffin, you could at least consider her reputation and be discreet about it."

Oh, God. Why hadn't she considered what Patricia might think before cavalierly allowing him to spend the night? And when had he actually left, anyway? "Patricia," she began, but Griff cut her off, laying a big, warm hand on her shoulder.

"I'm not sixteen anymore, Patricia. I don't sneak around. If I did, I'd park two blocks away like I used to when Candace and I met up at night." He stepped around the table and pulled out a chair. Patricia huffed but sat, some of the rigidity leaving her spine.

Next, he pulled out Evie's chair. As he guided her into it with a gentle nudge, he gave her a quick wink and she melted. He confused the hell out of her, but she wanted him more every day. Running her hands all over that incredible body the night before while knowing it was the closest she'd get to him as long as he was running for sheriff had about driven her crazy.

Patricia sipped her tea, but she wasn't through with her interrogation. "So if you don't call it sneaking around, what do you call it? Dating?"

"No!"

"Only because your niece is almost as stubborn as you are."

"We've been over this, Griff. The election—"

"Is county-wide and won't be decided on the basis of who I am or am not seeing."

Evie's hands shook. Her whole body wanted to follow, but she held herself perfectly still. "When did you decide that?"

"Last night, when I was inside Lila Renner's house and Clark was outside. Frankly, I wouldn't be at all surprised if he dropped out of the race."

Of course. Of course he would only see her publically if Clark dropped out. She'd insisted on it herself, after all. Still, her blood rushed through her body in a painful thrum and it was difficult to hear Patricia's question.

"Did something happen to Lila?"

"Yeah." Evie watched Griff's Adam's apple bob as he swallowed. Was he remembering the scene? Despite her own pain, the scream of betrayal clogging her throat, she laid a hand on his thigh beneath the table. "She killed herself."

"No," Patricia breathed. "What about the baby?"

"She's fine. She's with Frank's sister."

"Oh, poor thing." Griff and Evie's transgressions apparently forgotten, Patricia immediately began planning ways for the Ladies' Auxiliary to assist the Renners. Evie stood on the pretense of getting herself more tea, putting a bit of space between herself and Griff. He didn't say a word, but she could feel his eyes on her as she moved about the kitchen, bringing Patricia a phone to make the calls she needed to muster her troops and a pad and pen to give them their assignments and get commitments.

When they got to the church, the parking lot was filled with people talking in hushed tones. Word had obviously spread, as it was wont to do in Fairview. Evie spotted Clark Devane, his eyes red-rimmed and shadowed, his skin pasty, and suspected Griff had assessed him well—Devane didn't have the stomach for the job of sheriff.

Several groups turned to stare at them when they arrived, but for once their eyes weren't focused on her. No, they wanted the details—the painful, gory details—from Griffin. But he didn't say a word to anyone, merely ushered Evie and Patricia up to their usual spot and helped Patricia into the pew next to Candace.

The boys, perhaps sensing the mood, were more subdued than usual, but Teddy still managed to come up with a question for her. He scrambled to his knees and whispered loudly into her ear.

"How come you weren't here last week?"

"A friend of mine was visiting."

"You could have brought him. My mom brings Joey to church when he sleeps over."

"I'm sure she does. But this is Joey's church. My friend doesn't worship here and I didn't want to make him uncomfortable."

"Teddy, sit *down*," Candace hissed. "Jim, for God's sake, put him over here by me."

With an apologetic smile, Candace's husband picked up Teddy and moved him so he was sitting next to his mother. Then Billy had to move, too, because he didn't want to be separated from his twin. Which left Evie seated between Jim and Griff.

The bells tolled and people began making their way in from the parking lot, still murmuring, carrying the gossip inside.

Reverend Masters chose the perils of a faithless life

as his topic and while Evie was certain he'd written the sermon before hearing about Lila Renner's suicide, she hoped none of the woman's close friends or family were there to hear the glee in his voice as he described the torments awaiting those who ignored God's edicts.

Even Patricia was irritated by the time they left.

"You'd think, to listen to that man, that God had nothing better to do with His time than keep a big black book of every person's transgressions along with the appropriate punishment. I can't imagine what he was thinking to give a sermon like that today."

"Admittedly, I've only been here a few weeks," Evie said as Griff helped Patricia into the front seat of the SUV and she slid into the back, "but it seems the only message he knows how to deliver. Can't you—I don't know—petition to get him replaced?"

"You do like the big battles, don't you?" Griff asked with a snort.

"What do you mean?"

"He is a bit overzealous," Patricia admitted, "but that's hardly grounds for complaint. And he's the mayor's cousin."

"How very—"

"Fairview?" Patricia suggested as Griff started the truck.

"I was going to say irksome."

Griff laughed and a shiver went up Evie's spine. Damn, he needed to do that more often. Of course, if he did, she'd probably melt into a puddle of hormonal longing, so perhaps it was just as well he'd grown into a serious man.

At the house, Griff helped Patricia up the porch steps, but when Evie would have followed her aunt into the house, he put a hand on her arm. Immediately, goosebumps rose on her skin.

"I meant what I said this morning." Silver eyes stared into hers. "I want to take you out. Someplace proper. Someplace people will know we're on a date."

"Griff—"

His free hand came up to cup her cheek. "Just say yes, Evie. I'll be good, I promise."

That's what I'm afraid of. He would be good. Utterly, thoroughly, addictively good. Just being this close to him made her weak, sent her hormones into overdrive. What would it be like to sit across a candlelit table?

"No more excuses. I talked to Devane while you and Patricia were chatting with Candace after church. He's decided he's not ready to be sheriff. Let me at least take you to Cabot House on Wednesday night when the Good Time Charlies are playing."

"They're still around?" Firmly, she squashed the hurt that threatened at the reminder he'd waited to ask her out until after Devane had bowed out of the sheriff's race.

"Mmm-hmm. The membership changes, but the name remains. Still playing the greatest hits of the fifties through the eighties for your listening pleasure." He leaned even closer, so close that only a whisper separated their bodies, so close she could feel his heat and smell the musky scent of his skin. She shivered. "You do still like to dance, don't you, Evie?"

"Y-yes."

"Yes, you like to dance, or yes, you'll come out with me?"

"Both."

A slow smile spread across his face, stealing what little moisture was left in her mouth.

"Good. I'll pick you up Wednesday at seven."

It wasn't until he was driving away that Evie remembered the last time she'd seen him at Cabot House he'd had Hazel with him. She'd never managed to determine whether that had been a date. She didn't *think* so, but her judgment where men were concerned was notoriously poor.

As she entered the house, Patricia called out from the kitchen and Evie went to join her, bracing herself for more questions about Griff. But her aunt had moved on.

She was pulling baked items out of the freezer and stacking them in a reusable grocery bag.

"The Ladies' Auxiliary is meeting at Candace's in a couple of hours to discuss what we can do for the Renners. Beth Ann is bringing a coffee urn from the store and we will bring the food. That way we can be comfortable while we strategize."

"I thought you'd done that on the phone this morning." Evie gestured to the pad of notes next to the grocery bag on the table.

"Oh, sweetie, you've been gone too long. That's barely the beginning. When your mama died and you came to live with us, I didn't cook for a month. People showed up once or twice a week with food. There were fresh flowers delivered twice to keep the place cheerful, and before you even arrived a boxload of toys showed up so Candace wouldn't have to share hers.

"Frank Renner's a long-haul trucker. He'll need all kinds of help that Harry and I didn't. All I did this morning was start things rolling. This kind of emergency is what the Ladies' Auxiliary exists for."

Evie blinked away tears. "Have I told you lately how amazing I think you are and how grateful I am that you guys took me in back then?"

"Well, of course we did, Evangeline. You're *family.*"

And for Patricia, it really was that simple. No complex system of debts and balances, no treacherous morass of emotional quicksand, just doing the right thing.

THERE WERE ABOUT TEN WOMEN gathered at Candace's when Evie and Patricia arrived. A few looked vaguely familiar, but the only one Evie really recognized was Juliette Robbins.

"I got my package on Friday," she said with a wink. "So much fun opening it."

Evie grinned. "Just what you wanted?"

"Precisely."

"So tell me about the Ladies' Auxiliary. I am ashamed to admit it, but this is actually a younger crowd than I expected."

Juliette chuckled. "It's a dreadful name, isn't it? But it's tradition, and trying to change things isn't so easy. Once upon a time, the Auxiliary members were the wives of the volunteer firefighters. Now anyone who wants to help out can join. We do things like this, or we organize protests when Wal-Mart or McDonald's try to buy up big plots of land, or we raise money for programs at the school. Plus, of course, helping out the fire department."

"And what do you do with yourself when you're not fighting corporate giants?"

"I teach high school English."

"Wow, right back to your favorite place."

"I like to think I am making it better. I taught in Nashville for a few years, but I hated the lack of autonomy in the bigger schools. Every class has to read the same thing at the same time. Here I am the only Senior English teacher. Within certain bounds, I can write my own curriculum."

A little bell rang and the room quieted.

"Candace kills me with that freaking bell," Juliette whispered. "But it's better than giving her a gavel."

Evie snickered.

"As most of you know," Candace announced, "Lila Renner died last night, leaving her husband and small daughter behind. I will now turn this meeting over to my mother, who has some ideas on how we can help."

Patricia waved from her seat by the fireplace. "Sorry not to stand up. Do let me know if you can't hear me properly."

"Don't worry Patricia," one of the women said with a laugh, "you always manage to make yourself heard."

Patricia huffed in mock offense.

"All right, then. Do we have any idea where the

situation stands for the Renners? I know Mary has the baby right now. Is there more family?"

"Duane says they caught up with Frank last night," offered one of the women Evie didn't recognize. "He's in New Hampshire. It's going to take him a while to get back. Lila's folks are dead and Frank's father lives in Germany. The baby—Rosie, her name is—is staying with Mary for the moment.

"That's Deputy Duane Thomas's wife, Cynthia," whispered Juliette. "She prides herself on knowing everything that goes through the sheriff's office."

Candace spoke up. "Mary Renner lives in a small apartment in Greeneville and works as a dental hygienist there. She can probably take a few days off work, but I doubt she's at all prepared to handle a baby, nor do I imagine she has any desire to move into the house where her sister-in-law killed herself."

"We should see whether she wants someone to go with her to pick up the baby's things," said Patricia.

"I can do that. Duane will take me if Mary doesn't want to go at all."

"Bragging rights," whispered Juliette.

"Do you have something to add, Juliette?" asked Candace.

"Nope! I was just thinking we ought to organize a group of caregivers who don't have day jobs in case Mary can't get time off. Frank will have to work out a long-term solution himself, but I suspect that will take him a while."

"I've already set up food deliveries for this week," Patricia said. "Anyone interested in getting on the schedule for the future should let me know. Since Mary lives in an apartment, she won't have a chest freezer; we'll have to deliver the food every couple of days. Frank does have one, so once he's back living in the house we can stock that.

"It's hard to know exactly what they'll need until we have some idea of Frank's future plans, but for the moment we should set up a schedule to check in on Mary. Twice a day, I think, should be sufficient to let her know she's not alone."

Which was the point, Evie was beginning to realize. Sure, living in the Fairview fishbowl could be a pain, but perhaps it wasn't always such a bad thing.

And then an unfamiliar voice reminded her why she appreciated the anonymity of Vegas. "You know, Frank drinks." The woman who said it was about Evie's age, but as buttoned down and buttoned up as any old maid one could imagine. "Lila was convinced having the baby would save their marriage."

"Dierdre…"

"It's true, Patricia. I told her she'd end up raising that baby alone. Frank's been home less and less, and when he *is* home, he's drunk."

"Enough!" Patricia glared at the woman. "Right now, that's not our business."

Right now? When, exactly would it be the business of the town busybodies whether Frank Renner drank or not? What could they possibly do about it?

"At the moment, all we need to know is how long we have until Frank gets back to Fairview."

"Three or four days."

Evie whipped around at the sound of Griff's voice.

"Didn't mean to interrupt your meeting, but I figured you'd like to know. He's finishing this run he's on, then he'll be back. Until then, Mary's in charge of the baby."

"Thank you, Griffin, that is very useful."

Evie slipped through the crowd until she stood next to Griff. His eyes went from pewter to silver in an instant and he offered her a small, private smile.

"How you doing?" she asked.

"Better. Been a rough day, but seeing this helps."

Evie looked around the room. "It *does*?"

Candace glared at her. Ooops. That had been a bit too loud.

Griff took her hand and tugged her out of the room

and then out of the house altogether. Once they were safely away she tried to pull out of his grasp but he wouldn't let her go. Instead, he drew her closer. "Seeing the ladies in there come together to help one of our own, yeah, it helps. It restores a little—I wouldn't call it faith, exactly, more like balance I guess. Keeps me from getting burnt out.

"But it doesn't touch what you did for me last night."

A blush crawled up Evie's cheeks. "Anyone would have done the same thing."

"Nope. Not only wouldn't they, but they didn't. You did. It's been a damned long time since anyone took care of me like that." He bent his head and caught her lips with his own and heat shot straight through her. Her legs went weak and her arms slid around his neck practically of their own accord. His hands skimmed up and down her back, the light touch sending shivers cascading through her.

And then, suddenly, he drew back.

"Christ, woman, what you do to me. This is not exactly the time or place…"

Good God. They were standing out in front of Candace's house right in the middle of town. Anyone driving by would see them. And Evie needed to be inside, helping her aunt and her cousin. What had she been thinking?

Well, duh, she hadn't been thinking at all. Griff tended to have that effect on her.

"I have to get back inside."

"Yeah." He swallowed. "Yeah. I'll see you Wednesday." He kissed her again, and although this one was as light as the touch of a butterfly, it was just as potent. She had to wait a moment for her breathing to even out and her legs to start working again before she could open the door and face the crowd of women again.

Despite her attempt to be inconspicuous, several of the women stared at her as she re-entered the living room. The conversation had moved on from Frank's drinking habits to a more general discussion of childcare around town, and Evie gathered the business part of the meeting was at an end. She started to make her way over to her aunt, but Candace laid a hand on her arm to stop her and tugged her back out into the entry.

"I know you're not part of the Auxiliary, and you're not planning on staying in town, but you could at least be respectful."

"Respectful?" Evie kept her voice low, but she couldn't prevent the angry tremble. "Like it's *respectful* to treat me like your mother's servant rather than your own cousin? You do know the one about the pot and the kettle, right?"

"Gossiping with Juliette and playing kissy-face with Griff during our meeting is completely inappropriate!"

"Griff and I needed to talk, so we went outside. We didn't interrupt your precious meeting—which, by the way, contains more gossip than any conversation I might have with Juliette."

"Talk. Right. Is that what they're calling it these days?"

The thump of Patricia's crutches against the marble entry tiles cut off Evie's response. "Evangeline, I'm ready to go home. It's been a long day. You don't mind, do you?"

"Not at all."

"Is everything okay, mom?"

"Oh, yes." Patricia kissed Candace's cheek. "I was just up early this morning, and the tragic news has worn me out a bit. Will you come by once you've visited with Mary and tell me how she's doing?"

"Of course. I plan to see her tomorrow morning since I have the morning off, and I'll drop by the store afterwards."

"Perfect."

Yeah, perfect. Immediately, guilt hammered Evie for the unkind thought. She'd misjudged her cousin, assumed Candace had taken the easy way out of caring for her mother when she called Vegas. But that hadn't been the case. Candace hadn't wanted Evie around when they were kids, and it was pretty clear that hadn't changed, but it was time for both of them to pull up their big girl panties and learn to get along for Patricia's sake if nothing else.

CHAPTER 9

M ONDAY MORNING, EVIE THREW HERSELF into re-doing the store's display window with their new "A Good Yarn" theme. Patricia had brought a bunch of yarn and both knitting and crocheting supplies from home, and Evie ran down to the five and dime and found a small pirate's chest among the Halloween paraphernalia, along with more poster board for a sign. She filled the chest most of the way with packing paper from the storeroom, then covered the rest with a hand-knitted sweater from Patricia's collection, some knitting needles, a couple of crochet hooks, stitch keepers, and some pattern books.

Around the chest, Evie arranged more pattern books, plus stitchery-themed mysteries and romances, going for a combination of color, size, and style to make the display pop. She was still crawling around in the cramped space when Candace arrived. Rather than hurrying along to give the town less to look at, she slowed down, hoping to avoid her cousin altogether.

Candace stuck her perfectly-coiffed head into the opening. "Morning, Evie. Whatcha putting in?"

"Patricia has decided to do some stitch'n'bitch sessions."

"Sounds like fun. I have a half-dozen unfinished projects myself." She pulled back and Evie heard her talking to Patricia.

"Mary was really grateful for all the stuff I brought

over," she said. "She's freaking out. Was babbling about how they'd practically fired her for asking for the week off and how she couldn't possibly get any more."

"I'm so glad you were able to go over this morning. Not that I don't trust the others, but you grew up in the Auxiliary."

"Her apartment is really small. I understand why staying at the house isn't an option, but that place really isn't built for a baby. It's going to be tough to squeeze in the crib, let alone anything else. Cynthia's borrowing Duane's truck this afternoon to help bring the crib and a few outfits from the house over, but Mary isn't sure how much Lila even had. She says she tried to organize a baby shower when Lila was pregnant, but Lila didn't have many friends, so it didn't work out."

How sad was that? Griff's description of the condition of Lila's arms and legs slipped through Evie's mind and she rubbed her hands over her arms to subdue the sudden chill. Which had come first, the isolation or the cutting?

She stepped out of the window.

"Maybe during the first stitch'n'bitch, people who don't have current projects could think about making stuff for Rosie."

"Oh, that's a great idea," said Patricia. "We could start a yarn collection, too—everyone has yarn they bought for one reason or another and will never use. That way no one has to buy new to knit for a baby they've never met."

"You're not kidding," Candace agreed. "I have at least two unisex kits I bought when I was pregnant with the boys and never got around to making. Hat and mitten sets. One's red and the other's yellow, I think."

"Wonderful." Patricia smiled and for the first time Evie felt completely in sync with her aunt and cousin.

"I have to get going," said Candace. "The Medfords are closing on their house today. I have to admit, it will be nice to help people who are taking steps forward in their lives." With a wave, she left.

"Does Candace keep pretty busy? Hard to imagine much call for attorneys in Fairview."

"She and her partner, Craig Lawrence, are the only game in town, so they have plenty of work. She's been after me for ages to make a will. I suppose I should, but I don't see the point—you girls can figure it all out. It's not as if I have so much. But Candace does a lot of that kind of thing. Wills, medical directives, real estate. Craig handles divorces and child custody agreements. Candace has done it, too, and she's qualified for it, but she doesn't enjoy it."

"I completely understand."

"Those kinds of things are more lucrative, but I must admit I wouldn't want to spend my days immersed in all that acrimony, either."

The day passed quickly, with plenty of women stopping in to ask about the new window. One woman, upon hearing about the yarn donations, went home and returned with a large, linen-lined wicker basket.

"I bought this ages ago and never found a use for it," she explained. "I can't keep my own projects in it because my cats would destroy them, but maybe you could find a spot for it for collecting yarn?"

"Oh, it's perfect!" said Evie. "I'll put it at the edge of the window so people can drop their donations in."

It wasn't until dinner that Patricia brought up the topic Evie had been dreading.

"So, when are you and Griffin going on your date?" she asked casually as Evie cut into her brisket.

Evie's stomach lurched and she put her fork down slowly so it wouldn't clink against the plate. "Wednesday night. The Good Time Charlies are playing at Cabot House."

"So you'll be gone for dinner?"

"I hadn't thought about it." *Much. Only every other second.* "We talked about dancing, not eating. I'll have to check."

"Of course he'll buy you dinner. He was raised right."

No use arguing with Patricia about the onset of the twenty-first century, so Evie just nodded.

TUESDAY, EVIE SPENT MOST OF the day leafing through crochet pattern books and trying unsuccessfully to avoid thinking about Griff. Her mother had taught her to crochet a basic flat stitch, and because both Patricia and Candace were knitters, Evie had continued working with yarn on and off through her teens. But she hadn't picked up a hook in years, and in that time the world of crochet had seemingly exploded. One of Patricia's books was full of "amigurumi," little crocheted stuffed animals, and Evie fell so hard for a baby giraffe that she immediately went online and ordered supplies to make it for Rosie when the Good Yarn meetings started.

Isabelle stopped by with a yarn donation and when Evie showed her the pattern book, she laughed.

"Oh, God, once you start it's all over. When I was a kid, I swore I'd never be a knitter. And then one day I needed new legwarmers and my mom wouldn't buy me the ones I wanted because they were too expensive, but she said she'd teach me how to make them. The rest is history." She looked up from the book.

"I hear you and Griff are coming to see me tomorrow night."

Evie grimaced. "Word sure does get around. I only told my aunt."

"He made a reservation, which he never does. He knows he can stop in whenever and I'll find a place for him even if we're full. So naturally I asked what the occasion was. If it was supposed to be a secret, he should have taken you to Greeneville. Or maybe even further."

"I guess that's true."

"So you've finally realized you're not the destroyer

of careers?"

"Haven't you heard? Clark Devane's dropped out of the race."

"Oh, for God's sake!" Both Patricia and Beth Ann looked up, and Izzy dragged Evie into a corner.

"You seriously waited until Clark dropped out to go after what you wanted?"

"No. That is…Once Griff knew who I was, what I did, he didn't ask me out until after Devane was done."

A line formed between Izzy's perfectly plucked brows. "Really? That's not like Griff. I mean, he's not the same rebellious kid he was, but he still has an independent streak. I'd never have imagined he'd care about people's opinions. Maybe the timing's just coincidence. Or—did you tell him about your concerns?"

Evie nodded.

"That's it, then. He probably figured you had no excuse once Clark was out of the running."

Could it be? Evie tried to recall Griff's exact words the morning he'd asked her out. He'd only said that Clark dropping out meant that Evie couldn't damage his election chances. Might all her hurt have been misplaced? Might he simply have been trying to reassure her? And did it change anything if he had been?

"I'm not staying in Fairview, Izzy." Though it was becoming harder to remember why every day.

"Cart before the horse much? You haven't had a single date with the man yet. Maybe he'll be so boring you'll be ready to run screaming at the end of the night."

"And if I'm not?"

Izzy shrugged. "Then you reevaluate. Cabot House wasn't always my dream, you know. I'd have kept trying the dance route if I hadn't met George. I doubt I'd have been successful—I wasn't kidding about not settling for the chorus—but finding him brought my whole life into focus."

"I wish I could have met him."

"I wish you could have, too. He was a complete geek.

Showed me so many things I'd never seen in my own hometown when I brought him back to meet my parents. And when he saw Four Winds, he was full to bursting with ideas for it, so we bought it."

"Wow."

"He was nine years older, and I am pretty sure he knew even then he didn't have all that much time. We wanted children, wanted so many things we never got. But we finished Cabot House, and when I'm there, it's almost as if he's beside me." She touched Evie's hand. "Don't let logistics get in your way. Trust me on this, sweetie. There's nothing you can't overcome if you're with the right person."

Izzy's words kept coming back all afternoon. Could Evie stay in Fairview, even for the right person? Could Griff be the right person? Could she be right for him?

Griff himself didn't show his face all day, not even for his usual morning coffee and scone. Probably avoiding the storm of gossip as long as possible. At four, he texted to ask her whether he could pick her up the next day at seven-thirty. Patricia laughed and opined that he was too nervous to call because he was afraid Evie would back out, but Evie figured texting was just easier.

Wednesday morning, Griff continued to avoid the Nook, which might have made him feel better, but only served to ramp up the tension that had kept Evie up all night. She'd tried to sleep, determined not to go on her date a haggard wreck, but her eyes kept popping open and her brain refused to shut down.

By closing time, she was about ready to jump out of her skin. She practically shooed the last two lingering customers out of the store and didn't even bother with the usual tidying up or closing out, promising Patricia she'd come in extra early to do it in the morning. She took her aunt's lack of argument as tacit approval of the date.

She ran her tub while she ironed the pale blue sundress with tiny yellow stripes she'd picked out for her date. With a pang, she thought of Celia, who'd packed the dress among the other things she'd sent for Evie. If she moved back to Tennessee, her friendship with Celia would change. Like her friendship with Benny. Cart before the horse, she reminded herself.

She washed her hair with the hand-held shower and dried it with her new blow dryer. Little signs of her small successes. Her fingers trembled so badly she had to remove her eyeliner twice and start over. No matter how she tried to convince herself that this was just another date, she wasn't that good a liar. It was different. Griff was different. He always had been.

He knocked on the apartment door precisely at seven-thirty, just as Evie was blotting her lipstick. Swallowing hard, she gave herself one final glance before she went to answer.

Evie had seen Griff dressed for work and for church, but dressed for a date the man purely stole her breath. Black denim molded lean hips and clung to muscular thighs, a sky-blue Oxford shirt showed off his tan and made his sandy hair gleam like gold, and well-worn motorcycle boots added just a touch of the whimsical rebel she remembered.

"You sure you can dance in those?" she teased, nodding at the boots.

"I'm not planning on doing the Bunny Hop, so yeah. Between my teen years and the Army, there's pretty much nothing I can't do in a pair of boots."

A flood of images of Griff in those boots and nothing else robbed Evie of speech and set her blood on fire. Completely misinterpreting her little shiver, he picked up the jacket she'd hung on the closet door and held it out for her. As he helped her into it, lifting her hair from the back, his fingers brushed her neck and her mouth went dry. Eating dinner was going to be difficult.

GRIFF HAD BEEN NERVOUS AS hell, but dinner with Evie

was easy. He worried, after her presentation and hearing how she'd worked to get her degrees, that he would have to struggle to come up with topics she'd find interesting. But no awkward silences interrupted the conversation. Evie told him stories about the women—and men— she'd met dancing in Vegas, about how she'd met Benny, and a few of the more outrageous things that had happened at Goody's Goodies.

And she got him to talk about things he never discussed. Like the night he'd been arrested. And some of the truly crazy things he'd done in boot camp. And the afternoon they got a visiting USO celebrity to sign one of the on-base missiles after far too much caffeine, far too little sleep, and a long and mostly incoherent discussion of Dr. Strangelove.

"There's a lot of that time I don't remember, and even more I don't particularly want to remember," he admitted, "but some of it was great. And when people ask me if I regret it, given what happened at the end, well, the road I was headed down I was likely to end up just as badly scarred from a bike accident. I could have died the night my dad bailed me out."

"Thank goodness you didn't."

"Would you have missed me?" He reached across the table and touched her chin and she blushed. That had to be a good sign, right?

"I don't know. I guess it depends on how well you can dance."

He choked on a laugh. The first one that night had surprised him. He didn't consider himself a laugher. But her stories had kept him grinning most of the evening. "I guess that means you've finished eating?"

She glanced down at the plate that had once held a chicken breast with tarragon sauce, rice pilaf, and sautéed broccoli rabe. "Unless you want me to lick my plate, I think so."

He shook his head, stood, and held out his hand. "Then let's show 'em how it's done."

As soon as her fingers touched his, every muscle in his body clenched and he had to force himself not to pull her into his arms right there and make a complete and utter spectacle of himself. She was so damned sweet and soft, despite her very real tough side. He led her down to the dance floor on the far side, where the Good Time Charlies had begun to play about half an hour earlier.

"Good grief," she said as they got to the floor and the band finished up their rendition of "Jackie Wilson Said," "is that Max Brannigan?"

"Yep. High school music geek turned rockin' keyboard player. At least when he's with the Charlies. The rest of the time he's still the high school music geek, only now they call him the music director."

"Jeeze."

And then, as if he'd paid them to do it—which he would have if he'd thought of it ahead of time—the band segued into Eric Clapton's "Wonderful Tonight." He tugged Evie close and wrapped his arms around her.

In heels, she was just a couple of inches shorter than he, and pressed to his body she fit against him like a dream, as if she had been made just for him. A few other couples dotted the small dance floor, but he paid them no mind as he and Evie swayed to the music.

The song ended and the band picked up the pace, heading into "Suspicious Minds," and Griff let Evie ease away to a more appropriate distance for the song's speed. They'd only gotten one verse in when the phone in his back pocket buzzed.

"Oh, hell. Why did I bring that thing with me?" He pulled it out and glanced at the number. The office.

"Because you're the sheriff?"

"Christ." He dropped his head and rested his forehead against Evie's. "Maybe if I ignore them, they'll go away."

BUT THE PHONE CONTINUED TO ring, and with a sigh

Evie could feel, Griff led her from the dance floor.

"This better be good, Hazel," he said by way of greeting. He listened for a moment, then rubbed the spot directly above one eye with his fingertips. "She did what?" He waited. "Yeah, that's what I thought you said. Okay, tell them to back off and let her know I'm on the way."

He clicked off.

"I'm sorry, Evie. This is my fault."

"Your job, not your fault."

"No, this one's all on me."

"What happened, if you can say?"

"It's Sarah Branck."

"Mrs. Branck, the third grade teacher?" Though Evie'd been too old when she moved to Fairview to be taught by the woman, she was an institution.

"That's her. Her husband died about a year ago, and ever since she calls in every couple of weeks to report a prowler. My dad always went out personally, so when I took over the job, I kept it up. Tonight, Hazel sent Josh Melville because she didn't want to disturb me, and Sarah chucked a flowerpot at him."

Despite the pity she felt for the older woman, Evie couldn't help laughing. "Was there a plant in it?"

"Yeah." Griff grinned, then sobered. "She also called him by his father's name, which is a bit disturbing. But she's had episodes of confusion before, and she's always snapped back, so with a little luck we can get this all straightened out." He touched her cheek. "I just hate like hell to cut our date short. I'll drop you at home on my way out there."

"Don't. I'll come with you, if that's okay."

"Of course it is. This won't be an official visit—it's not like Josh is going to charge her with assault. But why would you want to?"

She wished she knew. Yes, she's always liked Mrs. Branck. And yes, she felt sorry for the woman who, from Griff's description, was obviously lonely. But the tug in her heart had as much to do with Griff as with Sarah Branck.

"I guess I don't want our date to end, either." Not wanting to answer any other questions he might come up with, she hurried on. "And maybe I can help."

"Well, okay, then." Griff grinned, dropped a twenty-dollar bill on their table, and took her hand in his. The scrape of his callused fingers against her own sent a thrill through Evie, and she struggled to keep her voice even as she teased him.

"Why, Sheriff, you don't pay your bills?"

"Nah. Izzy knows I occasionally have to take off in a hurry, so I leave a tip and she runs a tab for me."

At the car, Griff pulled her into a quick embrace. "I swear to you, Evie, it's not always like this."

She looked up into his eyes in the dark parking lot. Something in his gaze, in the fervency of his voice…he was promising more than his words indicated. More than she could readily accept.

"Come on," she teased, resorting to humor once more, "this is Fairview. I know what a hotbed of crime and corruption it is."

Griff laughed. "I guess you do."

The drive to Sarah Branck's house took only a few minutes. Josh Melville, who Evie vaguely recognized as having been a couple of years behind her in school, stood on the sidewalk talking to Rachel. Dirt clung to his hair and streaked his uniform.

"Thank God," he said when Griff stepped from the car.

"Go on home and get cleaned up," Griff told him. "I'll handle it from here."

"Do you want me to stick around?" Rachel asked.

"Nah, we're good. Go on with your rounds."

Rachel gave Evie a cheerful wave as she drove off. Josh didn't say a word, but she could feel his curiosity. Tomorrow, all of Fairview would be abuzz with the fact that Griff had brought her along on a work-related incident. If Devane hadn't dropped out of the sheriff's race, such gossip might have given him a serious edge.

"Shall we?" Griff broke into her thoughts, holding out his hand. Together, they walked up the path toward the house.

"Mrs. Branck? Sarah?" Griff called when they were a few feet from the door.

A curtain shifted in the front window and a minute later the front door opened.

"It's about time! I could have been killed!"

"You could have seriously injured Josh Melville. You cannot throw things at my deputies."

"Deputies?" The old woman frowned. "Ted Melville's no deputy. He's a mechanic. When he's not drunk."

"That wasn't Ted," Griff explained patiently. "That was Josh. His son."

Sarah's frown cleared. "Josh is a good boy. Terrible at math, though."

"Yes, he is. And you shouldn't throw things at him."

Sarah peered out at them. "Who's that with you?"

Evie stepped forward into the light spilling out of the house. "Evie Bell, Mrs. Branck. I'm Patricia Stewart— Patricia Bell's niece."

"Oh, of course. The pretty one's daughter. What was her name? Emma?"

"Yes, Ma'am."

By that time, both she and Griff were standing in the doorway. "Why don't we all go inside for a few minutes," he suggested.

"Oh, oh, of course." Sarah led them inside and she and Evie sat on the sofa. "I can't believe you're back in town. Such a shame what Marissa and Johnny did to those girls."

Evie had never met her mother's parents. Emma had rarely even mentioned them. How odd that she'd never noticed the silence.

"What did they do?

"All that nonsense about Patricia being the smart one. Too much pressure to put on a child. I tried to tell them children understand that sort of thing. But when you don't have your own, no one listens."

"You don't have children?" There went Evie's first idea of finding a son or daughter to help the woman.

"Oh, we wanted them. But we weren't so blessed. Still, I understand them." Sarah's rheumy eyes pleaded with Evie.

"Of course you do. Everyone in Fairview hoped their children would get you as a teacher."

"That's sweet of you to say." She blinked a couple of times, then frowned. "Why are you here?"

"I came with Griff— with Sheriff Barstow. You called to report a prowler."

"Oh, that's right."

Griff settled on a chair across from them and propped his elbows on his knees. "Sarah," he said gently, "I looked around. There's no one here."

"I know what I saw."

Evie shook her head minutely, begging Griff to let her handle Sarah. He leaned back.

"Do you think the prowler meant you harm?" Evie asked. "Did he feel threatening to you? Or did he just surprise you."

"Well, what else would he be?"

"It's just a thought, you understand, but I did wonder…do you believe in spirits?"

"You mean ghosts?"

"Not the chain-dragging, house-haunting type. I mean more the benevolent manifestation of a lasting love." Said aloud, it sounded ridiculous. But Sarah seemed to consider it.

"You think I am seeing a ghost. Of Joe."

"I don't know. But no one else can see him and I can't help wondering whether that's because we're not meant to. He appears to you when you're missing him most."

"Then he'd be here all the time." Sarah wrapped her arms around herself and Evie's heart clenched. She stroked the woman's back lightly.

"I understand. Even after all these years, I still occasionally do a double take because I think I see my mom out walking or in a shop. I still talk to her when I need advice."

"I talk to Joe all the time," Sarah admitted.

"He wouldn't want you to be so alone," Evie said. "Perhaps you could consider a dog? They're said to be very sensitive. A dog would bark if there were a prowler outside, but wouldn't concern himself with a spirit watching over you."

"My friends have suggested getting a pet for companionship, but I don't know."

"I could come by one afternoon when Patricia doesn't need me and we could go to the shelter and look. It can't hurt, and maybe one will call to you. If not, no harm, no foul."

"I suppose."

"Let me talk to Patricia, and then I'll give you a call and we can make a date. Okay?"

Sarah Branck nodded slowly and patted Evie's knee. "You're a good girl. Just like your mother. Big hearts, both of you."

Evie's throat clogged. "Thank you. That's very sweet of you to say."

"Well, then," said Griff, "are we all set here? Sarah, you're going to be okay for the rest of the night?"

"Yes, yes. I'm sorry for interrupting your date."

"Don't you worry about that. You know you can always call. Any time."

Sarah pushed herself to her feet and walked them to the door. On impulse, Evie leaned over and kissed her papery cheek. "I'll talk to you soon and we'll go looking at pound puppies."

"That sounds lovely."

CHAPTER 10

"Come home with me," Griff said as the door closed behind Sarah and they heard her shoot the bolt.

It shouldn't have shocked her. Not with the way the evening had gone so far. But it did, and she blurted out the first thing that came to mind. "And take the walk of shame tomorrow morning in clothes everyone will know I wore to Cabot House tonight?"

"Is that what you would feel? Shame? If people knew we were seeing each other?"

"Of course not." She swallowed, then met his eyes. "Is that what we're doing? Seeing each other?"

"I thought that was the point of dinner and dancing."

She tapped him on the chin to lighten the mood. "I thought that was just to soften me up. Maybe get me tipsy."

His lips quirked. "Okay, you caught me. That probably *was* lurking in the back of my mind."

Damn, that dimple really did it for her.

"I promise, I'll get you home before even the earliest of the early birds are up to peep and cheep to each other about our activities."

"What the hell. Your competition has folded, so you no longer have to worry about votes. As the song says, let's give 'em something to talk about."

A fleeting frown creased his forehead. "Evie—" but he cut himself off, shaking his head. He opened the passenger door to the SUV and helped her in, then reached over her slowly, deliberately, his shoulder just brushing her breast, to snap her seatbelt in place. "Wouldn't want you to get hurt," he said as he retreated. His lips touched hers so lightly as he passed her she might have thought she imagined it but for the searing heat that shot straight down through her body at the contact. Before she could respond, however, he was out and loping around the front to climb into the driver's seat.

Once they were moving, he took her hand again, this time gently, almost hypnotically tracing random patterns with his thumb. Evie couldn't remember the last time someone other than her mother had held her hand before she'd run across Griff. If she'd been asked, she would probably have said the idea held no appeal, that it seemed a trifle juvenile. But there was nothing childish about the rough glide of his skin against her own, nor about the tiny explosions of sensation slicing through her.

Neither of them spoke. Even when they arrived at the house and Griff helped her out of the SUV and led her up to the front door, he didn't say a word. Was he afraid he would break a spell? Afraid she would change her mind if he said the wrong thing?

And then, suddenly, as if conjured by her thoughts, apprehension swamped her.

"Griff," she said as they walked into the living room. "I need to explain something."

"C'mere. Let's sit." If her words—with their implication that she was backing out—angered or frustrated him, he didn't show it. "I'll get you a glass of wine and we can talk. I haven't been holding up my end of the 'get you tipsy' bargain." He winked and she felt a little of her fear dissipate.

He settled her on the sofa and then went into the kitchen. "I'd ask you whether you preferred red or white, but I only have red," he called. "Sorry." He came back holding two generously-filled jelly jars.

"The décor's not as nice as Cabot House, either," he said, setting the wine down on the coffee table and then sitting beside her. "My old man's a beer drinker. Well, that and bourbon. There aren't any wine glasses in the house." He slid an arm over her shoulders and pulled her close. Again, he brushed his lips over hers quickly, almost reflexively.

"Now. Tell me what's on your mind."

As if she could even think when he was pressed up against her side, the heat from his body surrounding her, sensation swamping her.

But she had to. She had to be clear. They both deserved it.

"Look. I don't…here's the thing: I haven't been with anyone in a long time." The words came out in a rush. "Idon'twanttodisappointyou."

He didn't dismiss her words, but he picked up her hand a pressed a long kiss into the center of her palm. "What makes you think you could disappoint me?"

Wine. She needed wine. She took a long swallow, then continued to hang onto the jelly jar with her free hand and stared into the ruby liquid as if it held tea leaves.

"People have expectations," she said at last. "You know. I'm a dancer, I must be flexible. I'm a showgirl, I must be experienced. I sell sex toys, I must be adventurous."

"And you don't think you are."

"Well, I guess I'm flexible enough. That's just biology. But it's been years since I danced and even longer since I slept with anyone."

That took him by surprise.

"You haven't had sex in four *years*?"

She shrugged. "After the surgery, I didn't want to for a long time. And then…well, working for Benny, most of the people I met seemed to think I would just jump into bed with them. I went out with a few men, but when I wasn't ready to hop into the sack after one date, they would be…disappointed."

"You mean you weren't easy, so they didn't bother to call for a second date?" He sounded so horrified on her behalf she almost laughed. Until she remembered Theo.

"Pretty much. One guy didn't even take it *that* well. He got really angry. That's when I stopped even trying. I figured the toys were easier to deal with."

"What do you mean, he got angry?" The words were a low, dangerous growl.

"Griff—"

"Did he hurt you? Dammit, Evie look at me."

She did, and suddenly everything in her stilled. His face was white, his eyes blazing with fury.

"Did. He. Hurt. You."

"A little. Not badly. By the time we got to that point on our date, I had a pretty good idea that he wasn't going to take rejection well, so I decided to end it at the casino where I used to work instead of letting him drop me at home. When I explained that I had no plans to sleep with him, he hit me—once—before casino security took him down. It was all on film, and it was apparently not the first time he'd gotten drunk and gotten into trouble, so he went to jail. And I switched to battery operated boyfriends."

"Jesus." Griff took the wine from her hands and laid it back on the coffee table with trembling hands, then dragged her into his lap and wrapped her so tightly in his arms she had trouble breathing. He buried his face in her neck and rocked slightly.

Evie didn't know what to do. Her hands stroked his thick, silky hair.

"Is he still in jail?" The words were muffled against her neck.

"I have no idea. I doubt it. That was two years ago."

"What's his name?"

She pulled back slightly to look down into his face. "What's going on, Griff?"

"I just want to check his status, that's all. I need to

know that when you go back there you'll be safe."

"It's been two years, Griff. He's not coming after me."

WHAT IF THE GUY WAS STILL inside and that was all keeping her safe? What if he'd only gotten out after Evie had left? She might believe she was safe, but she didn't know that kind of man, not the way Griff did. But he didn't really need the guy's name. He could find the case with the information he had. Just to be sure.

"You know, this was *so* not where I intended our conversation to go." Evie shifted on his lap and for a moment he feared she was going to leave, but she only reached for her wine glass, and his. "Maybe *I* need to get *you* tipsy."

Now she wanted him to joke, to flirt, when he was so torqued up by the idea of her getting hit, getting hurt, he could barely form a coherent sentence.

"But if, you know, you're not interested, I do understand. I mean, I sort of feel like I should come with a warning label about contents not as advertised or something."

He saw the flash of hurt as she started to scramble off his lap and it ripped through the fog in his mind. The hell was he letting her get away now. He grabbed her wrist with the hand not holding his wine and hung on until she met his eyes.

"I thought you were trying to tell me you didn't want to sleep with me. After all, you don't put out on the first date." *Weak, Barstow. Really weak.* But she smiled a little and the shadows faded from her gorgeous eyes.

"I'd hardly call this our first date."

"I promise, our next first date will be better."

At that, she actually grinned, and her body relaxed back into his, and he could breathe again. "That's not what I meant and you know it."

"Well, how many dates would you say we were at,

then?"

"I have no idea! Why does it matter?"

"Because if you don't put out on the first date, then there's a schedule. And I need to see where we are in it." Gently, he cupped one hand over her left breast. "Are we far along enough for this?" he asked, rubbing his thumb back and forth across the nipple that poked through the fine cotton of her dress.

"Oh." Her lids drooped and her breathing went slow and soft. She squirmed on his lap and instantly his dick reacted, sucking all the blood from the rest of his body. "Oh, yes. We definitely are," she murmured.

"Excellent." He took her mouth, tasting the wine mixed with that unique sweetness he'd noticed the very first time he'd kissed her. Slowly, he lowered her back until he was lying next to her, him on his side, her on her back, leaving his hand free to coax the buttons of her sundress loose from their holes.

It was like unwrapping the most delicious package ever. Each button revealed more tantalizing, tempting flesh, and each time he had to touch, to feel, to taste. Beneath his ministrations, her body arched and she moaned.

EVIE HAD NEVER EXPERIENCED ANYTHING like being with Griff. Everywhere he touched her—and that was *everywhere*—he left a trail of fire behind. Her skin burned, her blood boiled, and all she could think about was getting closer, getting him inside her.

He spread open the bodice of her sundress and pushed himself up on his elbow to look down at her. His fingers traced over her from collarbone to waist, then detoured up to circle her right nipple through the lace of her bra. Her thighs clenched with need.

"Pretty," he said, then bowed his head and sucked her breast into his mouth. His teeth scraped through the lace and her whole body tightened. She was on the edge of orgasm, and he still had all his damn clothes on!

Her fingers made quick work of the buttons on his dress shirt, only to be confronted with the tee he wore beneath it. With a growl of frustration, she slid her hands beneath that to the hot, silky skin beneath.

"Bed," he murmured. "Now." He levered himself off the couch and, before she realized his intent, lifted her into his arms and headed for the stairs. She wanted to tell him he didn't have to carry her, but she wasn't sure it was true. Her legs were shaking. And besides, what a rush to feel all that muscle all around her.

At the top of the stairs, Griff kicked open a door and she got a flash of masculine, gold-and-brown décor before he knelt on the bed and set her down and all her attention refocused directly on him. He kissed her again, and the whole world centered on her mouth, his tongue, their one spot of joining.

He made quick work of the cuffs of his dress shirt, then pulled both it and his tee over his head and rolled atop her, his legs pinning hers, his chest rubbing against her sensitized nipples, his mouth feasting on her neck, then nibbling her earlobe until she pushed him off and reversed their positions.

She ran her hands over his chest, over the scarred tissue that now seemed to embody perfection to her, down his flat abdomen, following the light trail of dark blonde hair to the top button of his jeans. His breath came harsher, louder in the quiet room and she saw the erratic movement in his abs as she pulled the button free and grasped the top of the zipper. Carefully, slowly, she pulled the tab down. Beneath, boxer briefs outlined his arousal.

Which twitched in reaction as she looked at it.

She ran a finger down his length and Griff hissed. He slid out from under her and disposed of the pants, then stood beside the bed, naked and stunningly, shockingly gorgeous, staring down at her, his silver eyes glowing with heat that spiked through her. With trembling fingers, she hurried to undo the rest of the buttons on her dress, then stripped it off.

For a moment, she hesitated, kneeling there on the bed in her bra and panties. What would he think of her body? Had she gained too much weight since quitting dance?

But with a low sound of approval, he pushed her back down to the bed, following her down so that he lay beside her. He flicked open the front clasp of her bra and spread it wide. Beneath the heat of his gaze, her nipples tightened to an almost painful pinch and liquid heat pooled between her legs.

"Evie, Jesus," he muttered, then bent his head and sucked her breast into his mouth, sending flames shooting through her entire body. His hand swept down her stomach and his long fingers slid beneath the waist of her panties. She spared a brief thought for just how thoroughly she'd soaked those panties, then one of his fingers slipped inside her and all thought ceased. He drove her crazy, his mouth lapping, tugging at her breast, fingers inside her, delving, pumping, circling until she flew apart into a million tiny pieces.

And then, while her heart still thundered, he bared her completely, and his tongue followed her scar down from her belly button, over her abdomen, still twitching and shaking in reaction, until he took her clit gently in his teeth. Which almost sent her right over the edge a second time. But she forced the reaction down and slid her fingers through his silky hair to pull him back up her body for a kiss.

God, he tasted good. Dark and rich and somehow sweet, like the very best chocolate, with the hint of red wine and, overlaying it, the tang of her own arousal. She could kiss him forever, if she didn't need something else more urgently. She pushed him onto his back and slipped one leg over so she knelt astride him.

"You're my prisoner now, Sheriff," she said. "What shall I do with you?" She scraped her nails lightly down his chest, watching the muscles jump and twitch.

"Anything you want." He fisted a hand in her hair and pulled her down for another kiss. "Anything."

"Ooh, right answer," she murmured into his mouth. Shaking him off, she began to move down his body, running her tongue over the shiny puckers of scar tissue and smooth warm skin, tasting the salt of his sweat and the faint hint of something soapy. She pressed a kiss to one sharply defined hipbone, then deliberately let her breasts brush across his erection as she switched to the other side. His hips came up off the bed in an involuntary move that made her grin. *Oh, yeah.*

She caught his eyes with her own and slowly, slowly took him into her mouth. As she sucked him deeper, he gave another little involuntary pulse. His eyes shut and his hands clenched in the sheets.

FOR A FEW MINUTES, GRIFF allowed her to tease him. Her mouth was hot and wet and every time she pulled back the slightest suggestion of teeth grazing along his cock had him jumping out of his skin. But damned if he was going to come this way. Not this time. He wanted to be looking into her eyes. He wanted to hear her shout his name at her own release.

On the very edge, he slid his fingers into her hair and tugged her back up his body. He flipped them both and in one smooth stroke was inside her. She sucked in a sharp breath and her inner muscles clenched tightly around him. *Oh, hell, yeah.* That was more like it. He held still as long as he could, letting her get accustomed to him, but when her fingernails bit into his butt, urging him on, his restraint snapped. He pumped into her hard, fast, and Evie met him thrust for thrust, locking her ankles around his back and digging her nails into his shoulders. He was almost gone, almost beyond his own limit when she sobbed out his name and her whole body tightened around him, her inner walls spasming so violently he could no longer contain himself. He came in a an overwhelming explosion that left him so weak he simply collapsed atop her, burying his head in the grapefruit-scented nest of her hair.

With the tiny bit of energy he could muster, he nuzzled her cheek and kissed her earlobe. She shuddered in a completely gratifying fashion.

"'m I crushing you?"

"Nnn." She squeezed him a bit. Also gratifying. Apparently he wasn't alone in being utterly wiped out. Still, he levered himself off, careful to pull her along with him so that when he rolled to his back, she was tucked neatly at his side, her head in the hollow of his shoulder.

This was how it should be. Every damned day and every night.

The thought should have scared him. If he considered it objectively, it did. Evie had no intention of staying in Fairview, and he couldn't imagine having this kind of reaction, this kind of connection, with another woman. He'd been kidding himself with his list of attributes of the perfect wife, the woman he'd someday settle down with. No wonder he hadn't found the right one.

He shoved the thought away. He had tonight; he couldn't waste it. He trailed his fingertips down her arm to her waist and over the sweet curve of her hip. She snuggled closer, letting her delicate hand rest on his chest, fingers moving in tiny circles as if she were trying to keep herself awake. He stroked her wild hair, smoothing the mess he'd made of it. Eventually, her fingers stopped moving and her breathing deepened into the even rhythm of sleep.

Still, he did not let her go, did not cease the slow strokes, even as he set his mind to work on the problem of how to keep her.

Evie might think she didn't belong in Fairview, but she was wrong. The people here loved her. If he were being completely fair, he'd admit that she obviously had people who cared about her in Vegas, too, but fairness didn't enter into it. Patricia needed her—not just physically, but emotionally—and Evie needed to learn what family meant. The Ladies' Auxiliary meeting had opened her eyes a bit to the positive aspects of small town life, but her childhood, and the less-than-welcoming reception she'd received upon her return, had scarred her.

He bore some of that guilt himself. The upcoming election and his fear of public disapproval had led him to treat her in ways that still shamed him. The memory of that day in the storeroom when he'd effectively deserted her at her weakest point absolutely gutted him. But that was the past. He would do better. He would prove to her that she could count on him, count on lots of people in Fairview. That she had reasons to stay even when Patricia had healed. His arms tightened around her and she shifted and muttered in her sleep.

But she was skittish. He couldn't just go announcing she should stay or she'd run for sure. If he wanted her to stick around, he'd have to be more devious.

Before allowing himself to fall asleep, he reached across Evie's body and set the alarm for four-thirty. He'd promised to get her home before the neighborhood woke up, and he intended to keep that promise. She needed to be able to face the local gossips without fear of further disapproval. Not that they wouldn't talk anyway, because they would. As soon as word got around that he'd taken her dancing, people would assume they'd slept together. Assumptions, however, didn't carry the same gossip currency as sightings. And he had no intention of allowing anyone to dismiss Evie on his account.

<h1 style="text-align:center">CHAPTER 11</h1>

GRIFF'S ALARM STARTLED EVIE OUT of a surprisingly deep sleep. Unaccustomed as she was to sharing her bed with a man, she would never have believed she could doze off in Griff's arms and sleep straight through. He rolled over, his big body covering her own for a moment, and shut off the alarm. Then he relaxed once again onto his back, pulling her against him.

"Morning," he said, voice rough with sleep.

"Is it really?" The sky outside was still dark, with not even the faintest glow of dawn.

"Afraid so. I need to get you home." He pressed his lips to her forehead, then put a finger under her chin to lift her face so he could kiss her properly. His mouth was hot and sweet, and the kiss went on forever. His callused hands slid over her skin, leaving a trail of goosebumps, and her nipples reacted immediately.

"Mmm." He rolled her over onto her back and dropped his head down to suckle each breast in turn.

"God, Griff." Her body was electrified, sparking and shaking. He'd taken her from half-asleep to soaking wet in seconds. She'd never experienced anything like it. She arched against him, demanding without words, but he merely grinned at her.

"Not sure we have time," he teased.

"Make time, dammit."

When he still didn't move, Evie reached down and grasped his cock, circling and squeezing. His eyes went black.

"Christ, woman." He freed himself from her fingers, then rolled so she was atop him. "You want me? Take me."

She'd never had such an offer. Didn't really know what to do with it. She drew her knees up so she knelt astride him, then took his erection in hand and positioned it at her entrance. His eyes never left hers, and as she sank down, she saw the dark flare of pleasure, the scalding heat she felt reflected in his gaze.

For a long moment, she stayed there, rocking slightly, feeling him so deep inside her it was as if they were a single organism. His hands came up to cup and fondle her breasts and she let her head tip back, arching into his touch. At last, though, she had to move. She began slowly, wanting it to last, but neither of them had the patience or control to keep to that pace. Who sped it up, she had no idea, but Griff's hands were at her waist, helping her move, pushing her to meet his thrusts, and moments later she tumbled over the precipice into a long, shuddering orgasm and felt his release flood through her.

She collapsed on top of him, completely done in, and felt his hand slide through her hair, petting her. It was the last thing she remembered feeling as she had fallen asleep and, oddly, the sensation this morning brought tears to her eyes. Sex was fine. It was great. But this kind of gentleness, it could be addictive. She forced herself to pull away.

"I guess we should get going."

"Maybe we should take a shower." Griff wiggled his eyebrows at her.

"I think I should probably wait to get home for that."

He gave a deep sigh and pulled her up for another kiss. "I suppose that would be best. Otherwise we might never get out of here." His fingers lingered on her body even as he drew away and crawled from the bed. He bent over to reach the clothes spread out on the floor, and

Evie couldn't help admiring the view of his long, strong legs and tight butt. Maybe they had time for that shower after all. *Down girl. Not for you.* Griff wanted a forever woman, a woman he could have a family with. Even if she could see staying in Fairview, she'd never be able to give him children. Theirs was a temporary arrangement, and she wouldn't embarrass Patricia or harm his future for a fling.

They drove back to Patricia's house in silence and Evie might have felt awkward if not for the fact that Griff held her hand the whole way. And then insisted on walking her up to the apartment.

"We have time," he said when she protested, "no one is watching."

She unlocked the door to the apartment and he pressed her back against the wall, his mouth covering hers for another scorching kiss.

"When can I take you out again?"

"I—" Her mouth dried up and she couldn't speak. She had to swallow and start again. "I don't know. I have to ask Patricia when it would be convenient for her."

"If it's not convenient during the day, I'll take you out late, when she doesn't need you. We'll go to the movies. We'll go to a bar. Places that stay open."

Public places. She understood what he was telling her. That these were dates. It should have thrilled her, his readiness to be seen with her, his open support. Instead, it terrified her.

"We'll see."

"Tell me you don't want this and I'll back off." He bent his head and brushed a kiss across her lips. "Tell me to go away, that you've had your fill."

Of course, she could do no such thing. He burned through her like fire, like an addiction. She'd seen friends lose their careers—even their lives—over drugs and never understood. But now she did. She would give him up eventually. But not yet. Not until she absolutely had to.

"I'll call you once I've talked to Patricia."

He grinned. "Do that."

Evie watched him walk back down the stairs before closing the door to the apartment. There was no point trying to sleep, so she ran a tub and slid into the steaming water, inching down until only her head and the tops of her knees stuck out. Her body hummed, fulfilled in a way she hadn't felt since, well, ever.

Which was *so* not good.

Food always tastes better when you're hungry. That's all. And then there was the build-up, the fantasy. She'd followed Griff around before she even understood what she wanted from him. Naturally, the consummation would seem more intense than with other men. The feeling wouldn't last.

She dunked her head beneath the water, then scrubbed shampoo into her hair and attached the hand-held shower to rinse it out, determined to rinse away obsessive thoughts of Griff at the same time.

Unfortunately, the ones that crept in to replace them were no less confusing.

Evie had attended her grandfather's funeral. She'd been six—no, seven—and her mother had driven them down to Fairview for three days. Hundreds of people had turned out for the service, all of whom had taken the time to express their condolences to her aunt and uncle, many even kneeling down to say a few words to Candace. When they got to Emma, however, they didn't have much to say. "Sorry for your loss," they'd mumble and then move on, casting pitying glances at Evie.

Was that the beginning of her resentment toward the town?

She climbed out of the bath and toweled off. As she dragged a comb through her tangled curls, she contemplated Sarah Branck's revelations. She'd called Evie "the pretty one's daughter," so even though she'd disapproved of Marissa and John Bell's treatment of their children, she'd internalized the distinction. How vindicated the Bells must have felt when Emma ran off to be a dancer and ended up a single mother. It probably never even occurred to them they'd predisposed her to such behavior with their low expectations.

And those low expectations had passed right down to her daughter.

More unpleasant thoughts to be pushed away. Evie picked up her new dryer and began to blow out a chunk of hair, running her fingers through it to separate the strands. The sensation of her fingertips against her scalp brought a sharp memory of Griff's hands in her hair the night before, but she ignored the image, as well as the tingling warmth accompanying it.

She should have bought leave-in conditioner along with the hair dryer. Shampooing too often would leave her with a head full of straw, and this was her second wash and dry in less than twenty-four hours. But after last night, it had been necessary. Otherwise she would have been certain people could see—could smell—what she and Griff had done.

And would that be so bad? She wasn't a child. Adults were allowed to have sex. Even casual sex. And now that Griff wasn't facing a difficult election, she didn't have to worry about hurting him.

But who was going to protect her? She had a sinking feeling getting involved with Griff might be the end of her.

Once her hair was dry, Evie dressed for the day and settled cross-legged on the bed with her laptop. She still had more than an hour before Patricia would be up, and she needed to start putting together the Nook's new website. They didn't need anything fancy—they weren't planning to compete with the big guys for online ordering—but customers had to be able to find out about upcoming events and sales, and email with questions and requests. Evie had learned the basics of website building in her degree program, but she hadn't had much practice.

Thus, she hadn't gotten very far when it was time to head down to the main house. She did, however, have a list of things she needed to get before the site could move forward, so that was a start.

WHEN SHE LET HERSELF INTO the main house, Evie could hear Patricia in the kitchen, and braced for an inquisition. Sure enough, even before the swinging door had shut, Patricia pounced.

"There you are! How was your date?"

"Very nice. The Good Time Charlies are still a lot of fun after all these years."

"I didn't hear you come in." Patricia switched on the burner under the kettle.

"I didn't realize you were waiting up. We had to go out on some county business. Mrs. Branck called the sheriff's office to report a prowler."

As Evie had hoped, that diverted her aunt. "Oh my goodness. Is she okay?"

"Oh, yes. It turned out to be nothing. But she was a little confused, which worried me. Josh Melville took the call first, and when he got there, she mistook him for his father."

Patricia frowned. "That's dreadful. I had lunch with her a few weeks ago…right before you got here…and she seemed perfectly normal. But she didn't make the Ladies' Auxiliary meeting at Candace's, which isn't like her at all. I should have called her right after that, but I was so caught up with the Renners' problems."

The kettle began to whistle, just as Evie heard the front door open.

"Are you expecting someone?"

Her aunt turned off the stove and poured water into three cups with tea bags. "That will be Candace herself. She's bringing over supplies for the Renners because Frank gets home today. I told her we could deliver them to the house after the store closes since she's got a PTA meeting for the boys tonight."

Candace pushed through the swinging door, bags in each hand. "There's more in the living room," she said. "Diapers, onesies, dry goods, formula. These are frozen casseroles for Frank." She laid the bags on the counter and began putting casseroles in the freezer. "I heard through the grapevine he got home last night."

"Oh, good. Has anyone heard what he plans to do about baby Rosie?"

"No clue." Candace shrugged and a childhood memory surfaced of her aunt screaming at Candace for answering every question with a shrug. Good to see her cousin hadn't lost all her rough edges.

But then Candace closed the freezer door and fixed her gaze on Evie. "I hear you and Griff went out last night."

Evie clamped down hard on the desire to tell Candace to butt out and instead turned her hand to putting three scones in the microwave and counted to ten. "That grapevine's been working overtime. Want to tell me every little detail in case I forget one or two?"

"This is *Fairview*. Word gets around fast. Especially given how many women are interested in Griff. Even before he became sheriff, people considered him a catch. Now, well, they're doubly interested."

"Speaking of Griffin's job," Patricia put in, "they had to go over to Sarah Branck's house last night. Did you know she was having memory lapses?"

"No, I had no idea! She always seems perfectly in control when I see her in town. And she always recognizes me, Jim, the boys…are you sure?"

The microwave dinged and Evie pulled out the scones and put them on plates on the table, then carried the three cups of tea over as well.

"Evie says she mistook Josh Melville for his father," said Patricia, settling into a seat. "Perhaps she only has trouble in the evening. It sometimes happens that way. And she wasn't at your house, even though I called and told her about the meeting myself."

"That's true. We'll have to figure out a visitation schedule to check up on her."

"I'm going to take her to the pound to see whether we can find a dog to keep her company," Evie offered.

"A dog? Like that's a replacement for human interaction?"

"I didn't say it was. But I think she's lonely, and the dog will give her a reason to go out and about and company when she's home."

"I think it's a lovely idea," said Patricia.

"Well of course you do. Your favorite child came up with it." Candace snatched the bags off the countertop and stormed out. If the swinging door could slam, it would have.

Evie stared after her. "What on earth was that about?"

Patricia sighed. "I think she and Jim are having trouble."

"Oh, no. They seem so perfectly suited." Evie collapsed into a chair.

"In some ways, they are. But I don't think I'm speaking out of turn saying that Billy's been going to a speech therapist. You've probably noticed he doesn't talk."

"I have. But I figured that was just because Teddy did all the talking for him."

"It partially is, but it also turns out he has some developmental issues. And that's very difficult for Candace and Jim. They're both quite accomplished. They don't know how to deal with an imperfect child. I could have told them no child is perfect, but it wouldn't help. When problems crop up, it's easy to blame each other. Harry and I certainly did a fair amount of it when Candace started acting out in high school."

"You and Harry were wonderful parents."

Patricia smiled and patted Evie on the shoulder. "We did our best. But it didn't escape my attention just now that Candace thinks we preferred you."

"She was just lashing out. I expect she feels like I've usurped her position with you now the way I infringed when I was a kid." And maybe, if she and Jim were having trouble, Candace was one of the women who had her eye on Griff. One more reason Evie should stay away from him.

THEY ARRIVED AT THE STORE and Evie ran over to the café for coffee. She didn't regret spending the money on the cheap drugstore coffeepot, but her own coffee just didn't come close to Beth Ann's brew and her stomach had been too jittery after Griff left to drink the stuff. Now, though, she'd need the caffeine to get through the day.

Of course, Beth Ann served up a side of gossip with her drinks, and she wouldn't be put off as easily as Patricia when it came to questions about Evie's night out.

"So how was it?" she asked as she handed over the cup. "Dierdre Beck was in earlier and said she saw you guys dancing. Is Griff a good dancer?"

Hell, yes. The man had all the right moves, both on the dance floor and off. "It was very nice. And yes, he is."

"She also said you left early." Beth Ann didn't bother to mask her curiosity.

"He got a call from work."

"So your date ended abruptly?"

Just Evie's luck, the next person in line was the deputy's wife, Cynthia, who she'd met at Candace's house. "I heard the call was nothing. Just Sarah Branck imagining a prowler again. And Duane said you went to the scene with Griff."

"As you said, it wasn't dangerous or anything. And I had no ride, so he brought me along."

"According to Josh Melville, you didn't just sit in the

car, though. You went into the house."

Evie resorted to Candace's patented shrug.

"So then what happened?" asked Beth Ann.

"Nothing. It was just, you know, a false alarm. So we chatted with Sarah Branck for a while and then Griff took me home."

"Really," said Cynthia. "So it was—"

"Sorry to interrupt," said the man who'd gotten in line behind her, "but do you think I could just have a large coffee? I'm kind of in a rush."

Evie could have kissed him. She took her own coffee and ran off to the bookstore side, getting while the getting was good. Not that Beth Ann wouldn't follow the minute café traffic slowed down, but at least maybe they'd have some privacy for the interrogation.

Behind the counter in the Nook, she pulled the list she'd made out of her bag, along with her cell phone.

"I want to take some pictures of the store so I can get started on a website," she said. "They won't be great with only the cell, but they'll do until I can get a better camera."

She was outside trying to frame the bookstore and the café in a reasonable-looking shot when the big, black Suburban marked with SHERIFF pulled up to the curb. Her stomach clenched into a tight knot and she had to swallow back the bubble of coffee-flavored bile in the back of her throat.

Griff unfolded himself from the SUV and strolled over to her. Without giving a clue as to his intentions, he wrapped his arms around her and planted a kiss on her lips.

"Morning," he said softly.

"You…I…What?" Evie struggled to get some semblance of control. "My God, Griff. People are already talking. You're just feeding the gossip beast."

"Let them talk. They're going to anyway, so might as well give them what they want." He still hadn't released her, and Evie could feel the heat of his body all around her.

"Easy for you to say." She forced herself to pull away. "I've already been questioned three times today. Women are a pain in the butt. I bet no one gave *you* a hard time when you went in to work."

"No, but then most of the guys I work with have to wait for their wives to tell them what they think."

"Well, one of the women in the café was Duane's wife, and she was basing her questions on our visit to Sarah Branck's house."

"See? That's what I mean. Duane has no idea what to think, so Cynthia will get the answers and then go home and tell him."

In spite of her frustration, Evie laughed. "You win."

"Let's go inside." Griff grabbed her hand. "Might as well be hanged for a sheep as for a lamb."

Evie let him lead her into the café, where he ordered his usual large coffee, finally letting go of her when he had to pay. She felt the stares of everyone there, all focused on her hand in Griff's. Their curiosity was a living thing and it made her whole body itch. But Griff didn't appear to notice at all.

"Thanks, Beth Ann," he said, toasting her with the cup before slinging a casual arm over Evie's shoulders and drawing her back toward the bookstore side.

"Good morning, Griffin," Patricia trilled when she saw them.

"Morning, Patricia. How are you doing?"

"I am just fine and dandy." Patricia looked around, then dropped her voice. "Evie told me about Sarah Branck. Is she going to be all right?"

"I hope so." Griff's arm tightened around Evie's shoulders. "Your niece was great with her. Much better than I would have been on my own. Did you hear she's taking Sarah to see about getting a dog?"

"She told me this morning. I think it's a wonderful idea."

"Me, too."

"Guys, I am right here." A blush burned in her cheeks and she swatted Griff.

"Yep. But I'm gone." Griff brushed a kiss across her temple. "Just stopped by for coffee. I have to get back to work. Patricia, do you think I could steal Evie for a few hours tonight? Our date got cut short last night and the Good Time Charlies are at the Roadhouse tonight. I figured I'd take her out after dinner."

"Absolutely. That sounds like a fabulous idea."

"Griff!" Evie squelched a curse. "I said I would ask."

He shrugged, giving her a charming smile. "Yeah, but I was already here, so the time was right. You can ask next time."

So confident there would be a next time. Of course, she hadn't exactly given him a reason to doubt. But what was she doing? Patricia would get her cast off in another week, and then there would be some PT, and then Evie would go home.

CHAPTER 12

THE MORNING WENT EXACTLY AS Evie expected; the Nook was full of women, all more interested in her date with Griff than in buying books. But Evie kept her lips sealed and her hands full of bestsellers, using all her wiles to be sure every customer left with at least one. Those who were least intrusive got tidbits of information along with their purchases.

"Yes, Cabot House was lovely."

"We danced twice before we had to leave."

"Yes, we're going out again." And both times she let that slip, she felt a little shudder of nerves go up her spine she hoped no one else noticed.

The first surprise came when the bell chimed at 12:30 and Evie looked up from explaining the concept of urban fantasy to a confused mother to see her cousin standing in the doorway. The two women standing in the mystery and thriller section debating the merits of James Rollins immediately quieted, and Evie realized they were waiting—possibly hoping—for a repeat of the scene Candace had made over the window display.

But Candace ignored them, giving Evie a brief nod before turning to Patricia. "I, um, have an hour off and I thought I could take you to lunch if you haven't already eaten."

When Patricia seemed to hesitate, Evie jumped in. "That's a great idea."

"You can handle the store by yourself?"

"Of course she can," snapped Candace. "She's not a child. And it's always been a one-woman operation."

"I'll be fine," Evie agreed. "You never get a chance to get out. Take it!" *Get things straight with your daughter before I leave and you go back to having to manage the place alone.*

"Well, that would be lovely," Patricia said. She took the cardigan from the hook behind the counter and joined Candace by the door. "I do have my cell in case anything comes up that you don't know how to do."

"Yes, Ma'am." Evie gave a mock salute, and turned back to the customer. A moment later, she heard the bell signaling that Patricia and Candace had left.

A few minutes later, the mother left with one Charles de Lint novel and one Jim Butcher novel, along with a long list of suggestions to get her teenaged son involved in reading.

The two women were still hanging out in the thriller section, no doubt waiting for Evie to get done with the mother so they could ask her about her date. Sure enough, as soon as the door shut, one of the women waved her over.

"What do you think of James Rollins?" she asked. "I'm trying to get Samantha to read him."

"I haven't ever tried him," Evie answered.

"I only ever read romance," said the other woman, presumably Samantha. "But I read a lot of romantic suspense and Gina here says I would like these."

"You have to get out of that romance gutter," said Gina.

"It's not a gutter! If you ever read one, you'd see that."

"I did read one. I read that *50 Shades* thing everyone was talking about."

"That wasn't romance."

"Why don't you guys make a deal," Evie suggested. "Samantha, you read a James Rollins. But you get to pick a romance novel for Gina to read."

"Do *you* read romances?" asked Samantha.

"Are you kidding? I grew up in a bookstore. I read romances, thrillers, mysteries, fantasy…you name it. Plus, when you get home from dancing in a show in Vegas, you're not ready to go to sleep, but there is *nothing* on television. Almost all the dancers I worked with were big readers. And since we didn't have money to buy a ton of books, and getting to the library wasn't always convenient, we traded books all the time—anything one of us had, all of us read."

"Huh," said Gina. "I suppose that makes sense." She cut a glance over at Samantha. "Does Griff read?"

"He says no. But I think he just hasn't found the right books yet."

Samantha snickered. "That's the attitude."

"My husband loves the Travis McGee books by John D. MacDonald," offered Gina. "They're a bit dated for me, but there's a sort of sweet undertone to all the macho BS. Maybe he should try something like that. Because I have to tell you, normally Tom's not much of a reader, either."

"Maybe I'll do that."

The door chimed again and Evie got her second surprise of the day: Hazel.

"Hazel! How nice to see you!" Evie left Samantha and Gina, who were moving over to the romance aisle anyway, and walked up to the front of the store.

"Where's Patricia?" Hazel asked.

"She went to lunch with Candace. Did you need her for something?"

"Oh, no, not at all. It's just so not like her to give up control of the Nook unless absolutely necessary. I know she just hated it when Beth Ann's cousin was here running the show. Several of the Ladies Auxiliary had offered to help out, but none of them could do it every day and Patricia didn't want a rotation. Of course, what she really wanted was *you*, but most of us didn't even know that was a possibility. We thought you were still dancing and that you wouldn't be able to get the time off."

"Even if I'd been dancing, I would have taken the time." She'd known, of course, that by not coming home for Harry's funeral, she'd be cementing any negative opinions people in Fairview had of her, but she hadn't thought it would matter. At the time, she couldn't see anything that would force her back to the town.

Joke's on you, Evie. As usual.

"But we didn't know that. Now, of course, we do." Hazel smiled, but held back whatever else she might have been going to say as Samantha and Gina approached the counter, books in hand.

"I can't wait to hear how this experiment turns out," Evie said as she rang up the James Rollins and the Suzanne Brockmann and took the women's money.

"We're fast readers," said Gina, "so we'll be back in to let you know."

"Maybe you guys should write things for our new website," Evie suggested. "Like 'Thrillers for Romance Lovers' and 'Romance for Mystery Lovers' or the like. We could post them up on the site and print them out for the store. Top five or top ten suggestions to get people interested in reading new genres."

"Oooh, that would be fun!" Gina tapped her fingers on the counter. "I bet I could come up with ten good ones."

"Me, too," said Samantha. "We'll get back to you."

"Thanks, ladies. Nice to meet you two."

As the women left, chattering about the possibilities of future columns, Hazel laughed. "Those two will make the Nook *the* place. Gina is married to Tom Geller. He's a big developer around here. She's invited to everything by everyone. She's even a member of the Ladies' Auxiliary, though she never comes to meetings. She can be a royal pain, but she's got a great sense of humor and if she actually writes you a column, it will probably be funny."

"And Samantha?"

"Sam's Gina's second cousin or something. Very different, but close as two peas in a pod. She was a year ahead of me in school, always with all the top scores and top honors. She went off to school at Princeton and everyone expected her to achieve great success—cure cancer, bring peace to the Middle East, that type of thing. A bit like you, actually."

"Me? My God, Hazel, I barely passed eleventh grade bio."

"True, but everyone assumed you'd be famous one day, that you'd put Fairview on the map. Maybe win Dancing with the Stars or whatever. And they felt…well, Sam was born here. If she won awards, the credit would go to her parents, her immediate family. But a lot of people in Fairview felt as if…" She shifted on her feet and wouldn't meet Evie's eyes.

"You can say it. They thought I owed them for taking me in."

"I doubt anyone thought it out that clearly, but yes. You belonged to the town in a way other children didn't.

"You know, Isabelle faced some of the same issues when she came home, especially from her old dance instructors, but she and George immediately began fixing up Cabot House, so they forgave her. They'll forgive you, too. Patricia and Candace and Griffin have been making sure people know you missed Harry's funeral due to illness. And when people see how hard you're working to bring the Nook back, the disappointment will fade."

"What happened with Samantha? I don't recall hearing about cancer being cured."

Hazel laughed, then sobered. "I'm not sure. She came home last year with a Master's in library science, of all things. She's working at the library now, though we still have ancient Eliza Stephens as head librarian."

"Good Lord. I mean, I don't want to sound harsh, but how is that woman still alive? She was older than dirt when I was in school."

"I know." Hazel grinned. "She's like the freaking Energizer Bunny of librarians. She keeps going and going and going."

"And shushing and shushing and shushing." Evie giggled, and suddenly they were both laughing. "Can't you just imagine," Evie gasped, "a clockwork bunny shaped like Eliza Stephens, finger to its lips, constantly shushing you?"

"Ohmigod, stop. I'll never be able to look the woman in the face again."

From the café side, Beth Ann glared at them, which set Evie off again. It took several minutes to get herself under control.

"Oh, I needed that," she said when she could speak.

"Tough day?"

"A lot of busybodies."

"That's Fairview for you."

"It is. Is that why you came, too? To ask about my date?"

"No." Hazel blushed. "Actually, I wanted to ask you about your friend Benny."

Evie gaped. She couldn't help it. "Benny?"

"It's ridiculous, right?" Her shoulders slumped.

"Of course not! Why would it be ridiculous? You just surprised me." *Understatement of the century there.*

"It's ridiculous because he's so…much… and I'm so…not."

Evie studied Hazel for a long moment while the other woman stood there, fidgeting. She wasn't Benny's usual type, it was true. He went for glamor and glitz, but those relationships—if they could even be called relationships—had never lasted.

"You are quieter than he is, that's for sure," she said at last. "But that's not such a bad thing. I've known him a long time, and I think you might be perfect for him. If he's what you want. Which is the part I am having a hard time with."

"Why?" Hazel frowned, and her slumped shoulders squared. "Just because you don't want him, doesn't mean he's not attractive."

How sweet that she would defend him. A woman like Hazel might really be exactly what Benny needed. But could he see that? Would he understand how precious the relationship was? Evie would hate to see either of them end up hurt.

"It's not that at all. But a relationship with Benny comes with lots of limelight. And lots of talk. People will speculate on your sex life, whether you guys test out all the Goodies, whether he's faithful or not. It's inevitable. Paparazzi will snap your picture when you're at your worst and cheap tabloids will use the pictures under headlines like 'Has the Sex Toy King Lost His Touch?' Benny's used to that kind of treatment. Could you live with it?"

"I wouldn't like it," Hazel admitted. "I'm not sure whether I could live with it or not."

"Then that's the only advice I can give you. Be sure. If you decide to go for it, I will be behind you one hundred percent, but I'd hate to see you guys crash and burn simply because you hadn't thought it through."

Hazel nodded slowly.

"Do you have any indication that he feels the same way?"

"He called me last night." She blushed again. "He wants me to come visit him in Las Vegas. I told him I couldn't get away until after the election because Griff needs me, and he said that was fine, that he could wait. We talked for almost three hours."

"That's awesome. Talking is good." Something she and Griff hadn't done nearly enough of. "And the fact that he called means a lot. Benny doesn't take steps like that unless he's thought them through. It's how he is."

"I kind of figured that. He sat with me at the dinner after the presentation. I mean, we all sat together, but he was next to me. And we talked a little bit, but I didn't think he'd actually follow up. So, umm, I thought maybe I would buy his books? If you have any in stock?"

"Of course. Why didn't you get them when he was here, though?"

"It's hard. Without an indication that he might feel anything, I couldn't…I would have needed an excuse." Hazel's face was so red, Evie worried she might burst a blood vessel. Was it possible for a woman so shy to withstand the media craze that always surrounded Benny?

"Hazel, don't get me wrong," Evie said as she pulled the books off the shelf. "Benny's a great guy. But fate's a bitch and she can give you the right guy in the wrong situation and there's nothing to do about it." *Like Griff. Right guy, wrong time, wrong place.*

As she handed the books over, Hazel surprised her with a smile. "I can be a bitch, too," she said. "Fate doesn't stand a chance if she tries to mess with me. And I don't think you ought to let her mess with you, either."

"Let's get you squared away first," Evie said, shrugging off the opening. She wasn't ready to discuss Griff. "Then we can worry about me."

GRIFF ANSWERED THREE CALLS AS he was doing his rounds. Luckily, none were particularly serious, as the vast majority of his mental energy was consumed with thoughts of Evie, not his job. How was he going to get her to stay in Fairview? How could he make her see that he was serious about her? How could he overcome her obvious resistance to a relationship?

The easy and obvious answer was sex. No question, she wanted him. And the way she had leaned into him this morning seemed to indicate that—at least physically—she was willing to stay with him for the remainder of her time in town. Despite her arguments about the gossips, she hadn't fought his possessive touches or the way he held her close on the street in front of the shop. Which was a damned good thing, because he had no idea how he might react if she did. Even now, his fingers itched with the memory of her skin. If she'd blown him off, he might have lost it.

But she hadn't. So she was okay with being his girlfriend—and what a weak fucking word *that* was for what he felt—while in town. She was still determined to leave once Patricia had healed, however. So many little things gave it away. She hadn't had her roommate ship any more of her belongings back to Tennessee. Hadn't opened a bank account. Hadn't even tried to throw a second Goody party after the one at Rachel's, though word at the station was that several women had expressed interest.

She wasn't putting down roots, and he was under no illusion that the tenuous relationship they had would be enough to hold her in Fairview.

And yet, she didn't love Vegas. She'd told him as much. She stayed for her job, for her friends. Well, she was making friends here. Rachel thought she was amazing, and even Hazel spoke highly of her. Hazel had been less than enthusiastic about attending the party when Rachel had invited her, but the next day she'd admitted to enjoying herself immensely and allowed as how the whole thing had been much less crass than she'd feared it might be.

Which nicely summed up how most of the citizens of Fairview were finding Evie herself. The town was slowly shedding its preconceptions and grudges, but Evie still hung on to her own.

He pulled up in front of his house and sat in the car, pondering. *Houses are for families*, he'd told her. And he'd meant it. If he told her he'd taken the time out of his schedule to look at a house he'd passed with a FOR SALE sign in the yard today, she'd bolt for certain. He didn't even dare put a name to the emotion that burned in him every time he saw her. She was too scared, too resistant to the idea of emotional commitment, and he couldn't figure out why.

But no time to worry about it now. He had a date with Her Fearfulness tonight, and he intended to make the most of it.

Inside, he cast a critical eye over the furnishings. Things he'd never noticed before suddenly stood out in light of the fact he intended to bring her home with him. The vague shabbiness of all the furniture, most of which he remembered from his own childhood. The layer of dust on the mantle that wasn't on the television. The fact that he'd never bothered to replace the two burnt-out bulbs in the overhead lamp.

He had a lot of work to do to show Evie he was worthy of more than a casual affair.

BY THE TIME THEY CLOSED the door behind the day's final customer, Evie was more than ready to head home and put her feet up for a few hours before her date with Griff, but she and Patricia still had to deliver the Ladies' Auxiliary's food and baby supplies to Frank Renner. After a quick stop to load up the trunk, Patricia gave her directions to the Renner place. Evie helped Patricia out of the car, then grabbed as many bags as she could carry and headed up the steps of the Renners' porch. Inside the house, she could hear the baby, Rosie, crying even before she rang the doorbell.

"We should have called before we came over," she said. "The poor guy is probably overwhelmed."

Patricia punched the doorbell. "No doubt. But I didn't have his number and the one Cynthia gave me is out of service. I would have had to call Frank's sister to get the number and that seemed a bit much. He'll be happy to have the help." As the crying continued unabated inside, she frowned and cast a look at the driveway. "His truck is here, so he's home. If he would answer the door, we could take care of the baby."

It seemed forever, but Frank did come to the door,

wailing baby in his arms. He was a short, wiry man with frizzled dark hair and a lined face that appeared far too old to belong to the father of an infant.

"Patricia?"

"Hello, Frank. This is my niece, Evangeline. We've brought over a few things from the Ladies' to help you while you get settled with Rosie. There's more food coming, too, now that you're home." Patricia stepped into the house as if she'd been invited. Frank hadn't, in fact, asked her in, but he stepped out of the way—not an unusual reaction when Patricia was in take-charge mode.

"Evangeline, why don't you put those things down and take Rosie?"

If there was anything she wanted less, Evie couldn't imagine what it might be. A baby. Another reminder of what she'd never have. But she reached out anyway and Frank handed Rosie off with an expression of profound relief.

"She won't...stop crying."

Why did it sound as if he was planning to say "shut up" before thinking the better of it? Evie cuddled the baby closer. Rosie smelled a bit sour, like curdled milk rather than the sweet, baby powder scent all the books Evie had read with babies in them described.

"When did she last eat? Is she wet?" Patricia reached over and tapped Rosie's diaper. "Evie, take those diapers in and change her. I'll fish out the formula and get a bottle started. Frank, can you carry all this for me?"

Change the baby? What the hell did she know about changing a baby? Of course, it couldn't actually be that hard. They showed it on TV ads all the time.

"Could you direct me to the bathroom?"

With his hands full of bags, Frank pointed down a hallway and Evie went. She found the bathroom behind the third door, but there was nothing resembling a changing table. So diapers in one arm, Rosie in the other, she headed back up to the kitchen.

"There's not a flat surface in the bathroom. Is there a

nursery? Or a changing table somewhere?"

Frank grimaced. "Hell, no. Lila just changed the kid on the bed, I think. Put a blanket under her."

Wow. Involved, much? And Lila thought having a baby would save her marriage? Not likely.

"Here, Evie." Patricia pulled a package out of one of the bags. "I noticed this earlier. It's a changing table pad. Just put that down under he baby with a liner on top of it." A small bag of liners followed the pad. Evie scooped them up and headed back down the hall.

The second doorway hid a guest bedroom with a twin bed. Evie laid Rosie down on the bed and unwrapped the pad and liners. Dammit, she needed wipes. And maybe powder and lotion or cream? This baby stuff was harder than it looked. At least the kid had stopped crying, probably curious about all the strange goings-on. Picking up Rosie once more, she went in search of the supplies. The master bedroom looked like a tornado had struck. Dirty laundry was piled everywhere, beer bottles cluttered the bedside table, and rusty stains the color of old blood marred the yellow sheets. Evie remembered Griff saying Lila had old cutting scars and her stomach clenched. How could Frank live in this? Granted, he'd only been home a day, but that was plenty of time to get a fresh start.

She turned her back on the disaster area and checked inside the master bathroom. Lined up on the back of the toilet were wipes, powder, and diaper cream. Evie snatched them up and hurried out.

Cleaning and changing Rosie took longer than expected, too. The baby was a squirmer. But at least she was happy. Evie carried her back up to the kitchen and found Patricia and Frank seated at the table. Patricia was rolling a bottle between her hands, warming it.

"Here she is," Evie said. "All bright and shiny."

Patricia held out her arms and Evie deposited Rosie into them. Her own felt curiously empty without the warm, wiggling weight.

"What are you going to do?" Patricia asked once Rosie was happily sucking on the bottle.

"No idea." Frank shrugged. "I gotta find some kind of day care. I can't exactly quit my job. I don't drive, the bills don't get paid."

"Well, you can't take a baby on the road with you. The Ladies' will help any way we can, but you're going to have to come up with a more permanent solution."

"Yeah, I know. I'm trying to get Mary to move in so she can watch her at night and we can find a sitter or day care during the day. But she says the drive to work is too long, that she needs to stay in Greeneville."

And she doesn't want to give up her life for her brother's kid. Evie didn't blame her. Had Patricia felt the same when she'd taken in her sister's eight-year-old? But bringing a child into an already-settled life, as Patricia and Harry had, was still easier than leaving her home and friends the way Mary would have to.

Patricia handed Rosie off to Frank. "Do you have my number? As I said, the Ladies' Auxiliary is here for you, so feel free to give me a call if you need anything. I'm either home or at the shop."

"Yeah, sure. Thanks." He rose and the bottle slipped from Rosie's mouth. She waved tiny fists around, looking for it, and Evie reached over and put it back in place.

When they backed out of his driveway, he was still standing in the door, watching them.

"I've never seen a man less prepared to be a father," Evie said after a couple of minutes.

"He'll learn. They all do."

But Evie knew firsthand that not all men looked after their children, and she wasn't at all certain Frank Renner had what it took.

WHEN THEY GOT HOME, EVIE told Patricia she'd be down in an hour to help with dinner, then climbed the stairs to her apartment. She felt bruised and beaten, all the tension of the day manifesting itself in sore muscles and a screaming headache. She needed to close her eyes, to lie down in quiet darkness and forget about nosy neighbors, irresponsible fathers, dead mothers, and all the babies she'd never have. Even her date with Griff held little appeal. Why start a relationship with no future?

For the sex, stupid. She could practically hear Celia's voice in her head and it made her grin for the first time in hours. Because, oh, yeah, the sex was amazing. And tonight they were going dancing. The man was a damn good partner, and not just in bed.

A little cheered, she texted Griff and told him to pick her up at 9:30, then set her alarm to take a half-hour nap and crawled under the covers fully dressed. She'd get ready after dinner.

The catnap helped, and Evie barely even flinched when Patricia brought up Candace at dinner. "It was nice of her to come over to the store. She rarely gets any time off in the middle of the day."

"How did lunch go?"

"Oh, you know your cousin. She wanted to apologize for this morning's little spat, but she couldn't bring herself to say the words."

Actually, Evie didn't know Candace, and for the first time that struck her as sad. "Did she say any more about what was wrong?"

"No. I doubt she wants to talk about her marital problems with her mother." Patricia frowned, then brightened. "But she did mention how pleased she was that you'd gone out with Griffin. I had no idea you had a crush on him when you were children."

Thanks so much, Candace.

"I wouldn't call it a crush. I admired his devil-may-care attitude. I wished I could pull it off."

"You? You were such a good child. What on earth made you want to be like Griffin? Not to say he hasn't turned out to be a fine young man, but he was a wild boy."

"And yet you didn't mind him dating Candace."

"Oh," Patricia laughed, "I minded. But I knew my daughter. If I'd told her to stay away from Griffin, she probably would have run off with him in the middle of the night."

Evie's stomach clenched rebelliously at the thought. It was a completely irrational reaction. Griff wasn't hers. And he *hadn't* run off with her cousin, despite the many nights Candace had crept out through their bedroom window. She spoke the words that haunted her without thinking:

"Well, maybe if she and Jim end badly, she'll run off with Griff yet."

Her aunt put down her fork slowly. "Don't say such things. First of all, Jim and Candace are just in rough patch. They'll get through it. And second, it takes two to tango, and Griffin only has eyes for you. Or hadn't you noticed?"

"I won't be here forever, Patricia. And what Griff wants I can't give him. We're just dating. Having fun while I'm here."

"So you're still thinking of going back to Vegas?"

"What would I do if I stayed here?"

"You're not a fool, Evangeline. You would find work. Starting at the Nook. Even before my accident, it was getting to be too much for me, as you well know having seen the books."

"I can make the Nook profitable enough to support you, Patricia. But I doubt it will ever support both of us." And how utterly, completely wrong that she wanted to believe it could.

"So you'll keep having those parties. Your friend Benny said both his mother and grandmother made their way selling Tupperware and Avon. You could do one of those as well as…the other kind of parties."

Evie pressed fingers against her temples. "Can we

talk about this another time? You get your cast off next week, and then there are weeks of physical therapy before I can even consider leaving. Okay?"

"You can't put off making decisions forever, honey."

"I know. But not today, okay?"

Her aunt nodded, but didn't speak for quite a while.

AFTER DINNER, PATRICIA REFUSED EVIE'S help tidying up, shooing her off instead to get ready for her date. In the apartment's small kitchen, Evie found a container of aspirin and after dry-swallowing a couple of them, she ran the tub, tucked her hair up in a clip, and crawled in to soak out some of the strain that had returned.

She meant only to let the warmth relax her a bit, but she must have drifted off, because she was startled awake by the ringing of the doorbell.

"Crap!"

She stepped out of the now-cold water, wrapped herself in a towel, and ran to the door, leaving wet footprints on the carpet. She yanked it open to find Griff standing there, dressed in black jeans and a blue chambray shirt. His eyebrows went up as he took in the view, and a grin creased his cheeks.

"I fell asleep in the bath," she explained. "Just give me a minute."

"Don't rush on my account." He stepped inside and reached for her. "I kind of like you this way." He pulled her up against him, kicking the door shut and tugging the towel loose.

"Griff..."

"Shh." He covered her mouth with his own and all her objections melted away. She slid her arms around his neck, soaking his shirt, and gave herself up to the pleasure of his body. With a groan, he pulled her even closer, sliding one denim-clad thigh between her bare ones. The rough fabric against her most tender skin set Evie's nerves aflame and she rocked against him, insanely attuned to him. He bit her lip and she dropped her head back, offering her throat even as she slid her hands into the waistband of his jeans, anxious to touch him.

But he pulled away.

"I don't think so," he murmured, sliding his hands to her hips and backing her toward the bed. "I quite like you all naked and wet and at my mercy." He plucked the clip from her hair and tossed it away.

Her knees hit the bed and he gave her a little push, then came down on top of her. The buttons of his shirt dug into her ribs. She didn't care. Power games had never been her thing, but damned if the way he held her down didn't turn her on. She put one hand under his shoulder to try and roll him over, but he just grabbed her wrist and held it above her head. A second later, he'd trapped the second with the first, holding them both easily in one big hand. His other hand covered her breast, and when he pinched the nipple, she almost came off the bed.

"You like that, sweetheart?" His mouth went to her other breast, his tongue making slow circles around the nipple without ever touching it.

"Please," she sobbed, twisting beneath him. "God, Griff, *please*."

"Nope." Keeping her hands manacled above her head, he looked down at her, silver eyes black with hunger and something she did not recognize. "If I let you go, you promise not to move?"

She shook her head.

"No, you won't move, or no, you won't promise."

"I can't."

"Well, now, see, that's a problem. Because I need both hands to take care of you properly." As if to emphasize his point, his free hand slid between her legs and he brushed over her clit with one long finger. She arched off the bed, but his legs kept her in place. He brought the finger to his mouth and sucked it, his eyes never leaving hers. "Where are those pretty, pink, girly handcuffs you showed me the other day?"

"In the box under the desk." Her voice came out a shaky whisper.

He eased slightly off her, then pushed her up the bed until her hands reached the spindles of the headboard. "Grab on," he ordered and she did. "Now, you stay just like that 'til I get back." His fingers trailed fire as they coasted down her neck, between her breasts and over the long scar below her belly button.

She could move. She could just get up and follow him across the room and to hell with his stupid command. But she didn't. Instead she watched as he bent over and pulled out the box, rummaged through it, and came up with the fuzzy handcuffs. He strolled back to the bed, apparently in no rush, and dropped the little keys on the bedside table. She wanted to scream, but all that came out was a strangled sob.

Slowly, careful not to let his body touch hers, Griff knelt on the bed and hooked one handcuff over one of her wrists. As it snapped shut, a shuddering breath forced its way out of her body and he looked down, a question in his black eyes. In answer, she merely held the other wrist in position. He slid the chain behind the spindles and snapped on the other cuff.

OH, FUCK, HE WAS IN trouble. She was the sexiest thing he'd ever seen in his life and she'd given herself over to him with utter trust. Bad enough he'd jumped on her like a dog in heat instead of taking her dancing like they'd planned, but then he'd fucking chained her to the headboard. Okay, the chains were covered in pink fur, but still. This was no way to win a woman's love.

He'd just have to make it so good for her she'd forgive his complete lack of couth.

He let his palms graze over the tips of her budded nipples and she immediately arched her back, pushing into his touch. He pulled back, punishing them both.

"Stay still," he ordered.

She gave a mewling little cry, but subsided.

Again, he touched her. Lightly, barely allowing the tips of his fingers to brush the skin of her face, her neck, the sides of her breasts. He watched the muscles in her stomach ripple, but she held still. He allowed himself to bend down and lick the dark pink areola around her left nipple, carefully avoiding contact with the tight little knot at the center.

"Damn you, Barstow."

"What? You want me to stop?" How he managed to grin at her, he had no idea.

"No! Hurry up."

"Sorry. Not on the agenda." He bent over her again, this time laving the actual nipple, tasting the sweetness of her skin, the tang of perfume from the bath she'd still been in when he arrived. He blew on the damp bud and her muscles contracted again. His dick throbbed, urging him to get on with it, but he tuned out the needs of his own body, focusing all his attention on Evie. Everywhere he touched her, goosebumps rose along her pale, soft skin. Her eyes were closed, her breathing ragged.

Oh, yeah.

He knelt between her legs, letting his hands slide up and down her muscular calves before bending over to plant a kiss just above her bellybutton, where the thick rope of scar tissue began. It hurt him to look at, that scar. To think about what she'd suffered: the pain, the loss of her job, the judgment of those who had never questioned why she might have missed her uncle's funeral. Tiny pinhole scars shone faintly silver at regular intervals along the length. He recognized those, too. Staples. Carefully, he kissed each tiny dot, weaving back and forth across the longer scar, working his way down to the thatch of blonde curls where the marks disappeared.

Evie shivered beneath his ministrations. She was on

the edge. He knew it. And he would send her over, but he wanted a few more minutes. He let his fingers trail over the tops of her lean thighs. Hands on her knees, he pushed her legs further apart, then curled over to press his lips to her inner thigh. The scent of her arousal almost undid all his good intentions, but he ruthlessly throttled back his own desires. He nipped the tender spot, then soothed it with his tongue.

God, nothing on this earth tasted like she did.

He turned his attention to the other thigh, giving it the same treatment. Evie's whimpers of pleasure were the sweetest music he'd ever heard.

At last, he allowed himself to touch the soaking wet curls at her center with the tip of his tongue. Her hips twitched upward, encouraging, even pleading, and he couldn't hold back. He plunged his tongue inside her, immersing himself in the sweet honey taste and scent of her. Her thighs clamped about his head and she sobbed incoherently. Griff wedged one hand between her legs and slid one finger, then two, into the sweet, dark, cave of her body, replacing his tongue. He curved them up, seeking the spot that would send her flying, and when he found it, when her breath came in short, sharp pants and her inner walls clenched around his knuckles, he let his teeth toy ever so gently with her clit.

Evie exploded. She bucked and arched so high she almost threw him from the bed, and her muscles clenched around his fingers in a way that almost had him coming in his jeans. He hung on by a thread, determined to make it last.

And then she burst into tears, and cold chased all the heat from his body. He scrambled up and grabbed the keys from the bedside table, but his hands shook and it took three tries before he could get the cuffs off her. "Baby, I'm sorry. Please don't cry. Evie, please. I'm sorry." He didn't even know what he was apologizing for and he didn't care.

When he released her hands, he half expected her to

shove him away, but she didn't. She wrapped her arms around his neck and held him so tight he could barely breathe. Which was fine. Or would be if she'd stop crying. He stroked her hair, her back.

"Evie, sweetheart, tell me what's wrong."

"Nothing." Her words were muffled against his neck. "I'm sorry. I didn't…I've never done this before."

"So we won't do it again." A panicked feeling chased across his heart. He wanted to beg, to promise her anything so long as she gave him another chance.

Her next words came so quietly he almost missed them. "We could do it again. I liked it…right up 'til the end."

"The end?"

She looked up at him, her green eyes drenched with tears. "I was alone."

The simple statement shredded his heart into a thousand tiny pieces. He hadn't even considered she might feel shut out by his devotion to her pleasure. He'd been trying to keep her from touching him in order to allow him to last longer, but she had no way of knowing that. She'd been *alone*. The very last thing he wanted for her.

He rocked her slightly, then took her hand and pressed a kiss to her palm. "You're not alone, Evie. I swear."

She drew in a long breath and her hands crept to the buttons of his shirt. "No?"

"Never."

His shirt unbuttoned, she tugged it from the waistband of his jeans, then slid cool fingers beneath his tee. As her hand encountered the massive swath of scar tissue from his burns, she slowed. "Can you feel it when I touch you here?"

"Sort of." He sat forward and pulled off both the tee and overshirt. "When I first got out of the hospital, I used to spend hours poking at my skin, trying to figure out what I could and couldn't feel. But touching yourself is different. You can always get the sensory input from your fingers you're not getting otherwise."

"And experimentations with…other people?"

Other women. Might she be just a little jealous? "I haven't experimented with other people much. The scars freak them out for the most part." He picked up her hand and laid it dead center on the scar tissue. "Try me."

Her fingers explored while he related what he experienced.

"It's a strange sensation. I can see your hand. I know what I should be feeling. But there's nothing there. The other night, when you were giving me a massage, my muscles could feel it, though. Press harder."

She did.

"See, I can feel that. Not in my skin, though. It's like you're touching me, but there's an inch of numbness before it hits."

She bent her head and pressed her lips to the nipple just above the scar tissue on his left side. He tugged her up for a proper kiss.

"That I felt," he whispered against her mouth.

"I wanted to do that the first night we were together. But you needed comfort."

"I needed *you*. I still do." *I always will.* He forced the words back.

"Yeah?" Her hand went to the waistband of his jeans, which was when he realized he hadn't even taken his boots off. He pulled away and divested himself of boots, jeans, and briefs, then rejoined her on the bed.

Her tears had dried, and passion glazed her emerald eyes. A faint flush rode her cheeks as she watched him, and the visible evidence of her desire ramped his own back up to full in an instant. She reached for him and he pressed her down into the mattress, connecting their bodies at every possible point. She'd felt alone? Not this time.

He took her mouth, sucking her full lower lip between his teeth and caressing it with his tongue. She shivered and her hands coasted down his back, a peculiar, uneven sensation given the large patches where no nerves survived. Still, he'd heard it said that sex was in the brain, not the body, and he believed it. He could see her hands in his head, even where he couldn't feel them, and the contrast turned him on as much as the actual sensation of skin on skin.

And then her fingers wrapped around his cock and he forgot everything but the need to be inside her, to be one.

He grabbed her hand and brought it up to his face so he could suck her fingers into his mouth.

"If you touch me like that," he murmured, "I'm going to embarrass myself."

"But I like touching you." Her lips quirked.

He closed his eyes and let his forehead rest on hers for a second. She was joking with him. That had to mean she was better. If they were joking, she wasn't alone. He pressed his mouth against her neck, sliding first one knee and then the other between her legs. She bent her own knees so that her feet were flat on the bed and reached for him again, but this time she simply held him in position, an invitation to take what he wanted.

So he did. He surged forward at the same time as he recaptured her mouth, tongue and cock invading at the same time. But his Evie was not the type to be conquered. Her nails dug into his butt, urging him on and her own tongue dueled with his. He reached back and positioned her long, strong legs around his neck, desperate to reach same spot with his cock he'd found with his fingers, to make her feel the burning urgency slashing through him.

Her breath hitched and she grabbed for his shoulders. With a fierceness that surprised him, she pulled him down on top of her, so that she was folded practically in half. Thank God for her dancer's flexibility. He needed to kiss her. Needed to taste her. Needed everything. His balls tightened. He had to get himself under control. He had to take her with him but in this position he had no access to her clit.

He tried to pull back enough to get his hand between their bodies, but Evie wasn't having any. She bit his lip, pulled him down closer to her, and he felt the trembling beginnings of her orgasm. He thrust harder, deeper, and felt her go over, felt the spasming clutch of every single muscle in her body holding him fast, which sent him flying straight into the stratosphere.

When he came down, he was still on top of her. He had to learn not to crush her. Next time, she'd be on top. He rolled to the side, grinning at the memory of the last time they'd tried that position.

"What's so funny?"

"Not funny. Happy. Planning for next time."

"Already?" Her fingers traced patterns on his chest. "What are you, eighteen?"

He laughed. "I didn't say I was ready for it. Just that I was making plans."

She snuggled into him. "You do that. Me, I'm going to sleep. Wake me up when you figure it out."

"Evie?"

"Mmm?"

I love you. "Sweet dreams."

EVIE WOKE CURLED INTO THE heat of Griff's body. In the darkness of the apartment, there was no hiding from her own thoughts. She couldn't imagine another man ever affecting her the way Griff did, taking her the place he did. She'd gone and fallen in love with the least appropriate man in the world. So damned unfair. Why couldn't he have remained the feckless bad boy? Why did he have to become a man who wanted a white picket fence, a house filled with children of his own and a respectable position in the community? The exact things she could never hope to give him?

She propped herself up on her elbow and looked at

the clock. 3:18. He'd been parked in her aunt's driveway for almost six hours. No doubt the whole neighborhood was already talking. He took the gossip in stride, but she'd face the firing squad at the store in the morning.

"Stop worrying." His voice was husky, filled with sleep, and when she looked down at him, his outrageously sexy eyes remained closed.

"I can't."

He blinked a few times, then met her gaze. "Tell me what's on your mind."

"Fairview. Patricia. Candace."

"Candace?"

He would pick up on that. "I'm tired of making people angry."

"And aside from the store window, which I thought you guys got through, what have you done to upset Candace?"

"This."

"*This*? How in the hell is what's between you and me any of Candace's business? Any of *anyone's* business?" He flipped her over so she lay on her back and he loomed over her. "Evie?"

"It's not. Candace is in a bad place right now. I think she just feels as if I am stealing her…friend. Her shoulder to lean on."

"Candace is as much my friend as she ever was. She and Jim are struggling. A blind fool could see it, but I am not involved in that in any way, shape, or form. And I don't want to be."

"I get that." And she did. "Still, it doesn't change Candace's…irritation. And I get that, too. I'm disrupting an ecosystem that worked for everyone until I got here."

"It didn't work for Patricia. It didn't work for me." He brushed her hair away from her face and bent down to kiss her. "Sweetheart, you can't live your life trying to please everyone. Every once in a while, you have to do what's right for *you*."

She went for humor. "You mean I should do you."

He didn't bite. "I'm serious. You remember telling me in the closet at the Nook that you were used to disapproval?"

"I lied."

"I didn't believe you even then, if you remember. But I don't think it was a lie, exactly. I think you may have been used to disapproval from people who don't mean anything to you. But what that tells me is that Fairview is different. Patricia, even Candace, are different. You care about them. You care about their opinions."

"Okay, so I care."

"Then why are you leaving to go back to a city, a life, that doesn't mean anything to you? If you're tired of upsetting people, stay here. That will make me happy. It will make Patricia happy. I could be wrong, but I think it would make you happy, too."

Tears clogged her throat, her nose, welled up in her eyes and dripped down her face. "It's not that simple."

His mouth twisted and his eyes dimmed. "I can't take it when you cry. Tell me what's not simple, and I'll fix it."

If only. But she just shook her head and reached up to pull him down on top of her. His arms curled around her and he rolled to his back, bringing her up against him and tucking her head into the hollow of his shoulder. He offered comfort rather than sex, and Evie sank into it, shutting out the outside world and focusing on the rough warmth of his big hand stroking her back. Eventually, she fell back to sleep.

When her alarm clock scolded her awake the next time, she was alone. A complicated mix of relief and disappointment rushed through her. *Stay,* he'd said. But what did that mean? If she moved to Fairview, did he see a future for them? *Houses are for families,* he'd said at his father's place.

You could adopt. But it wasn't the same. Ask the numerous couples who went broke every year with fertility treatments and IVF. People wanted their own kids, not someone else's. Ask Patricia. As much as she'd loved Evie, only Candace had been her daughter.

But maybe Griff didn't mind. Or, more likely, he figured they could just heat up the sheets for a few more months. Tears sprang to her eyes and she forced them back. Dammit, she'd cried more since returning to Fairview than she had since her mother's death. It wasn't until she reached for a tissue that she saw the note.

Still never went dancing. Maybe tonight?
XOXO
-G

Yes. Hell, yes. And if she had to pin her hopes on a couple of X's and O's, well, they'd had less support than that in the past. Before she could talk herself out of it, she reached for her cell phone and texted him:

🖐9:30. This time I'll be dressed.

Less than a minute later, she had his reply.

🖐Not on my account, I hope.

She laughed aloud in the empty apartment and went to take a bath.

Chapter 13

PATRICIA'S MORNING FROWN TOOK EVIE'S good mood down a notch. *Here we go. Watch your reputation. Blah, blah, blah.* But her aunt surprised her with a completely different question.

"Have you decided to stay in Fairview?" she asked, settling down in a chair with her arms across her chest.

"I'm not sure. Didn't we just have this conversation yesterday?"

"We did. But that was before Griff's car was parked outside all night."

"Sorry about that—" Patricia raised a hand, forestalling Evie's explanation.

"I don't need an apology."

"I know you're worried about people talking."

"Is that what you think? Evangeline Lorraine Bell. I am ashamed of you. You believe I'm so small-minded as to worry about gossip? Especially at my age?"

Chastened, Evie sat opposite her aunt.

"You're a grown woman, and you'll do what you want. But have you considered Griffin's feelings in this?"

"Clark Devane dropped out of the race. Being with me won't hurt him."

"Not his career. His heart. The boy's in love with you. What will it do to him when you up and leave?"

Evie's heart stopped. She couldn't breathe.

"Do you know how many women he's dated since he

came home?"

I haven't experimented with other people much. She shook her head.

"None. Not a single one. And plenty of women have tried to turn his head, believe you me."

"He hasn't dated at all?"

"No." Patricia seemed about to expound further, and Evie leaned forward, but then the front door slammed and she heard Candace's voice calling hello.

"I'm just on my way in to work," Candace said, swooping into the kitchen, "and I figured you'd be up. Cynthia called this morning and said Duane's feeling poorly so she can't go over to Frank Renner's house tonight like she was supposed to. Can you take her spot?"

"What time?" Evie asked.

"Oh, eight, eight-thirty. Mary says Frank has trouble getting Rosie to go to sleep and she won't be there tonight. Does it matter?"

"Yes, it matters. I have a date and Patricia can't go by herself."

"Oh, a *date*. God forbid the needs of a child should come before your *date*."

"Candace!"

"She's not really interested in Griff. She only wants him because he was mine."

The coil in Evie's gut, the one that kept everything together, wired up and pulled into place, snapped. "What the hell are you talking about? I have never in my life taken anything from you. *Never*."

"Right. Like all your good behavior shit as a kid wasn't so you could show me up? Take my parents' love?"

"As if I could! I *had* to behave. *Had* to. At any damn time they could have thrown me out and I would have gone into foster care. So don't you *dare* talk to me about having things taken from you."

The kitchen was still and silent as a morgue.

God, where had that come from?

Patricia's face was white and even Candace seemed frozen.

"Evangeline…"

"I'm sorry," she blurted out. "Please, just…" But the words would not come, and she fled.

After a quick stop in the apartment to grab her keys, she slid into her car and drove away from Patricia's house. Tears blurred her vision, but she kept going. As long as she was moving, they couldn't catch up to her, pin her down, ask for answers she didn't have. Her cell phone rang, but she ignored it. It rang again, but she had nothing to say.

Ten minutes later, her cell buzzed with a text from Griff.

↳Where are you? Patricia is worried.

She pulled over.

↳Driving. Clearing my head.

His response was immediate.

↳Let me come get you. Please.

She'd been nothing but a leaky faucet with him. She couldn't do it again.

Call you in a little while. Look after Patricia?

This time, the response took a minute.

↳Of course. But whatever happens, I need you to promise me you'll come home.

Home.

↳I promise.

GRIFF STARED ACROSS THE TABLE at Patricia and Candace, who sat holding hands. Both had red eyes, and Patricia looked older than he'd ever seen her. Even at Harry's funeral, she'd stood proudly, her shoulders back, never wearing her grief publically. Now she sat slumped over, defeated.

"What happened?" Patricia hadn't explained when

she called, and he hadn't waited. He'd left for the house the minute she said Evie's name.

"All those years," Patricia said shakily. "All those years she was the perfect child because she was afraid we'd send her away if she misbehaved. How could I have let her think that?"

Jesus. Oh, Evie. His heart folded in half. No wonder she'd cried when she felt alone. "She was a little kid, Patricia. She didn't tell you what she was going through. You did your best."

"It wasn't good enough. How could she not understand that we loved her regardless?"

"Because she didn't have a lot of experience with love. Her dad left. Her mother died. Kids take stuff like that the wrong way. They feel like it's their fault. You and Harry were great parents to her. I was there, remember?"

"Yeah, well, I was a lousy sister."

"Hell, Candace. We were kids, too. I figure the way you reacted was probably par for the course. The situation was far from ideal."

"I'm not a kid now." Candace blinked back tears. "And I have treated her terribly since she came back. I started the whole fight this morning."

He reached across the table and covered Candace's free hand with his own. "So you'll fix it. Just like you'll fix things with Jim. And as for starting things…seems to me you are all better off knowing what's at the root of the problem."

"What if she leaves again?" asked Patricia.

"She won't. I won't let her. But I'm going to need your help."

"Of course."

"You need to open the store today. You need to go on as if nothing is wrong. If anyone asks where Evie is, just say she's running errands, had to go into Greeneville…make up an excuse. When she comes back, she won't want to explain where she's been or what you guys talked about."

"And me?"

"You'll help me," Patricia said. "Griffin will go about his business and wait for Evie's call. You will take me to the store, and then if you can get away from the office—"

"I'll manage."

"Then you can stay at the store and we can work together. We haven't done that in ages."

Candace nodded, and Griff patted her hand once more before standing up to leave. "Hang in there," he said. "We'll work it out."

He climbed into the SUV and set his phone in the cup holder so he'd hear the buzz of vibration as well as the ring when she called.

EVIE DROVE AIMLESSLY UNTIL SHE found herself in front of the Branck house. A trip to the pound, that's what she needed to restore a little sanity to her life. But first she had to check in with her aunt. After several deep, steadying breaths, she dialed Patricia's number.

"Evangeline? Hang on, I just want to step outside. A bunch of knitters are here."

"I can call you back."

"No! Don't be silly. Candace can handle the ladies for a few minutes."

"Candace is at the store?"

"Yes. She took the day off work. Now, tell me were you are. How you are."

"I'm in front of Sarah Branck's house. I thought if you could do without me for a couple of hours, I'd take her to the shelter and see if we could find her a dog."

"That's a wonderful idea. In fact, ever since you mentioned taking her, I've been thinking…while you're there, why don't you see if there's a calm pup who could spend his days at the Nook?"

"The Health Department wouldn't object?"

"I doubt it. We don't do any actual cooking at the café, and the two sides are quite separate. I've always loved dogs, but your uncle Harry was terribly allergic."

"I'll see what I can do."

A puppy. Evie's heart lightened. Of course, her aunt would need help taking care of the dog until she'd fully recovered. Even while undergoing physical therapy, she probably wouldn't have the strength or balance to walk and clean up after a dog. Evie's return to Vegas was being pushed further into the future and she didn't care. Benny would be fine. And if he and Hazel really did hook up, he might even be persuaded to make regular trips back to Fairview, so Evie would still get to see him.

And she'd have longer to figure out what was between herself and Griff.

She texted him.

⮱Taking Sarah Branck to get dog. Back later. Feeling better. Promise.

He wrote back almost immediately.

⮱Sounds good. Here if you need me.

And he would be. Griffin Barstow was rock solid. And, according to Patricia, he was in love with her. It was a thrilling, terrifying idea. So she tucked it away and went to knock on Sarah's door.

"Evie," the woman said, stepping aside to invite her in. "How lovely to see you again. But…did we have a date?"

"No. I'm sorry. I meant to call you, but I suddenly found myself at loose ends and wondered whether you might be up for a trip to the pound? Turns out, my aunt thinks we should have a dog, too, so I am in the market."

"Oh, perfect! Let me get my sweater and we can go."

On the way to the shelter, Sarah regaled Evie with stories of Rover, her childhood dog. "That dog would— and did—eat anything. The year he got into the Halloween candy was the worst. He puked rainbow-colored effluvium for two solid days."

"Oh, no! But you never got a dog as an adult?"

"No, I went into teaching right out of college, and Joe went to work for the electric company. It didn't seem fair to lock up a dog all day while we were at work. We had cats for a while—they don't mind being on their own so much—but after the last one passed, we never got around to finding another."

No wonder the woman was lonely.

When they entered the trailer that housed the shelter's office, a cheerful young man with hair as shaggy as a sheepdog's introduced himself as Kevin.

"Looking for a new friend today?" he asked.

"Yes, actually, two."

"A two-fer! Totally excellent." He handed each of them a clipboard and motioned to a couple of chairs. "This part is kind of like a dating service. We need to know that the dogs we introduce you to are the right temperament for you and that your home is the right kind of home for them."

Both Sarah and Evie took about ten minutes filling out the forms. Only the last question gave Evie pause: *What would you expect to spend on a dog over its lifetime (food, medical, etc.)?* The answers were less than two thousand dollars, two to five thousand dollars, five to ten thousand dollars, or ten thousand dollars plus. She knew the answer. Vet bills racked up insanely fast. Could Patricia really afford a dog?

But Griff had said that Candace was doing well financially, so if anything happened, Candace would help. Evie had to stop painting her cousin with such a black brush. She checked the ten thousand plus box and handed the form back to Kevin. He read through it and made some notes, then did the same with Sarah's.

"I have a few dogs to introduce to each of you. If you'll wait here, I'll go get our first contestant."

He returned minutes later with a big, skinny dog with floppy ears and the color markings of a German Shep-herd.

"This is Gentleman Jack. He's mostly Vizla, we

think, but as you can see, some Shepherd snuck into his lineage. He's four or five years old, fully housebroken, neutered, and walks great on a leash. And despite his size, he's very gentle. He does, however, have one really bad habit."

Kevin let the dog off leash and he came over to them and sniffed both Sarah and Evie. Then he sat next to Sarah's chair and plopped him enormous head onto her lap. "Oh," she said, "he's wonderful." She stroked the mutt's bony head.

"Yeah, well, go sit on the couch and see what happens." Kevin gestured to the loveseat against the wall. No sooner had Sarah settled there than Jack leapt up next to her and once again appropriated her lap for a pillow.

Sarah laughed aloud.

"It's a problem," Kevin said. "Lots of people don't want dogs, especially dogs Jack's size, on the furniture. And he's apt to shove people out of the way if he wants to be with you."

"That doesn't matter, does it Jack?" Sarah asked. "I believe we'll do just fine."

"Excellent!" Kevin turned to Evie. "Don't worry, I have someone smaller in mind for you." Once again, he left the trailer. Evie walked over to the couch and knelt down to say hello to Jack.

"Isn't he amazing?" Sarah asked.

"He really is. You're a good boy, Jack. And now you're going to have a real home, where I bet you'll be spoiled rotten."

Sarah blushed. "I'll have to be careful about that."

"You'll do fine. Besides, he's had a rough few years. A bit of indulgence won't hurt him."

The door opened and Kevin carried in a squirming mass of brown fur.

"This is Cocoa," he said, setting the dog down. "She's a Poodle and Terrier mix. We're not sure what kind of Terrier, possibly Lakeland or Fox. She can be…excitable. I know you said you wanted a calm dog, but I think she might be better for your needs than our more relaxed guys. She's happy enough to sleep all day if you put a bed in your store, though she will want to get up and greet everyone, but after that she'll generally go back to bed. The thing with some of the less active dogs is that they really don't want to be disturbed. Cocoa won't nip a child who pulls her hair or snarl at a visiting dog who wants to play with her toy."

"Oh, yeah, that would be bad." Evie patted her thighs and the little dog came over and put her front paws up on Evie's knees.

"Well, aren't you just adorable?" Evie bent to look the pup in the eye and Cocoa's tiny pink tongue swept out to lick her chin.

"Aww, you want to come home with me, don't you?"

Cocoa yipped and Kevin laughed. "I'd say that's a yes."

Kevin sent them on their way with instructions, recommendations, and bags of the food the shelter used that they could mix with whatever they planned to feed the dogs at home to help with the transition.

Evie drove straight downtown to Norm Bennet's pet shop to introduce the new dogs and pick up toys, beds, and food.

"My treat," Sarah said when Evie pulled out her credit card.

"Oh, I couldn't—"

"It's the least I can do for taking me out to meet my new best friend."

"Never argue with Mrs. Branck," Norm said. "She'll make you sit in the corner and recite multiplication tables."

"I would never!" But the elderly woman's eyes twinkled.

Evie dropped Sarah and Jack at the Branck house and helped carry the oversized bed into the living room, though she doubted the dog would spend much time on the cushion when the couch was more to his liking.

Then, able to avoid it no longer, she drove to the Nook. When she entered the store with Cocoa in her arms, two men stood in the nonfiction section. Patricia and Candace looked up from behind the counter and Candace squealed.

"Ohmigod! How cute is he? She?"

"She. Her name is Cocoa."

"Oh, my, look at her little face," said Patricia, making her way around the counter to pet the dog.

Beth Ann abandoned the café and came over to pay homage to the little princess as well.

"Can a guy buy a biography in this place," one of the men joked, approaching the checkout, "or is it just the puppy appreciation society?" He rubbed Cocoa's curly head. Candace hurried back to the register and took his money.

Evie explained what Kevin at the shelter had told her about Cocoa's personality and, indeed, every time the door opened that afternoon, Cocoa sprang to her feet and rushed to see who had arrived. Which kept her pretty busy, since everyone in town wanted to come in and meet the Nook's newest addition.

Evie snapped a picture of the pup with her cell and sent it off to Griff.

☙Mrs. B's?

☙No, Patricia's.

☙Wow, didn't see that coming. We still on for tonight?

Yes. It was time to get on with her life.

☙10pm? Promised I would check on Renners after dinner.

She hadn't actually promised, but at some point she'd decided to give Fairview a shot, and that meant becoming more active in the community. Including the Ladies' Auxiliary.

☙10 it is. XXOO

GRIFF DELETED AND RETYPED THE last four letters three times. He hoped they didn't frighten Evie, but it was high time he made his move. Her disappearance, Patricia's panicked call, had put the fear of God into him. Patricia's cast would come off any minute and Evie would run unless he could convince her she had a future in Fairview. To that end, he had quite a bit of work to do.

His first stop was the hardware store. Martin Waters had already put suggestions from Benny and Evie into place successfully. He might want to expand on those ideas, might appreciate a little professional help.

"Hell, yes, I'd pay for that," Waters said when Griff explained his plan. "That girl's a pistol. Got great ideas. I've never sold so many bits and bobs in my life since word got out women could come in and make up honey-do lists and I put the doodads by the registry area."

"Great," said Griff. "I figure all I need is about a half-dozen clients to prove to her it's a viable business."

"You go get 'em, then. This place wouldn't be the same if she left."

Next, Griff visited Norm at PetWorks.

"Have you had a chance to try any of the things you talked about at the seminar with Benny Silver?"

Norm shrugged.

"Didn't they make sense to you?"

"Of course they made sense. But I'm not computer whiz to set up a system like that."

"Would you be willing to hire Evie to set it up and teach it to you?"

"What would it cost me?"

"Hell, Norm, I don't know." Griff flattened his hands on the counter and stared the other man in the eye. "Look, I'm doing my best to get her to stay here in Fairview, but you heard her at that meeting—she's a go-getter. She wants a career, not a job selling books for her aunt. All I'm trying to do is show her opportunities for using her expertise right here."

"Why on earth didn't you just say so? Of course you can add me to the list of folks who'd take a class with her or whatever. Have you seen her new puppy? She and Sarah Branck brought their new dogs straight over from the shelter."

"I saw a picture. Haven't had the pleasure in person."

"She'll charm you right out of your shoes. And, being as there's a bit of terrier in there unless I'm mistaken, she'll probably run off with those shoes, too. Now, do you need me to sign anything?"

"No. I don't want it to feel like we're ganging up on her."

Two down. And he could count on Izzy, too. She'd said as much at the presentation. So that was three. Gritting his teeth, he drove to one of his least favorite places in town, the Cut and Run Beauty Shop. Gossip ran like hair dye through the place. He had no idea whether Evie could improve Marta's bottom line with her marketing expertise, but he did know Marta hated to be left out of anything happening in Fairview. Her agreement was a foregone conclusion, but he needed her to say so explicitly.

"So it's true," Marta said slyly when Griff outlined his idea. "You are dating her."

"I am."

"I saw her at the Auxiliary meeting, but I didn't get a chance to meet her. She hasn't been in for a haircut."

"I'm sure she will be."

"Her cousin goes all the way to Greeneville for her color."

"Well, maybe Evie could figure out a way for you to encourage people to stay here in town for what they need." Of course, it was probably only that Candace got tired of being pumped for information, but Griff wasn't about to volunteer that opinion.

"Perhaps. You tell her she can come in and talk to me about her new business. No guarantees."

Good enough. "I'll tell her."

It took Griff several hours to sign up the last two people on the list—one jewelry shop owner and Mark Davis of Davis's Department Store—because both of them asked him a thousand questions. But both of them had been at the seminar and had seen firsthand that Evie knew her stuff, so eventually both agreed they'd at least give her a shot at improving their bottom lines.

The sun was setting when, on his way home, he passed the little house he'd first seen a few days before. Now, next to the FOR SALE sign in the yard, a box of flyers had been hammered into the ground. He stopped and pulled one of the flyers out. Three bedrooms, two baths. Not so different from the house where he'd grown up. The image of sharing such a place with Evie and a couple of kids assailed him. Coming home to her every night, waking up with her every morning....

He didn't have a lot to offer her—the sheriff's position came with an SUV, but not a great paycheck—but if he'd learned one thing that morning it was that Evie didn't fear financial ruin, she feared abandonment. So maybe all the shying away from commitment had less to do with him than with her need to be sure he wouldn't take off on her.

Well, no problem there. He wasn't going anywhere. And he'd prove it. Starting when he took her dancing tonight.

COCOA HAD BEEN AN ENORMOUS hit at the store, and Evie had managed to avoid talking about her breakdown all afternoon by focusing attention on the dog. But just as they were locking up, Beth Ann approached her, looking grim, and she could feel all the tension of the day rising up once more.

"There's something I need to tell you," Beth Ann said.

"Candace and I can go…" Patricia offered.

"No. It's important for all of you to hear." She took

in a deep breath and let it out slowly. "It was Leah who painted your window."

"Your cousin?" In all the time they'd spent at the store, Evie had never met the woman who'd been running the place for Patricia until Evie got to town.

Beth Ann nodded. "She told me last night. Everyone in town knew you and Griff had a date and she was over at my place talking about what was going on between you two and it just sort of slipped out. I'm so sorry."

Evie's stomach clenched, but she tried to be fair. "It's not your fault."

"It sort of is." Beth Ann shrugged her shoulders and rubbed a hand over the back of her neck. "When you first arrived, I was…angry. Why did Patricia need you? She had us. You just seemed determined to change everything. And…" she took another deep breath. "And it was pretty clear Griff was interested in you. So, yeah, I was bitter. And I ran off at the mouth to Leah. And she took it upon herself to act. If I had known, I swear I would have stopped her."

"Of course you would have," said Patricia.

"I can't believe it," said Candace. "Leah. What a—"

"Candace!"

"Sorry, mom. But seriously. What did she think she was going to accomplish?"

"She wanted me to leave. Everyone else did, too. Doesn't make her anything special. She just went a bit further than most." It was hard to keep the bitterness out of her voice.

"That is simply not true." Candace sounded precisely like Patricia, and it almost made Evie grin. "Look, I know we weren't all that welcoming, but we didn't know you. You'd been gone a long time. We didn't want you to leave, we just hadn't figured out where you fit in yet."

"And you've got that down now?"

"Sure. You're the quirky relative who sells sex toys." Candace winked at her and Evie felt a little of the tension leave her body.

"That's me." She turned to Beth Ann. "Thanks for letting us know about Leah. I wish she'd apologized for herself, but I guess that's too much to ask."

"I'm afraid it is. I got angry at her, but I still think she doesn't believe she did anything so very wrong.

"Well, that's it. I guess I'll get going. Again, I'm sorry for my part in the whole mess."

Evie touched the back of Beth Ann's hand. "It's okay. Really."

After Beth Ann left, Candace said she had to go home to feed the boys before the PTA meeting. "But before I do, I need to apologize, too." She grimaced. "When mom got hurt, I wanted to get her an aide to help her out until she was back on her feet, but she wouldn't let me. She insisted I call you. I guess it reactivated a lot of stuff from back when we were kids."

"Candace, I promise, I never tried to take your mom from you."

"Oh, I know that. I knew it then. I was just a pissy teenager, and I guess I grew up into a sort of pissy adult. So I apologize."

It was a perfect apology, and Evie wanted to laugh and cry at the same time. "No problem. Just get over it, okay?"

"Done. Now, I have to go. Are you going to be able to get to the Renner house tonight?"

"Yeah, I can do it. I told Griff to pick me up later so I would have time."

"Great. I really appreciate you pitching in."

GRIFF STARED INTO THE REFRIGERATOR, waiting for food to miraculously appear. Unfortunately, he hadn't made it to the grocery store, and no kitchen fairy had magically filled the fridge. The cupboards weren't much better. Some canned tuna, a couple of cartons of soup, packaged mac and cheese. Lovely. He glanced at his watch. He wasn't picking Evie up til ten, so he still had two hours. Plenty of time to run to the diner to eat and then come home and clean up. He'd even bought a new shirt while at Davis's Department Store that afternoon.

The diner was crowded, but sitting at the counter suited his itchy mood. He needed to keep moving, to have people to talk to, or he'd obsess on Evie for the next two hours. The big, juicy burger and fries and the constant flow of people were doing the trick until the radio he still wore on his belt crackled. Tossing a twenty on the counter to pay for everything, he headed outside.

"We need you at the station, Sheriff," said Hazel. The wording and the fact she'd called him by his title clued him in that whatever she had to say wasn't suitable for public ears.

"On my way," he said. In the truck, he thought about calling her back, but he was only a couple of minutes from the station so there wasn't really any point.

When he arrived, an ambulance sat in front of the building, lights flashing. Inside, Hazel waved him back. Both Rachel and Josh were in the bullpen, while EMTs saw to a woman in his office.

"What's going on?"

"It's Mary Renner," said Josh. "Frank beat the crap out of her. She drove over here and Hazel called for the ambulance, but she wouldn't go without talking to you first."

Frank...oh, shit. Evie was headed over to Frank's house. He checked his watch and dialed her number.

C'mon, Evie, pick up. But she didn't.

"Rachel! Josh! We're headed over to Frank's. Right now."

"But Mary—"

"No time, Hazel. Tell her I understand and I'll catch up with her later. But I want Clark, Duane, and whoever else you can get hold of to meet us there. No sirens. I don't want to spook the guy. Evie and Rosie are both there."

Hazel's face paled. "I'm on it."

EVIE PULLED UP BEHIND FRANK'S truck in the driveway and climbed from the car, her mind already on her date with Griff. So what if they didn't have a future? They had tonight, and she intended to make the most of it.

Once again, as she reached the porch, she heard Rosie crying. And once again, it took Frank an age to answer the door.

"Yeah?" His breath was a beery slap in her face and she almost turned on her heel and left, but concern for Rosie stopped her. She stiffened her spine and adopted her most Patricia-like expression.

"I am here from the Ladies' Auxiliary to look in on Rosie." So what if she made the Ladies' Auxiliary sound more like Social Services than a volunteer civic organization?

"Well, by all means come on in." Renner swayed a little as he held the door open. Not even nine at night and he was already blotto. Lovely.

Rosie had been settled in her carrier, which rested on the kitchen table. Her tiny face screwed up, fists flailing as she howled.

"What's the matter, kiddo?" Evie lifted her from the seat and jiggled her in her arms.

"I've been trying to feed her," Frank said. "She keeps shoving the bottle away."

"Is she wet?" Evie checked and sure enough, the diaper needed changing.

"I just fucking changed her!"

Evie winced. Not that she hadn't heard—and said— her own fair share of four-letter words, but Frank's tone was so harsh it was no wonder Rosie was upset. Evie carried her back to the guest room and cleaned her up and by the time they were ready to go back to the kitchen, the baby was cooing happily and pulling on the long strands of hair that had escaped Evie's ponytail.

"That's a good girl." Evie tickled Rosie's tummy.

"She likes you."

Of course she does. I don't yell at her. Evie picked up the bottle and settled Rosie in the crook of her arm to feed her.

"You should come over more often." His crafty, calculating tone, set Evie's nerves—already frayed—on edge.

"As my aunt explained, the Ladies' Auxiliary will help any way we can. But you have to find a permanent solution. I have my own job, as do many of our members."

The doorbell rang, but Frank remained in the kitchen, staring at her.

"Shouldn't you get that?"

"They'll come back."

If Evie had learned one thing as a showgirl, it was how to deal with men like Frank Renner. She stood, Rosie still in her arm. "If you won't get it, I will. I am expecting my cousin, Candace." She strode toward the door. The atmosphere in the Renner house had gotten too thick—whoever had rung the bell was coming in, whether they knew it or not. But just as she was reaching for the knob, Frank grabbed her arm.

"Don't touch that door."

"Get your hands off me!" If she hadn't been holding Rosie, Evie would have put an elbow into him, but as it was all she could do was pitch her voice loud enough so whoever stood outside could hear. Which, of course, set Rosie off and she began wailing like a siren.

"Open the door, Frank."

Griff.

Apparently, Frank recognized the voice, too. "You got no call to be bothering us here, Sheriff."

"Open up, Frank, and we can talk this through."

Talk what through? How had Griff known she needed help?

"Like hell." Frank's arm shot out, the flat of his hand

hitting her in the center of her chest and slamming her into the wall. The double impact knocked the breath from her lungs. Instinctively, she struggled to hang on to Rosie as her legs went out from under her and black edged her sight. There was a tremendous crash and Griff appeared in her narrow field of vision. He touched her face with one finger and cursed.

"Call for a bus," he said over his shoulder. "And get them outside." He stepped over her legs, moving toward the hallway.

Rachel knelt beside her. "Here, give me Rosie."

Evie handed the baby over as more deputies stepped around and over them, crowding into the house.

"Come on, Frank," she heard Griff say. "Locking yourself in isn't doing anyone any good."

Rachel helped her to her feet. "Let's get moving."

An ambulance had pulled up behind the police cars outside and Rachel led Evie over to it.

"I'm fine, really. Just had the wind knocked out of me."

"Griff wants you and Rosie—" The blast of a shotgun drowned out the rest of her words.

Griff. Instinctively, Evie started toward the house, but Rachel held her back. More gunfire followed, and Evie clutched at Rachel's hand.

What if Griff got hurt? What if Frank shot him?

It seemed hours before a commotion by the front door resolved into Duane and Josh hauling a bleeding and handcuffed Frank Renner outside. Griff followed behind them, along with two deputies Evie didn't recognize. One carried a short-barreled shotgun. The group headed toward the ambulance, and Rachel urged Evie away.

"They'll need to get Frank checked out," she explained, "but they need to keep him contained and away from anyone else, too."

Evie barely heard her. Griff moved too slowly, too carefully, and under the strobing colored lights, his skin looked bloodless. Keeping her distance from Frank, she hurried around and approached the group from the side. As soon as he saw her, Griff broke away, but when she would have flung her arms around him, he held her off.

He cupped her cheek. "You okay?"

"I'm fine. But you…what happened?"

He grimaced. "Pretty sure I cracked a rib."

"Cracked a—?" She ran her fingers over the thick, heavy vest he wore, found the impression. "You were shot!"

"Yeah. Guess I'm not as good a negotiator as I thought. We knew he had the sawed-off, his sister warned us. Didn't realize he had a couple pistols as well."

Evie wanted to wrap herself around him, but had no idea how to do so without causing him pain. She covered his hand where it rested against her cheek with her own and turned her head to press a kiss into his palm. "I've never been so terrified in my life."

He drew her in closer and pressed a bone-melting kiss to her lips. She wanted to sink into the sensation, to drown in him so she'd never have to come up for air. But reality wouldn't be denied. The fantasy of being able to let him go after a brief affair had died with the sound of the shotgun. If she didn't end things right away, losing him would cripple her.

"I can't do this. I'm really sorry, Griff. I thought I could, but I'm not cut out for the short-term affair."

He dropped his hand from her face and stepped back, face stiff, eyes blazing in the darkness, but his words came low and even. "And that's how you see us? As a fling? A little entertainment while you're stuck in Fairview?"

"No! You know that's not true."

"No? Then explain it to me, because I don't get it. I thought we were building something."

"Building what?" Evie wrapped her arms around her waist. "Pretend for a minute I tried to stay here. Found a job. I wouldn't want to give up my work for Benny. I like selling sex toys. They make people happy."

"And? When are you going to realize I don't have a problem with what you do? In fact, I'm rather fond of those fuzzy pink cuffs."

She felt the heat rise in her face. "Me, too," she admitted. "But being involved with a woman like me wouldn't be good for you."

"It's not about women like you, Evie. There are no women like you. There's only you. And I don't want to 'be involved with' you, I want to marry you."

It was like Frank's blow all over again. Her lungs collapsed and her knees went to jelly. But Griff didn't seem to notice, his words continuing to hammer at her. "Hell, I spent all afternoon finding ways to convince you to stay. I even looked at a house I thought we could live in. But we obviously haven't been on the same page."

"You don't understand," she whispered.

"Damn straight."

He started to walk away, but she reached for him, catching his sleeve. "Please."

He looked back over his shoulder. Sighed. "I know when you first came, I was the one who wanted a fling. I accept that. But things have changed for me, Evie. I can't do a short-term thing, either. Not with you."

"And what about that house?"

"What do you mean?"

"Houses are for families, you said. I can't give you that."

"You mean you don't want to."

"Griff, I can't have children. I told you that."

All the anger cleared from his face and he stepped close, resting his forehead against hers for a minute before lifting it.

"Evie, sweetheart, look over there." He jerked his chin at Rachel, who was dancing around with Rosie in her arms, trying to keep the child quiet. "Do you have any idea how many children like Rosie there are in the world? We can have as many kids as we want."

"You mean it? You won't mind that they're not yours?"

"They will be mine. They'll be ours. I love you, Evie. Madly, crazily. Not some hypothetical children I might or might not be able to have with someone else, just you." He wrapped his arms around her.

"Your rib…"

"Will be fine. Later on, you can kiss it better. Right now, I need to hold you."

She buried her face in his neck. "I love you, Griff. Madly, crazily."

"And you'll marry me?"

"If you're sure."

"Never been more sure of anything in my life. Marry me, Evie."

"Yes." She kissed his neck. "A thousand times yes."

CHAPTER 1

When Momma died, Timmy and I ran. The way I saw it, any man who'd stab a woman five times, then slit her throat and leave her lying on the floor, blood soaking into the worn carpet and running in rivulets down the ancient grout between the kitchen tiles, wouldn't hesitate to get rid of any other little inconveniences in his life.
from *A Bad Day to Die* by Lucy Sadler Caldwell [DRAFT]

EVERY BATTLE CALLED FOR A specific weapon, and over the years Lucy had become accustomed to carrying at least one at all times. Now, without the weight of a pistol at her hip or back, the reassuring bite of a sheath at her ankle, or even the knowledge of a can of Mace in her purse, she felt supremely vulnerable. But she could hardly walk into a police station armed to the teeth, no matter how much she might prefer to.

So instead of checking the bullets in a magazine, she patted the tight bun restraining her wavy hair, spritzed her neck with a touch of eau de toilette, and gave her appearance one last once-over in the rearview mirror. Good to go.

Sliding out of the Range Rover in a pencil skirt and high heels wasn't easy, but when she turned to walk up the steps to the station house and caught a man on the sidewalk doing a double take, satisfaction swirled through her. The costume had been worth the effort. As she swung open the heavy iron-and-glass door, she nodded at the man, who narrowed his eyes and frowned. The disapproval radiating from him almost made her laugh, and she entered the building on a wave of renewed confidence.

Her first challenge sat behind a long counter directly ahead of her and just inside the door, ostensibly guarding against unauthorized personnel. In reality, the barrier— and guardian—were flimsy. Lucy could have vaulted the counter and knocked Marge Bollingham flat on her butt in less than a second. Marge looked up from the crossword puzzle in front of her, and Lucy saw recognition darken her eyes and pale her skin.

"May I help you?" Marge asked, her voice stiff and decidedly unhelpful.

"I'm here to speak to Chief Donovan." Lucy kept her own tone as friendly as possible.

"He's busy."

Indeed, behind the counter, beyond the six desks that comprised the bullpen of the small department, Lucy could see what had to be the chief's office. The door was open, and a dark-haired man sat behind a desk talking to a uniformed officer.

"I'll wait," she said.

Marge's lips flattened. "I'll buzz him," she said at last. And then, as if it had only just occurred to her, "Who shall I tell him is waiting?"

Games. Why did everyone have to play games? But if Marge wanted to waste time, Lucy would oblige. "Lucy Sadler Caldwell," she said. Then she glanced ostentatiously down at the nameplate on the counter between them. "Marge."

The woman stiffened, but didn't reply. She pushed some buttons on the phone in front of her and Lucy saw the man in the office pick up his phone.

"Someone's here to speak with you, Chief," said Marge. "Her name's Lucy Sadler."

At the name, the cop who'd been talking to the chief whipped around. Lucy was too far from them to make out anything distinctive, but she was surprised to see feminine features beneath the short blonde hair.

Donovan must have asked her to come back, because without further word Marge hung up and pushed a button beneath the counter and a section swung inward to let Lucy pass. Lucy carefully closed the barrier behind her and gave Marge a smile before walking back toward the office. The uniformed cop had disappeared, and Donovan was standing when she arrived.

Christ, the man was tall. Even in three-inch heels, she had to look up to him, a fact she vaguely resented. Black hair fell in a shock over the front of his forehead and grazed the neck of his khaki uniform shirt, and for a split second furious heat blazed in his green eyes. But it was gone so fast, she might have imagined it.

He held out a hand. "Ms. . . . . Sadler, is it? I'm Ethan Donovan, Dobbs Hollow's chief of police."

"Actually, it's Lucy Caldwell. Lucy Sadler died a long time ago." She took the hand, willing her own to stay cool and steady as Donovan's gaze sparked with interest at her statement.

The phone buzzed, and Lucy turned to look out at Marge. But Donovan hadn't released her yet, and he had to have felt the involuntary clench of her muscles when she saw the man standing in the bullpen as if he owned it.

Donovan let go of her hand, his calloused palm sliding against her own where every nerve in her body had suddenly focused. "Excuse me just a minute," he said, stepping out from behind the desk and leaning out the office door.

"I'm busy at the moment, Mayor Dobbs," he said, his body blocking the doorway. "Can I get back to you in an hour or two?"

Lucy couldn't hear the mayor's response, but it went on for quite some time. Eventually, Donovan nodded.

An Excerpt from TWISTED

"That'll be just fine." A moment later, still blocking her view, he asked Lucy whether she minded if someone else sat in on their meeting. "A precaution, you understand," he said with a disarming smile that slashed deep grooves in his cheeks. "I'd like to close the door against interruptions, but nowadays that's not such a smart move, even in small-town departments."

Laughter bubbled up in Lucy's throat. Was he worried about being accused of sexually harassing her? *Her?* In *this* town? Far more likely, *she'd* be accused of seducing *him*. But he'd find that out soon enough without her enlightening him.

"Not a problem," she replied. "I completely understand."

"Excellent." He waved to someone in the bullpen, and a minute later the same blonde cop who'd been in his office came to the door. It took Lucy a full second to recognize her.

"Tara Jean!" She leapt from her seat, practically tripping over the blasted high heels in her shock. "Look at you!"

Tara Jean grinned back at her. "Look at *you*," she retorted. "The famous author returns."

"Hardly. You don't get famous writing true crime." And then the words sank in. "How did you know?"

"Why don't we all sit?" Donovan suggested, drawing her attention back to him.

For a moment, she'd forgotten he was even there, forgotten the whole point of her visit to the police station. "Of course." She took her seat, and TJ settled in the chair next to hers while Donovan went back around the desk.

"Shall we start again?" he asked.

"Sure." She swallowed. "Would you like me to go first?"

"That might be best."

"You asked my name. When Tara knew me, it was Lucy Sadler. Now, it's Lucy Caldwell. I had no idea anyone knew Lucy Sadler of Dobbs Hollow and Lucy Caldwell, true-crime chronicler, were the same person."

"I recognized you from the author picture in your third book. In fact"—she broke off and looked at Donovan, who nodded—"I was talking to Ethan about you when you came in."

"You were?" Lucy recalled the way Ethan had reacted to Marge's message, cutting short his meeting and double-checking her last name when he introduced himself.

"Ellen Wilson recognized you this morning driving through town. She called me to see if I knew why you had come home. I wanted to explain who you were, since Ethan's only been here a few months."

And he'd be getting complaints the minute word got out she'd returned. "How far did you get?"

"Not far. She only called a minute or two before you arrived." Tara Jean reached over and laid a hand over hers. "I hadn't gotten past the fact that you used to live here, and now you're a famous writer."

"I can't believe you actually read my books."

"Of course I did. They're incredible. I bet even Ethan's read them."

Lucy glanced across the desk, and Donovan's lips twisted into a wry smile. "'Fraid not. I surely will, though. But name and occupation aside, was there a reason you came to see me today? Something you wanted to talk about?"

"Yes." Lucy pulled a sheaf of papers from the black tote bag she'd laid next to her chair and pushed them across the desk at him. "I wanted to give you these: copies of my permits, the concealed-carry license, and the registration numbers."

Donovan didn't look down. Instead, he held her gaze with his own. In the deep, forest green of his eyes, she saw that same spark of interest he'd shown when she declared Lucy Sadler dead burn even brighter.

An Excerpt from TWISTED

She dropped her eyes, squelching the urge to fidget by spreading the papers across the desk with a fingertip. "The rest are from departments I've worked with over the past few years. The names and numbers are for people there who can attest to the quality and legitimacy of my work."

She leaned down and reached into her bag once more, pulled out four books, and laid them in front of him, covers up.

"If you skim them, you'll get an idea of what I'll be doing while I'm here."

"I'll read them." Still, he never even glanced at the books, never took his eyes off her. "But how 'bout you give me a little preview."

Lifting her chin, she met his gaze solidly with her own.

"I'll be investigating my mother's murder."

ABOUT THE AUTHOR

Laura K. Curtis has always done everything backward. As a child, she was extremely serious, so now that she's chronologically an adult, she feels perfectly justified in acting the fool. She started teaching at age fifteen, then decided to go back to school herself at thirty. And she wrote her first book in first grade. It was released in (notebook) paperback to rave reviews, and she's been trying to achieve the same level of acclaim ever since. She lives in Westchester County, New York, with her husband and a pack of wild Irish terriers, which has taught her how easily love can coexist with the desire to kill.

To find out more about Laura and her books, please visit her online:

Website: laurakcurtis.com.
Twitter: @laurakcurtis